I0761820

fyi...

This is a mystery set in a group home for teenage girls who have been convicted of minor crimes. I've tried to make it realistic and impactful, which means addressing topics that may be triggering to some readers, such as:

- negative interactions with police & other authority figures
- drug abuse
- self-harm
- bullying

The crime involves a severe allergic reaction.
These are not graphic.

POISON IN THE *SYSTEM*

JACK A. ORI

Cover design by Jack A. Ori

Interior design by Jack A. Ori (generated via Vellum)

For more information, visit https://authorjackori.com

First edition, April 2025

ISBN: 978-1-7345211-9-1

Printed in the United States of America

one

TASHA AND HER friends block the doorway so we can't escape. I reach for a fork from the pile on the table, wondering if I'd really have the courage to use it as a weapon if need be.

Nah. That'd just get me sent back to juvie. I put the fork carefully down next to the paper napkin Elizabeth's folded, pretending I don't know Tasha's there even though I'm counting every footstep I hear as they stomp toward us.

"Keep setting," I whisper to Elizabeth, who's standing there frozen, holding tight to a plastic cup in her pale white hand. "Don't give her power she doesn't need."

Elizabeth nods, but her hand is shaking as she puts the cup down. I turn back toward Tasha and her little posse to see what's what, and slide over, moving so I'm in between them and Elizabeth just in case.

Tasha's really the only one to be afraid of; the other two are nothing but pathetic little girls who imitate her every move. In Morgan's case, she's literally a child, barely thirteen with skin a darker brown than Tasha's but lighter than mine and hair she recently put in cornrows for the first time.

Vanessa's closer to my age but with half the sense. She's thin as anything and has blonde highlights that are starting to fade out, bronze skin, and a perpetual smirk. Her eyes dart away when they meet mine and I'm probably imagining it, but her cheeks darken slightly.

Nah. That's me wishing I wasn't the only bi girl in this place. No way Vanessa and her bully-wannabe ways would be into me.

“What do you know?” Tasha says, her voice grating on my ears for a change. “Looks like she does have friends, huh?” She nods at me, making it clear who she’s talking about. "I mean, it's weird being as big as us and hanging out with babies, but whatever floats your boat, am I right?"

Vanessa looks away as Morgan puts her hands on her hips and says, "Yah! Losers attract losers."

My eyes dart all over the room. No one’s gonna help me and I know it, but I can’t help wishing Ms. Carter would be better than the teachers I used to deal with at school and actually *do* something.

Why are there no adults in the room?

“Leave Brianna alone!” Elizabeth pipes up, her voice shaking.

Tasha imitates her in a high-pitched voice. Morgan doubles over laughing. Vanessa shoves her hands in her pockets. She's smiling slightly — does she actually LIKE Elizabeth standing up for me?

Nope. When she catches me staring at her, she snorts loud as can be and laughs hard. Too hard, like she's trying to convince someone she thinks this is funny.

Elizabeth blinks hard, too close to tears for my liking. I put my hand on her shoulder, “Do me a favor and grab the salt and pepper shakers from the kitchen, okay?”

Elizabeth nods slightly. She gives me a watery smile before she turns and walks away, flipping her red hair over her shoulder and walking with her head up like I taught her.

Soon as she’s gone, Tasha lunges forward and grabs a fork off the table.

“Give me that.” My voice is so strong it surprises me. I reach for the fork, but Tasha pulls her hand back, holding it over my head.

“Relax,” she says. “It’s only a fork. So what if you're so weak you can’t stop someone walking off with it?”

I jump for the fork, but she pulls it away again, laughing, and gets ready to toss it to one of the other girls.

“HEY!” Ms. Carter’s voice bounces off the walls from behind me, making me flinch.Her heels click on the floor in time with my heart pounding, and within seconds, she's standing between me and Tasha. "Do you girls have jobs to do to help us with dinner tonight, or do I need to find some for you?"

Tasha snickers. "Our job's to chill, dawg," she says, snapping her fingers.

"That's what the day room is for," Ms. Carter crosses her arms, tilting her head up at Tasha even though she's half her size. Where does she get that courage from and can she bottle some up for me? She goes on, "Brianna's working. Help out or go."

Tasha's eyes narrow. I stand frozen, clutching a knife so tight my hand hurts and wishing for the second time in as many minutes I wasn't scared to stab someone in the heart with it. I swear I'm not a violent person, but I can't stand girls like Tasha who think they rule the world.

Tasha blinks first, rolling her eyes and saying to Vanessa and Morgan, "Let's get out of here." She smirks at me. "Later, Bri. Have fun babysitting or whatever." She and her friends saunter out the room, their hands on their hips in the exact same place, but don't think I didn't catch that Vanessa's half a second behind the rest of them.

I feel like throwing that knife down on the table hard enough to make it bounce, but I control myself. I've heard rumors about Security dragging girls to the office in cuffs. It's not worth it. My real arrest was bad enough.

Instead, I hurry to finish with the forks and knives so Elizabeth won't have to do much when she gets back.

Ms. Carter puts her hand on my shoulder. "Don't let her get to you, Brianna," she says, her voice soft and measured. She's not any older than my mom, but she always feels grandmotherly to me when she tries to be comforting. "You did the right thing, trying to stand up to Tasha without getting in trouble yourself." She frowns. "Where's Elizabeth?"

"Kitchen," I manage to get out. "I sent her to get the salt."

Ms. Carter nods. "It's wonderful you have her back," she says, "but it's her job to set this table. Please go get her."

"Yes, ma'am," I mumble. I always try to show extra respect in the hopes it makes a difference in those progress reports the house has to send to the judge every month, even though it probably doesn't.

As I turn, Ms. Carter says, "One more thing, Brianna. I think it's important Elizabeth learns to fight her own battles. Simone too." Simone is the smallest girl in here, so I try to look out for her. I'm not sure she's even 13 yet, which is supposed to be against the rules, but if the judge didn't care the rules don't matter. "I don't think you're ready to supervise yet. Tomorrow we'll try you in the kitchen instead."

My shoulders slump. I don't want to leave Elizabeth alone with Tasha, and it sure doesn't sound to me like anyone's doing anything about that situation. But what choice do I have but to let it play out? Too many wrong moves and I get shipped off to juvie instead of living in a group home, and I'm not about to let Ms. Carter play that card.

I stop at the hand-washing station outside the kitchen and scrub up then put on gloves even though I'm not gonna be touching the food. Can't be too careful with germs, especially in a place like this. Then I push open the heavy kitchen door and slide in, looking for Elizabeth.

The kitchen's so full of activity it gives me a headache. Molly's at the counter next to the stove, drizzling oil from a dispensing bottle over a pan full of broccoli and next to her, there's another glass pan full of potato slices and some kind of sauce boiling on the stove. On the other side of the room, a couple girls from another cohort are running back and forth, getting stuff from the fridge for their dinner — every cohort has to make a side dish just for them — and Lisa's chopping salad vegetables.

My eyes dart back and forth, looking for Elizabeth.

"Where the hell is that salt?" Lisa says, squeezing the handle of her knife tightly.

I look away. I've had a thing about knives since I was little. Mom had a time getting me to help set the table in kindergarten cause I wouldn't touch them.

There! I've finally found Elizabeth. She's at the counter across from the stove, measuring salt. Ashley's helping her. Her long, light brown finger is so perfect as she points to the tablespoon that my heart almost jumps right out my chest. I breathe in and out, focusing on the red headwrap that covers her hair completely.

I look away before she can catch me staring at her.

"Ashley's getting it!" Molly calls to Lisa, and I flinch before it hits me she's talking about the salt and not my secret crush.

Lisa smirks as Molly slides over to stir the sauce for Ashley. My stomach feels tight and I have to look away before I throw up.

"Good luck to her," Lisa says. "Trying to get through to that —"

"Shut up!" Elizabeth says. "You know, this would have been done already if anyone would let me do it my way. I'm telling you, I know how to eyeball a tablespoon in a measuring cup."

"Ignore her," Ashley says under her breath. "She's all bark, no bite." Aloud she says, "Don't try to tell me this isn't easier. Go ahead and pour that tablespoon into the dish there, all right? We're almost done already."

I clear my throat. "Sorry for interrupting," I say, my cheeks burning up when Ashley's eyes meet mine. "Ms. Carter wants Elizabeth out there on table duty." I look away, shyly. "But I could help you with whatever it is you put her to work doing."

"It's cool," Ashley says. "We're about done. I was just helping her get some salt measured for Lisa is all. You know she measures a tablespoon and a teaspoon by eyeballing it in a one cup measure?" She puts her hand on Elizabeth's shoulder. "Go ahead and do the last one. Soon as it's done you're free of this kitchen."

Elizabeth's cheeks are as red as her hair. She dumps the salt into the bowl as hard as she can. "Can I go?" she asks, her voice hard.

"Sure can," Ashley says. "You did good." She picks up the bowl. "I'll go give this to Her Highness over there. And remember what I said. Lisa's no one to be scared of." She starts to walk off, then turns toward me. "Hey, be sure to try the potatoes tonight. Ms. Carter finally approved my recipe and I'm sure you'll love them."

I'm sure they're amazing. "C-course I will," I stammer. Shit. I thought I was better at hiding my feelings than that. "Come on, Elizabeth," I mumble, my shoulders slumping.

I only half hear Molly calling for Ashley's help with the trash as I put my arm around Elizabeth and lead her back out.

At six o'clock almost on the dot, the girls on kitchen duty begin announcing dinner. Ashley's voice is first. "Good evening. Tonight all cohorts have baked chicken or vegetarian baked chicken and steamed broccoli. Tiger Cohort has scalloped potatoes by me and salad by Lisa. Here's Robyn with your Lion Cohort sides..." She passes the mic to another girl who announces what her cohort is getting instead of potatoes and salad.

Elizabeth washes her hands at the washing station in front of the kitchen and goes inside to help bring the food to the serving table while everyone else lines up at the handwashing station. When we're done, we go to our chairs and stand at attention behind them with our hands behind our backs like we've got invisible cuffs on. I know without looking the other cohorts are doing the same at their tables. There's five of them cause Water Bear doesn't eat with the rest of us.

Tasha comes to our table. Instead of putting her hands behind her back, she crosses her arms against her chest. Her eyes are hard as they dart around the table, lighting on me then moving on to Simone, who is on the other side of the empty chair where Elizabeth will sit. Simone's staring down at her clasped hands, blinking hard like she wants to cry.

"Simone?" I whisper, leaning over Elizabeth's chair. "What's wrong?"

Simone's eyes dart to Tasha, then away. Lisa, who is on Tasha's other side, pokes Molly with her elbow and whispers something in her ear. Molly's eyes narrow — is she just listening or is she annoyed?

"Forget them," I tell Simone. "Talk to me, okay? What's going on?"

"I... I saw..." Simone blinks hard. "Never mind. I'm being jumpy over nothing."

I'm about to call her on that BS when Elizabeth's footsteps pound on the floor behind me. She stomps over to her seat and throws her hands hard behind her back. Her jaw is set, but her face is trembling like she's trying not to cry.

Now what? I'm almost glad the only little girl I got at home is my cousin and not my sister, cause looking out for these two is draining my battery fast.

"To be continued," I say to Simone, who shrugs and bends her head over her plate. I turn toward Elizabeth. "Your turn. What's wrong?"

"Patrice!" Elizabeth says under her breath. "I was gonna take the potatoes and — "

She cuts herself off cause Mrs. MacGregor, the program director, comes in. Lucky us, we get her sitting at our table, while other cohorts have lower level staff who probably let them get away with a lot more.

Patrice what? I think, my heart pounding, as Mrs. MacGregor's green eyes light on her, then on Tasha, who is still glaring at nothing. Mrs. MacGregor stares back for long enough I think she's gonna say something, but then she shakes her head, making her too-heavy earrings clatter and her grey-streaked hair bounce, and goes to her seat at the head of the table.

Typical. Tasha has a whole other set of rules than the rest of us. Mainly, Rule 1: Tasha does what she wants. Rule 2: See Rule 1.

Behind my back, I squeeze one wrist with the other so hard it hurts.

"I think you'll do better sitting next to me, Tasha," Mrs. MacGregor says. "Please switch seats with Ashley."

What? An actual consequence for Tasha? I can't gloat too hard, though, cause Ashley's beautiful brown eyes are far too wide and her face is drawn and tight.

She's scared to move.

"Ashley," Mrs. MacGregor says, her voice quiet. "Did you not hear what I just said?"

Tasha smirks. "She doesn't want to move and neither do I."

"It is not up to either of you." Mrs. MacGregor turns back toward Ashley while I stare, my mouth falling partway open before I get ahold of myself so I don't speak out of turn. This seriously isn't a hill for anyone to die on, Mrs. MacGregor included. And if Ashley keeps it up, she could be removed from the table in cuffs over nothing.

Please don't let it get that far. Please.

Mrs. MacGregor looks Ashley right in her eyes."Is there a reason that you are not cooperating, Ashley? That's not like you."

Ashley's eyes dart to Tasha, then away. She shakes her head. It's obvious that she's scared of Tasha — is Mrs. MacGregor only pretending not to get it or what?

"Then do what you're told, please," Mrs. MacGregor says. "You don't want to spend the dinner hour in my office, do you?"

Ashley blinks back tears as she stands. She shuffles down to her new seat as slow as can be, dragging her feet and staring at the ground.

Tasha purposely bumps against Ashley's shoulder as she moves over.

Ashley's knees buckle like she's going to fall, but somehow she rights herself before she comes close to hitting the ground.

I look around. I can't be the only one who saw that, right?

Molly's whispering something to Lisa, who's next to her. Second time. What's up with those two?

"Stop staring, Brianna," Vanessa says. "You're too good for certain bitches around here."

My head jerks up. I don't even like anyone that way except Ashley, but that never stops Vanessa from broadcasting to the world that I like girls so I get picked on twice as much.

"Excuse me," Mrs. MacGregor says, "but that comment is inappropriate as well as unnecessary, Vanessa. When I send the servers to the buffet, you may get an apron and gloves and join them so that you can learn the value of doing something for people other than yourself."

Like she cares. She just has to do something once every three times or so to make it look like she's standing up to bullies.

Tasha doubles over laughing, drowning out the voice in my head that's mad all over again about me being sent here when it wasn't even my drugs I was caught with.

Vanessa glares at her. "Stop it! You were thinking this the same as me."

Mrs. MacGregor clears her throat. "I suppose I can find something for you to do too, Tasha. Now both of you be quiet and let me finish what I was saying."

Tasha leans back in her chair, tipping it, with that same ugly smirk she has every time she gets away with some nonsense.

"Now," Mrs. MacGregor says, "Before the servers head to the buffet table, I want to take a moment to thank those girls who helped with dinner tonight, especially our cooks, Ashley, Molly, and Lisa." Ashley's cheeks darken and she looks away, staring at the tablecloth. Her shyness is so adorable it makes my nerves get all jangled in the pit of my stomach.

I turn quickly away to kill that.

Molly's staring down too, but it doesn't look right on her. She's never been shy like Ashley.

I can't take Lisa's smirk any more than I could before, so I look at Ashley again instead. Much better. I could stare at that petite little ballerina body all day long, and she's not looking at me so I don't have to stop. Yet.

Mrs. MacGregor thanks the servers, even Vanessa — wasn't that supposed to be punishment? — and thanks Elizabeth for setting the table.

"Brianna helped me," Elizabeth says, and Tasha snorts. Elizabeth glares at her and adds, "She also protected me when some people were being bullies."

Mrs. MacGregor frowns. "Maybe I should talk to you two about that after dinner," she says. "In the meantime, I'm glad to hear you worked as a team. All right, servers take your places, please. Brianna, you may go with the cooks to get your food if you'd like."

I don't like being singled out. It's only gonna invite trouble.

I look around to see who's gonna try to mess with me before I get up. Ashley's eyes are also darting everywhere. Tasha pushes her chair out so Ashley can't get past and she has to go the other way around the table. No one tells Tasha to move, of course,just like no one tells Lisa to keep her hands to herself when she throws her arm around Molly's shoulders. Molly's eyes are pointed toward the floor but she raises her head and forces a smile when she sees me looking.

I'm so busy trying to make sense out of that I almost trip over Morgan's foot in the aisle. The only reason I miss it is Simone breathes in sharply and I see it in my path when I turn my head to check on her.

Morgan giggles anyway. I ignore her, taking the biggest steps possible to catch up with Ashley. It's not hard cause she's moving in turtle mode and staring at her feet like she wishes the floor would open up for her to fall through.

"What's wrong?" I ask her.

Ashley shrugs. "Don't mind me. I'm in my feelings about... stuff."

"Stuff, like whatever's going on with Tasha?"

Ashley stiffens. "Just stuff," she says, her voice flat. "Some days I miss my foster parents even though they're the ones called the cops on me. How fucked up is that?" She blinks hard. "Anyway, forget what happened with the seats. It's not worth your energy." She grins, but her eyes have no light in them.

My throat tightens with anger that Mrs. MacGregor lets Tasha get away with messing with Ashley. But at the same time, that fake smile makes my heart pound so hard I can't think. I pull my eyes away from her before I do something dumb like try to kiss her.

"Um," I say, trying to think of a way to change the subject. "You know what happened between Elizabeth and Patrice? Elizabeth was spitting fire when she came out the kitchen but she seems over it now."

Ashley glances at Elizabeth, who's standing behind the chicken, wearing an apron and plastic gloves. Her eyes narrow. "That girl's got too many moods, that's all I can say. And they put Vanessa right next to her too. What she do to deserve that?"

Vanessa's tapping her gloved fingers on the edge of the buffet table like she's counting down the minutes til she can call it a day and get her food. Gross. And she's supposed to give us food after touching that dirty metal over and over? I deliberately turn toward Elizabeth to ask for the regular chicken and some potatoes.

There's a faint odor of peanuts in the air as Elizabeth dishes the food out, but that's impossible. Peanuts aren't allowed in here cause someone could be allergic. Must be imagining it cause I've been craving a PB&J the whole six months since my arrest.

"Leave some for everyone else," Vanessa says to Elizabeth. "Though I'll stick to the salad. I don't like sharp flavors." Her eyes meet Ashley's as she says the word 'sharp.' What's that about?

Ashley's eyes narrow. She looks away, just like she did when Tasha didn't want her to switch seats. "Up to you," she says, her voice shaking so slightly that if I didn't know her as well as I do, I wouldn't notice. "Just so you know, I followed the recipe exactly." She squeezes the edges of her tray tightly as she walks past.

I bite my lip, feeling like a coward for not standing up for her. That right there makes me not girlfriend material even if it was allowed in here, which is an absolute HELL NO.

I tell myself that's on Ashley cause she won't tell me what's up. Like she said, Tasha and her crew just aren't worth the energy. But that's a big pile of BS and I know it. It feels all sorts of wrong to stay silent.

I do anyway. Not like telling Vanessa to shut it's gonna do a damn thing for me or anyone else.

. . .

Mrs. MacGregor doesn't let anyone start eating until we all have food, which means I have to sit there worrying that my dinner's gonna go cold. My stomach growls while I stare at my plate. Ashley's potatoes look especially good. She cut them into small circles and made them with some kind of white sauce that shimmers on the plate. I bet there's cheese in them, too.

"Those potatoes must have taken some work," I say to her.

Ashley's eyes light up. "It was nothing, really." She glances over her shoulder. "Sure wish everyone else would get back so you can try them. I'm on pins and needles here for your verdict on how they taste."

"She'll say anything to impress her little girlfriend," Tasha says, coming back, and all the light drains from Ashley's face just like that. "Better let me be your taste tester."

Ashley's eyes dart back and forth while I stare at the head of the table.

I make a point of digging into the potatoes at the same time as Tasha does, determined to undo the hold she's got on Ashley's mood. They're good, with just enough cheese in the sauce, though I'm smelling that weird peanut smell again.

Morgan doubles over with laughter as Tasha begins coughing. I glare at Tasha, wishing I had the courage to tell her to cut it out.

Tasha coughs harder. I've had about enough but as I open my mouth I notice her face is swelling up.

She claws at her throat.

"Stop laughing!" Mrs. MacGregor snaps. She turns to Tasha. "Tasha? What..."

"Epi...Pen..." Tasha croaks. She has tears in her eyes. "Can't... breathe..."

Mrs. MacGregor jumps up, grabbing her walkie-talkie. "Go get the nurse," she tells Ashley, who is staring at Tasha, her eyes wide with fear. "Hurry!" Ashley's lips part slightly while Mrs. MacGregor uses her walkie-talkie to radio for medical help. She's talking but no sound's coming out.

Mrs. MacGregor whirls toward her. "What are you waiting for? Go tell the nurse that we need an Epi-Pen right now!"

Ashley flinches, then turns and bolts out of the room.

"You don't have one on you?" Mrs. MacGregor asks Tasha. Tasha shakes her head and tries to say something, but all that comes out is a raspy, wheezing sound. She has tears in her eyes and her face is flushed. It's the first time I've ever seen her scared of anything, ever, but what does that matter now?

She's dying.

Where the hell is Ashley with that nurse?

Around me, everyone's talking at once. Mrs. MacGregor is trying to ask if anyone else has an Epi-Pen on them so she can save Tasha's life, while half the girls are trying to guess how this happened and the other half of us are sitting frozen in our seats. Simone's eyes are wide as they dart toward a girl on the other end of the table and then back to Tasha. Elizabeth's eyes are squeezed shut and her hands are clasped while she prays silently. Molly's staring at Tasha, her eyes wide with fear and her mouth half open in surprise. She looks so much like a pasty white version of the shocked emoji that I feel laughter coming on and bite my lip hard to stop it cause this isn't the time.

Next to Molly, Lisa's staring into her plate, so I can't see her face, but I hear her say under her breath, "She only ate potatoes."

My head jerks up, remembering the fear in Ashley's eyes whenever Tasha was nearby and how she didn't argue when Tasha said she'd be her taste-tester.

No. Ashley wouldn't. She couldn't.

But what about that weird thing she said to Vanessa?

NO. It's not Ashley. I know it.

I look around at Tasha's friends, hoping they don't blame Ashley even though I know their rule is what one thinks, they all think.

Morgan's twisting the end of a cornrow, her eyes darting back and forth, and Vanessa's staring into her plate, her hands clasped like she's praying.

What do any of them know?

I put my hand on Elizabeth's shoulder, wishing I had octopus tentacles so I could comfort Simone too. "Hey," I whisper. "You don't think Ashley..."

Elizabeth shakes her head. "N-not her. But someone..." She swallows hard. "Everyone hates the way Tasha pushes them around. Someone was going to hurt her eventually."

A bunch of EMTs come running in. Ashley is behind them, holding the Epi-Pen. She's got sweat on her forehead and her breath's coming fast like she's been running.

I shiver at the thought of her in a tank top and sweats at a track meet, then bite my lip hard. What's wrong with me, thinking thoughts not suitable for church when someone just tried to kill Tasha and still could get their way?

"Got it," Ashley says. "The nurse had trouble finding one."

Simone's head jerks up. "S-she had a spare?"

Is that relief I see written all over her face? Those wide eyes, that breath she lets out?

What? No. Sweet little Simone wouldn't hurt a fly, never mind Tasha, even if she was getting picked on all the time... right?

"Let me have that, hon," one of the EMTs tells Ashley, interrupting my thoughts. That's fine. I wasn't thinking anything worthwhile anyway.

The EMTs take over as Mrs. MacGregor steps back. They grab Tasha and lay her flat on the floor. As much as I hate what she's done to me and everyone else, especially Ashley, I can't help feeling bad for her. That floor's got to be as cold as it is dirty.

The EMTs pull down Tasha's jeans. My head turns too fast, trying to give her some privacy. The whispers all around me get louder, but too late now to fix how that looks.

"Stay with us, sweetheart," one says. "We're gonna put an oxygen mask on you and you're gonna catch your breath in a sec, I promise."

Tasha nods slightly, but her eyes are already glazing over and I'm not sure she understands.

The EMTs quickly get her on a gurney and hooked up to oxygen. "Deep breaths... that's a good girl," one says as they attach a blood pressure cuff.

"She's stabilizing," an EMT tells Mrs. MacGregor, "but we're not out of the woods yet. We're gonna take her to the hospital and the doctors will take it from there."

"Of course," Mrs. MacGregor says. "Thank you."

Tasha's head lolls to one side as the EMTs begin wheeling her away. Is she gonna make it? Her eyes flutter open and she jerks her head up, trying to sit, and she lifts one finger, pointing at the air in between Ashley and Lisa. Her mouth moves under the oxygen mask, but nothing comes out.

One of the EMTs helps her lie back down and says, "You need to rest, sweetheart." They roll her away.

My hands throb from holding so tight to the table. I let go as girls begin whispering, "What did that mean?"

"Isn't it obvious?" Vanessa says. "She was saying Ashley poisoned her."

Ashley blinks back tears. "I didn't!"

"All she ate was your potatoes," Vanessa says. "How did she get peanuts in her if it wasn't you?"

"That is enough!" Mrs. MacGregor's voice is firm. "This incident is terrible enough without anyone making accusations." She lets her breath out slowly. "Tasha will make a full recovery," she says softly, but I got this sinking feeling she's trying to convince herself. "I-in the meantime, I need to make some calls. Try to eat something, girls, and please....don't spread rumors about how this happened. We're all going to need each other in the coming days." She walks off, her shoulders shaking.

Vanessa glares at Ashley, who slides her chair back a little, hugging herself tightly and staring at the ground like she wants to disappear.

This isn't right.

There's no way Ashley did this. I don't care what anyone says. I know she didn't.

But I gotta admit, Vanessa has a point. Everyone saw the way Tasha was treating Ashley and how much Ashley was bragging about those potatoes. So if Mrs. MacGregor calls the cops...

...Ashley will lose everything.

two

I PUSH THE potatoes around my plate, trying to think, while all around me the room buzzes with conversation. I don't need to make out the words to know what they're saying. It's all lies and rumors about Ashley.

I know cause she's the only one not talking. She's slid her chair away from the table some and she's hugging herself tight while she stares at the ground.

She's close to tears.

I shove my plate away and push my chair halfway out, then stop myself.

What am I gonna do? Throw my arms around Ashley in front of everyone?

That'll make things twice as bad for her. Can't do that no matter how much my body's screaming for it.

I grab my plate instead.

A quick look around the room shows me all the other cohorts are sneaking glances at us while trying to pretend they're focused on their own dinners. Only four adults, one for each table... if I play my cards right I can make it to the kitchen without getting caught.

Elizabeth's eyes widen as I stand. "Where are you going?" she whispers.

I bite my lip. I don't have time to talk. And I don't want to risk being overheard. But I know Elizabeth. She'll take it personally if I ignore her.

"Kitchen," I say under my breath, so quiet I can barely hear myself.

I glance over my shoulder at Ashley as I walk off. She looks so small, so defeated, with her shoulders slumped and her head bowed. It takes everything not to stop and tell her that I'm about to sneak into the kitchen and find proof she didn't do this.

Footsteps echo behind me as I hurry away. Shit.

I look over my shoulder. Elizabeth. Of course. She's running awkwardly, lurching forward with each step like she can't quite manage running and holding her plate at the same time.

I clench my jaw as she gets close. "Go back to the table," I say through my gritted teeth.

Elizabeth's face trembles. "No. You need me." There's a hardness in her voice that tells me she's getting stuck on something. I know her warning signs same as I know my cousin Vicki's. The next step is starting to cry, and then a full-blown tantrum.

And if that happens, it's game over. This girl has a set of LUNGS on her. One scream and I'll be lucky if I just get sent back to the table and not taken to the office in cuffs to explain myself.

Nope. Can't risk it. Besides, standing in the middle of the dining room like this is a bad idea. We're too exposed.

"Fine," I say, my voice clipped. I don't like letting her use tears to get her way. I'd never let Vicki get away with that. But right here, right now, I don't have a choice. "Hurry up," I say in that same no-nonsense tone. "Put that plate on the belt and be quiet about it." I turn my back on her. It's the only way I got to make it clear she needs to get ahold of herself.

Elizabeth's jaw tightens. I can't tell if she's mad or scared. But I guess I got through to her cause she does what she's told without another word except a whispered, "Okay."

I glance over my shoulder to make sure we're not in trouble. Shit. Molly's coming this way.

"We were — " I begin, planning to tell her we were only clearing our plates.

"You don't have to lie. I know what you're really doing." Molly's talking way too fast. She pushes her hair behind her ear. "I don't care that you're trying to get evidence in the kitchen. I mean, I do, cause I could be falsely accused, but um... I want to help."

I cross my arms. I don't like this one bit. "You gonna tell if I say no?"

Molly looks away. "Maybe," she mumbles. I bite my lip to stop from laughing at her. She's trying to act all tough, but it's obvious she doesn't have the balls. "Look, I was working right next to Ashley. A-all it takes is someone remembering wrong and I'll go down for this. So if I can clear my name..."

I stare at her. The fear is real, I'm sure of it. But what I don't know is whether she's innocent or if this is all an act.

Still, she might snitch on us if we don't let her have her way.

"Three in the kitchen's too many," I say, my voice hard. "You wanna help, you stand guard out here, okay? Signal us if anyone's coming."

Molly's face falls, but she gives me the same forced smile she had at dinner. "Sure," she says. "Whatever you need. Um..." She fidgets, interlocking her fingers and twisting her hands toward her then away again. "Share with me what you find? Please?"

I barely nod. Mom always says you got nothing if you don't have your word, so I don't want to speak any.

I push the kitchen door open and slip inside before Molly can grab it, gesturing to Elizabeth to do the same. The door creaks as it swings shut. I flinch.

If anyone heard that...

I bite my lip hard. I can't think like that.

The kitchen is eerily silent except for the hum of the fridge and the clacking of the conveyor belt. I look around. I don't know how anyone had time to clean, but the pot Ashley used is already in the sink.

"Wait," Elizabeth whispers as I reach for it. She opens a closet door and grabs plastic gloves. "No prints."

I give her a grateful smile as I slide the gloves over my hands. Guess she was right that I need her.

I grab the pot by the handles and examine it. It's full of soapy water, nothing else. I can't tell if there's a faint peanut smell coming from it or not cause the soap smell is so strong.

There's a metal spoon drying in the dish rack next to it. I let Elizabeth be the one to pick it up as a reward for thinking to get gloves.

“Look,” she says. “Yellow specks, like someone tried to wash it off but didn’t do a good job.”

“You think that’s peanut oil?” I whisper.

Elizabeth sniffs the spoon and nods. "Peanut oil isn't allowed," she says flatly. "This shouldn't have happened." She rocks back and forth on her heels, breathing hard.

My heart's racing and my breath's coming fast, but I hold the air in and count to five before forcing it out, just like they make us practice in group. Gotta keep it together for Elizabeth's sake.

"It shouldn't, but it did," I say quietly, squeezing her shoulders to try to calm her. "We're gonna catch whoever did this and that's a promise."

Elizabeth nods. "Gotta find the poison." She begins walking around, slowly. Anxiety rises into my chest as she says, "Lisa was here... Ashley and me were here..."

Hell, no. We don't have time for this. I hurry over to the trash and dig through it, hoping to find something. I can't stand the smell of rotting trash — when was the last time the girls on cleanup crew bothered changing the bag? I hold my breath and keep digging anyway.

My hand hits something small and plastic. It's got a small opening on top.

A bottle.

I pull it up slowly, almost like reeling in a fish, not that I've ever gone fishing. My heart pounds with excitement. This could be it. The poison bottle.

And then my heart sinks as sure as if I'd let a huge fish get away.

The label says "OLIVE OIL."

Not peanut.

Useless.

"Oh yeah," Elizabeth says, cocking her head. "Molly asked Ashley to throw that out for her." She holds her hand out. "I'll take it to her and ask if it's the same bottle."

"Don't!" I don't mean to be that snappy, but I gotta get Elizabeth's attention. She breathes in sharply and I explain, quickly, before she can slip into tantrum mode, "We can't carry this around, not when they might search every girl in the cohort to make sure she doesn't have anything on her that contributed to this."

"You mean like Tasha's Epi-Pen?" Elizabeth's voice is very small. "She always has it on her but it was missing. Y-you don't think someone stole it, do you?"

I stiffen. That would mean this is even worse than I thought.

"I hope not," I say, keeping my voice even for Elizabeth's sake. "You remember seeing anything while you were in here with the salt?"

Elizabeth nods. "My back was to the stove," she says, walking over to the counter and turning around. "I took the salt shaker from here and then Lisa said, 'Hey, I need that.' Except..." She looks away from me and mumbles, "She put another word in between that starts with R and is mean."

My throat tightens with anger. "You're not a retard," I tell her. "Don't ever let Lisa's words get you like that."

Elizabeth nods, blinking back tears.

Shit. Gotta get her back on track.

I say, "Forget her. What'd you see while you were measuring the salt?"

"Oh. Right." Elizabeth lets her breath out slowly. "Um, so Lisa was over there chopping vegetables." She frowns. "No, that can't be right. Why did she need salt if she was making salad?"

"Maybe she was roasting veggies," I suggest. Uncle Kevin always salts them just right before he puts them on the grill. I can almost smell them cooking.

I swallow hard. I don't have time to miss him right now.

"We didn't have roasted vegetables at dinner," Elizabeth says flatly. "Molly made broccoli while Ashley was helping me with the salt."

I frown, a dim memory coming to me. "Was Molly ever at the stove?"

Molly whistles twice before Elizabeth can answer.

That's our warning. Adult coming.

I'm in such a hurry to get out I almost forget I'm still holding the stupid olive oil bottle. I toss it in the trash at the last second and shove my way out of the kitchen.

three

MOLLY IS NOWHERE TO be seen when Elizabeth and I slip out to the area with the conveyor belt. Course not. She cares more about saving her own ass than ours.

No one's around at all — was she lying? Scaring us for no reason?

A quick scan of the room and I find her: she's sitting in her spot at our table, her hands clasped in front of her... and Mrs. MacGregor's heading that way from the other side of the room.

I shove my hands into my pockets so I won't be tempted to grab Elizabeth's like she's a little kid I need to walk through a parking lot and move as fast as I can. Halfway through the dining room I realize what a bad move that is.

My ankles are killing me and I'm breathing hard. That just screams suspicion, doesn't it?

"Listen," I whisper to Elizabeth as soon as I can catch my breath. "When we get to the table, Mrs. MacGregor's gonna question us hard. Let me handle it — you don't say a word. Deal?"

Elizabeth's jaw tightens, but she nods slightly. Maybe she's scared enough to actually keep her mouth shut.

I remember being her age all of a sudden, maybe younger, and Auntie Nan sitting me down for an important talk. *"I know your parents already talked to you about how to act around cops," she said. "But I want you to know your rights just in case you ever have any negative encounters.*

Now, you have what's called the right to remain silent. You understand what that means?"

My eyes burn now. I'm not sure what that's about — do I miss Auntie Nan or am I feeling bad about how disappointed she must be that I got myself arrested after all those warnings?

Mrs. MacGregor crosses her arms as we approach. "Brianna. Elizabeth," she says quietly. "You two should not have left the table. Where have you been?"

"C-clearing our plates," I stammer.

Mrs. MacGregor raises her eyebrows. I put my hands behind my back like I'm standing at attention, but it's mostly so she won't see them shaking.

"Clearing your plates?" she repeats, her tone as clipped as mine was with Elizabeth earlier. "This table is a crime scene, Brianna. You should not have removed anything from it."

I bow my head. Sometimes being meek and apologetic stops her from punishing me. "I didn't realize. I'm sorry. "

Mrs. MacGregor's eyes dart from me to Elizabeth and back again. "Take your seats," she says. "I have some news for the entire cohort."

I sneak a glance at Elizabeth as I pull out my chair. Her eyes are wide with fear. My stomach sinks. I feel terrible putting her in the middle of all this, even if she insisted on it.

"Listen carefully, girls," Mrs. MacGregor says. "I have several updates about the incident to share with you."

The incident? Is that what we're calling attempted murder these days?

"Tasha dead yet?" Vanessa asks, her voice hard. She turns and stares Ashley down.

Ashley looks away without saying a word. I could never hate her but I'm low-key aggravated. This would go better if she would stand up for herself.

Stop judging, Brianna. It's not like you stood up for her before all this started. I suddenly want to cuddle Ashley as if she was as small as Simone.

I look away before I get myself in trouble.

"That is inappropriate, Vanessa," Mrs. MacGregor says quietly, "but

I will let it go because I know that everyone in this room is having a difficult time with seeing Tasha collapse in front of them." She clasps her hands on the table. "To answer your question, fortunately, Tasha is still with us. She is currently in the Intensive Care Unit in the hospital and is getting round-the-clock care."

"Better be," Vanessa says. "I want to see her. And when I do, I'm gonna find out who did this to her and whoever it is..." She draws her finger across her neck, imitating slitting someone's throat.

Ashley gulps.

I stare at Mrs. MacGregor. Even she can't ignore that, can she? Vanessa more or less just threatened to kill Ashley. That's GOT to be the kind of thing that earns you a trip to the office to find out what in God's name you're planning, doesn't it?

But Mrs. MacGregor only says, quietly, "The investigation into how Tasha came in contact with peanut oil will be handled by us, not by you. Each of you girls is innocent until proven guilty, and for now, Ms. Carter and I will be in charge of finding out who did what. I sincerely hope that this was the tragic result of a prank gone wrong, but if someone did try to hurt Tasha, they will be turned over to the police."

Simone gasps audibly. I turn toward her. Her eyes are wide and she's sweating.

"Something wrong, Simone?" Mrs. MacGregor says, but her tone says, *Something you want to confess?*

Simone shakes her head. "I was j-just remembering when I was arrested," she stammers.

She's lying. And it better not be cause she's guilty, cause I don't think I could take that.

Mrs. MacGregor sighs. "I know that many of you have had very traumatic encounters with the police," she says. "That's why I will not bring them in until I have solid evidence that someone committed a serious crime." She crosses her arms. "To that end, I've asked Ms. Carter to come back in and as soon as she gets here, we are going to begin talking with each of you girls about what happened tonight." Her eyes linger on me as she adds, "I hope that anyone who knows anything will be completely honest with us. Lies only make you look as if you have something to hide, and I don't want to waste time going down the wrong path."

Why is she looking at me? I didn't poison Tasha.

I hold her gaze, refusing to look away even though I know that's what she wants. If she wants to accuse me, she can go ahead and straight-up say so instead of playing these stupid little games.

She blinks first, looking away. "Line up, girls." Mrs. MacGregor's voice is heavy. Tired. "I need you all to wait in the day room for us to call you to the office. Please remain there until your name is called. "

"What if we gotta piss?" Morgan asks, and a couple of younger girls double over giggling.

"I am going to take that question seriously even though I don't think you meant it," Mrs. MacGregor replies. "There will be adults in the day room who can escort you across the hall if you need to use the facilities." She stands. "All right. Go ahead and get in line. And girls, I need you to be on your best behavior. This evening has been terrible enough without having to discipline anybody for not controlling themselves at a time like this."

We're supposed to line up quietly, but almost nobody does. Everyone's whispering and shooting glances at Ashley, who's standing at the end of the line, putting a little space between her and the girl in front of her. Dr. Osborne, the adult who Mrs. MacGregor's put in charge of escorting us, makes her close the gap. She drags her feet but she does it. Dr. Osborne walks up and down the line, making sure we're standing at attention and not running our mouths. After forever, she lets us start walking. The day room's only around the corner and halfway down a short hallway, but it feels like it's ten thousand miles away.

The room's the same as always, with couches in front of the TV, shelves full of books, and a Ping-Pong table in one corner. There are three or four staff members hanging out in there, which is a lot more than usual. Most of the time, this room's as close to unsupervised as we get.

"All right, girls," Dr. Osborne says. "You all need to hang out here til you're called, so you might as well make the most of it. We'll put on a movie for those who want to watch and you can use the game tables."

I look around. I need to get Simone talking — where is she? She's sitting by herself on a chair in a corner, that's where, hugging herself tight. Ashley's even worse, sitting and staring at her feet.

I don't know who to talk to first. Simone, I guess. If I can get her secret out of her, maybe it'll crack this thing wide open so Ashley's name gets cleared. Course, that's never gonna happen 1-2-3 like I want, and Ashley looks like she could use a friend. And yes, I do mean friend, not anything else. Obviously.

I go over to her first. "Hey," I say, sitting down. "How you holding up?"

Ashley shrugs. "I'm holding." Her lashes are damp and clumped together, and somehow that hits me harder than anything.'"Um, it's really nice of you to check on me. Really. But I... I wanna be alone, okay?"

Her voice is soft, but I hear the way it trembles at the edge. I bite my lip, torn between respecting her space and pushing her to talk... or letting our fingertips meet, just for a second, like an accident on purpose.

"Fine," I say, disguising the hurt in my voice as best as I can. "But so you know, I'm working on clearing your name. So if you can think of anything weird that went down tonight..."

Ashley shakes her head. "Nothing," she said. "Only Elizabeth needing me to help her measure the salt, and that doesn't mean a thing." I can't help noticing the outline of her perfectly-shaped collarbone under her sweatshirt as her shoulders slump. "Sure wish that girl wouldn't wear her emotions on her face all the time, though. That stupid Patrice came running through and knocked her over and she burst into tears. You know what that does? It sends out a signal to all the bullies in this place to mess with her."

Like she should talk when she won't stand up to Tasha. Gotta let that go for now, though. "Patrice knocked Elizabeth over?"

Ashley nods. "She came running in at the top of her speed, screaming she had gossip about Tasha. Don't ask me what cause I wasn't listening. I went to help Elizabeth get up and tuned her and her nonsense out."

That's peak Ashley Woods. Quiet and sweet, always there to pick you up when you fall even though from what little she says in group, I know she's survived shit I can't imagine. I hug myself tight to stop her from seeing me shiver.

Focus, Brianna.

The important thing is what Patrice did to Elizabeth. No wonder she was in her worst mood when she came to the dinner table.

But does it mean anything? I doubt it. Patrice was acting the way Patrice always does, in so much of a hurry to spread someone else's business she's not watching where she's going. But still, maybe she saw something. Knowing someone was messing with someone else... that's the kind of thing a girl like Patrice wouldn't be able to wait to announce to the world.

"Can I ask you something else?" I say, keeping it chill even though my heart's going like a racecar on the track, so fast I'm almost dizzy. "What was that between you and Vanessa?"

Ashley's eyes narrow. "I-I don't know what you're talking about."

It's total BS but I don't dare call her on it. "You know," I say, "when she said she hoped the potatoes weren't too sharp."

"Oh." Ashley pushes her hair behind her ear, nervously. My breath catches in my throat and I have to force my eyes away from her. "Um..."

A security guard interrupts, calling, "Ashley Woods."

Damn it! Just as I'm getting somewhere.

Ashley stands. Her hands tremble as she smooths out her shirt. I stuff mine into my pockets so I won't be tempted to reach out to steady her. "That's me," she says nervously. "Figures they want to question me first, huh?" She gulps. "Wish me luck, I guess. I-if they think anything dumb, I just want you to know, it was nice knowing you."

"Ashley — " I begin, but she's already gone.

I stare at the space she just was standing in.The scent of her cinnamon-vanilla perfume lingers in the air. I breathe it in, trying to burn it into my nostrils in case...

God damn, I should have said something. What harm could it do now to tell her I love her? If they take her away I'll never get the chance.

I stand up straighter. The time for pity partying's over. They're not taking her away. I'm not letting her.

And what is it she knows that she's so scared to tell, anyway? Maybe she was letting her guard down just a little when they called her away but...

Nah. She started out this convo wanting to push me away. She doesn't trust me and she never will. Maybe she knows how I get every time I'm around her. Any straight girl would get freaked out about that, especially in here. No wonder she tried to shut me out.

I shuffle over to the other side of the room, holding my head high. Like I just said, the time for feeling sorry for myself's over.

I go to find Simone and see what I can get out of her.

four

SIMONE FLINCHES WHEN I sit down next to her. "Oh," she says, her small shoulders relaxing. "Hey."

"Hey." I pause, considering my next words carefully. I don't need Simone getting so spooked she clams up on me, but I do have to put her on notice that I know she's been lying and that I need the truth. "It was scary seeing Tasha rolling around the floor like that trying to catch her breath, huh?"

Simone nods. "I thought she was gonna die," she says, her voice breaking.

That's it. This is no killer. She feels too much to have started the ball rolling. But what's her secret then?

"Me too," I say softly. "That's why I'm trying to find the truth of what happened to her. I know she messed with all of us, but — "

"I didn't do it!" Simone says. "I'd rather she bully me every day than... that."

I raise my eyebrows. "No one said you did, baby," I say softly. "You scared they're gonna think so anyway?"

Simone nods. Without warning, she tries to climb into my lap. I freeze. If the staff sees this... but Simone is still such a little thing. There's rumors she gets sent to some sort of alternative grade school instead of middle or high like the rest of us. And if she needs to be held the way a little kid does, I can't turn her away.

I take the risk, putting my arm around her while she clings to my chest. After a minute, she looks up. "Someone framed me," she whispers.

I hold her closer. "Framed you how?" I whisper.

She shakes her head but doesn't speak.

I rub her back. "Listen," I say. "I'm trying to get to the bottom of this. But you gotta tell me what you know, okay? Cause that's the only way I can get you out of it."

Simone swallows hard. She reaches for her hair, reminding me so much of Vicki it hurts. Vicki tugs on her ponytail when she gets upset. It's an autism thing that comforts her somehow. And now here Simone is, wrapping a curl around two fingers and twisting.

"I want to," Simone says, "but I can't. If I tell I'll go to prison. With grown-ups."

I hug her, my heart racing. I want to tell her that's not a thing, but how can I? They threw her in here with Tasha and them, who are practically adults. And me. I was arrested driving home two months shy of my seventeenth birthday. I'm not exactly grown — far from it — but compared to this tiny girl...

"I don't get it," I say. "You're innocent, right? So how can telling..."

Simone shakes her head. "Please don't make me," she whispers.

I stroke her back while I try to think. "Tell you what," I say. "How about we play a game? Ping Pong or something? And if I win you gotta tell me one piece of your secret. But if I lose, I gotta tell you a secret instead."

Simone's eyes widen, but she says, "I'm bad at Ping Pong."

"Something else, then," I say. "Chess?"

Simone shakes her head.

She's not gonna make this easy for me. "I know," I say, grabbing onto the only idea I have left. "How about 20 questions? I'll ask you yes or no questions about this thing and all you gotta do is nod or shake your head."

Simone's eyes dart around the room. She's looking to see if someone's watching, but who?

"That's not a fair game," she says. "You can't lose."

This girl's tougher than she looks. I'll give her that. "How about I tell you a secret first, then?"

Simone looks away. "K," she mumbles.

I lower my voice. "I was arrested cause a bad girl put drugs in my car." My own words hit me as I hear them come out my mouth. A bad girl. Wasn't that long ago I thought Natalie was my first girlfriend, though she would have said otherwise. To her, the kissing and stuff we did when she was high was just messing around.

Simone's eyes widen. "I was innocent too. I didn't throw that egg at the cops' car. I was trying to get home with a bag of groceries for Mama. That's it."

I breathe in sharply. This poor baby got picked on even worse by the cops than me when all she was doing was living.

"Sucks," I say. "Bet someone else did it then ran and left you to get dragged off in cuffs, huh?"

"I guess." Simone looks away. "I didn't see who it was."

I nod. Have I said enough to make her trust me? I hope so. "Now," I say. "What is this about you going to grown-up prison?"

Simone swallows hard. "She signed my name," she whispers. "But they'll think it's me for real."

I squeeze her shoulder. "Signed where?" Simone shakes her head and I say, my voice low and urgent. "Simone. I can't help you if you don't tell me everything."

Simone bites her lip. Then she says, flatly, "Nurse."

I'm gonna have to drag this out of her one word at a time. "Something happened at the nurse?"

Simone nods. She makes a fist and sticks her thumb under two fingers. It's an ASL sign but I can't remember what letter it is. M? T? S?

What the hell is that supposed to mean?

"Simone," I say, trying to keep my voice even. "You gotta give me more than that, baby. I don't get it. Now what happened? "

The guard's voice comes loud and clear, cutting through the tension in the air. "Brianna Hunter."

Shit. That's me.

I don't know anything. They're making me miss my chance to get to the bottom of this shit for nothing.

But what choice do I have? I help Simone off my lap, stand slowly, and start to walk off.

All of the sudden, Simone throws herself at me so damn hard she almost knocks me over. I can feel her heart pounding hard as she clings to me, and when I hug her back, she's shaking.

She doesn't say a word but I know she's trying to scream, "*Don't tell. Please don't tell.*"

Dr. Osborne clears her throat so loud I flinch. "Simone. You can't do that, baby. Let her go." She looks me in my eyes. "You know the rules, Brianna. Please do not encourage this."

My throat tightens. Can't they see that Simone is terrified? But again, not up to me. I pull her off me as gently as I can. "I gotta go, Simone, okay? Hang in there."

Simone nods, but I can see how hard she's fighting tears.

I put my hands behind my back. I hate myself for it but what can I do? I just hope that if Security cuffs me, they have enough humanity to wait til I'm out of Simone's sight to do it.

I bow my head slightly as I follow Dr. Osborne to the hall where Security's waiting to take me to the office. Someone's eyes are on me the whole way and it doesn't hit me til Dr. Osborne hands me off to Security that it was Vanessa.

Her eyes hadn't just been on me, either. She'd kept glancing at Simone, then back at me. Am I crazy or was she actually... on Simone's side?

"I have to pat you down real quick," Security says, cutting into my thoughts. "Mrs. MacGregor's orders. Turn around, please."

I do as I'm told. I'm barely aware of Security pinning my arms behind my back while she pats down my shirt, my jeans pockets, my waistband. The sound of cuffs clicking around my wrists during my arrest echoes in my ears, competing with my thoughts about Vanessa.

"You're clean. Good. Let's go." Security puts her hand on my arm and leads me away. No cuffs, but she's in control anyway.

I argue with myself about Vanessa the whole way to the office so I won't freak out about what's about to happen to me.

five

SECURITY MAKES ME sit on the bench outside Mrs. MacGregor's office while she checks in. I put my hands in my lap and stare down at them, taking in every detail while I breathe in and out so I can try to clamp down the panic rising from my stomach. Staring at my long, thin fingers makes things worse cause now I keep feeling the weight of cuffs on my wrists while I remember how I heard one cop say to another after they made me hit the ground, "No burns on her hands. She's not using. What the hell?"

I take another breath and push it out hard while my throat tightens with anger that the cops couldn't figure out that me not using meant those drugs weren't mine.

Mrs. MacGregor's door creaks open. Ms. Carter sticks her head out and says, "Come on in, Brianna."

I half expect Security to be standing in the corner, watching, when I walk into the office, like they do on TV when someone's visited in jail. She's not there at all; I must have missed her leaving cause I was too wrapped up in my memories of getting arrested.

I sink into the chair in front of Mrs. MacGregor's desk. I feel like I've been sent to the principal in my old school. That only happened once, a few weeks before the cops got me, when she tried to talk to me about my slipping grades and what I was doing to my future.

I lift my head to look Ms. Carter in her eyes. How many times do I have to tell myself the pity party's over before it sinks in?

"Here," Ms. Carter says. "You're gonna need this cause you're gonna be doing a lot of talking." She hands me a water bottle.

I mumble, "Thanks." I put my hand around the bottle but don't open or drink. The plastic bottle is ice cold, so much so it burns my fingers, but somehow the icy feeling calms me.

Ms. Carter takes a seat next to Mrs. MacGregor, who is sitting with her hands folded on the desk.

"Remember what I told you earlier," Mrs. MacGregor says, her voice clipped. "The only thing that is important is the truth. One of your peers was seriously hurt tonight. So if there is anything you know about what happened to her, I hope you'll come forward about it."

Her eyes meet mine. I stare into them, refusing to blink first. If she's accusing me, she needs to come out and say it. "Any way I can help, I will," I say. "Did anyone shed any light on this already?"

"These conversations are confidential," Ms. Carter says. "So let's focus on what you can tell us."

So they're not gonna let anything slip. Got it.

Ms. Carter goes on, "I know you were helping Elizabeth set the table and then you sent her into the kitchen to get the salt. Was she gone an unusually long amount of time?"

Oh. So this is what we're doing — getting me to pin this on Elizabeth. Yeah, not happening. "Not any longer than it took you to kick Tasha and them out so it was safe for her to come back," I say coldly.

Ms. Carter and Mrs. MacGregor exchange glances. Was I too sharp for them? Too bad if I was. If they dealt with bullies the right way, I doubt we'd be in this mess.

"I know Ms. Carter sent you to get Elizabeth after she dealt with Tasha's misbehavior," Mrs. MacGregor says. "What did you see when you walked into the kitchen?"

I cross my arms. "Lots of things," I say. "There were a lot of people in there. Girls from other cohorts, too, running back and forth to the fridge. Ashley by the counter helping Elizabeth measure salt. Molly at the stove and Lisa doing salad."

"I see." Mrs. MacGregor makes a note on her pad. "Why was Elizabeth measuring salt? She was supposed to be on table duty."

"You'd have to ask her." I keep my voice even. They'd better stop pushing me about her. Elizabeth gets it even worse than Simone cause she's... different. She's never said it, so I don't want to assume she's autistic, but she's so much like Vicki I suspect it. Her brain gets stuck on something stupid and won't let go and sometimes I've caught her playing with a drawer, opening and closing it. I have a time trying to help her with her ELA homework, too cause she doesn't see the point to metaphors and spends the first hour of her study session complaining how she shouldn't have to read things that don't say what they mean. And worst of all, she and Vicki have in common trusting people they got no business trusting. "Lisa wanted it," I add bitterly. "She kept yelling for it even though all she had over there was salad."

"You're sure about that?" Ms. Carter asks. "That doesn't make any sense, Brianna."

"I heard what I heard and saw what I saw." I mean to keep my voice even, but it rises slightly. I don't like being gaslit.

"We're not saying you didn't," Ms. Carter says quickly, even though that's exactly what she said a second ago. She glances at her notes. "Wait... Ashley was with Elizabeth? So she wasn't at the stove watching her potatoes?"

Here we go. The real reason they brought me in here is so they can use me against Ashley. Well I'm not here for that. Ever. "Before you start making mountains out of molehills, that's cause she's got a big heart. She wanted to help Elizabeth measure real quick."

"So the answer is yes, then. The potatoes were left unattended." Mrs. MacGregor's voice is hard.

"Not entirely." I have to breathe hard through my nose to keep my voice from matching her accusatory tone. "Molly was at the next station, and she stirred it for her once in a while. Besides, she couldn't have been gone that long."

"Right." Mrs. MacGregor leans forward. "Tell me, Brianna. Are Ashley and Molly close?"

My heart pounds, half cause I don't like what she's insinuating and half cause the idea of Ashley being Molly's girl instead of mine hurts.

She calls Molly her best friend, but it's not like I don't know what that's code for, and it hurts twice as bad cause Molly didn't even stand up for her or check on her or anything. Where was she when Ashley needed her most?

"How should I know?" I say, my voice hard.

"You have eyes," Ms. Carter says softly. "You might have seen something." She sighs. "I know you have certain feelings..." She glances at Mrs. MacGregor and adds, quickly, "That are inappropriate to act on. But we need the truth, even if Ashley did something you wish she didn't."

I glare at her, trying to ignore the high pitched ringing in my ears. If I'm that obvious that the staff knows, no way Ashley doesn't.

"Ashley's not like that," I say, trying to keep the tremble out of my voice.

"Are you sure?" Ms. Carter's voice is still soft. "Can you look me in the eye and tell me that there is no possibility that Ashley asked Molly to stir peanut oil into the potatoes for her and Molly went along with it?"

My throat is so tight I can barely breathe. I lift my head as high as I can and look her in her eyes. "There's no possibility," I say, "and you're not gonna get me gossiping about someone I... about stuff I got no knowledge of."

Mrs. MacGregor turns a page in her notes. "You're right, Brianna. We shouldn't talk to you about Ashley. We need to talk about you."

"Me?" My heart pounds. Here it comes. The false accusation.

Ms. Carter sighs deeply. "Brianna," she says gently. "We know you took Elizabeth to the kitchen to snoop around after Mrs. MacGregor left the room. We heard it from at least one witness. So you really need — "

My head shoots up. "Who said?" I demand even though I'd bet anything the answer is *Molly*.

"That doesn't matter," Mrs. MacGregor says, her voice even, "and anyway, it's confidential. But you know what does matter, Brianna? You taking a younger resident into the kitchen when you knew neither of you should be there, and on top of that, lying to me about it. Yes, I was aware you two weren't merely clearing your plates. I had too much I needed to do to confront you then. But I am doing it now, and it would behoove you to tell me the truth. Why did you and Elizabeth go into the kitchen?"

My stomach tightens. I didn't make Elizabeth do anything. In fact, I tried to send her away and she wasn't having it. But if I keep the lie going, it's an out for her. It'd kill her to know it, but if I let them think I was Natalie 2.0, influencing innocent little Elizabeth to do the wrong thing, then I get all the punishment and she gets off scot-free. It's not fair, but at the same time, I can take it better than she can.

"I asked you a question, Brianna," Mrs. MacGregor says, "and I expect an answer. Why did you and Elizabeth go into the kitchen? And please have enough respect for me not to lie to my face."

A pulse starts up behind my eye on top of my throat being so tight I'm not sure anything will come out. "I wanted to find proof of who did this to Tasha."

Mrs. MacGregor's eyebrows shoot up. As much as she's been pushing for the truth, she obviously wasn't expecting me to actually tell it. "So you could clear Ashley's name," she says, and it's not a question. It's a statement of fact. "I am sure your motives were pure," she goes on, "but you have to realize how this may look to people who don't know you the way we do. The state could send inspectors, and at some point I may need to involve the police, and any of those people might see your behavior as an attempt at a coverup."

"That's called obstruction of justice," Ms. Carter adds, "and it's a very serious crime. That is why if you know anything about what Ashley or anyone else did, you have to tell us."

Crime. The word hits me hard. I brace myself, but the memory burns me before I have a chance to prep for it.

"Those drugs aren't mine, I swear they aren't! I didn't even know —"

"Out of the car! Hands where we can see them!" A dozen cops, all barking orders at once, like they just caught some gang leader with a thousand kills under her belt. "Show us your hands! Other side. Drop to one knee. Drop to both knees. Get on the ground! Hands behind your back!"

My heart pounds as I obey. Please God, don't let me have missed a step, not when I'm surrounded by a tight circle of cops, every one of them pointing a gun in my direction.

"Please," I whimper. "I didn't..."

"STOP RESISTING!"

A knee in my back, pinning me down, squashing me. Am I really unable to breathe or is it just fear they're gonna press the life out of me?

Cuffs clicking around my wrists. The cops fingers squeeze my elbows as they get me on my feet. "You're under arrest," one says, as if it's not obvious when the cuffs are so tight they cut into my skin and make my fingers tingle. He's triumphant, too, like he just won a big battle. "Let's go."

I bite my lip to force myself back to now. "I didn't..."

"We're aware," Mrs. MacGregor says, "but what you did do was break program rules." She takes the handbook off a shelf and opens it. "Read this aloud, please."

My heart's pounding so hard I can barely think but I have no choice. Mrs. MacGregor makes me read aloud a rule saying residents aren't allowed in the kitchen except if they're doing meal prep and another saying we're supposed to stay put during emergencies.

"So," Mrs. MacGregor says, leaning back. "You broke two very important rules, Brianna. Your presence in the kitchen was unauthorized, and this was minutes after a crime was committed in there. You also should not have gotten up from the table."

"I'm sure her intentions were good," Ms. Carter says. She leans forward. "You did this because of your feelings for Ashley, didn't you? You thought you'd show her how you feel about her by finding and eliminating any evidence against her, right?"

Always stay silent. They'll charge you if they want, but that doesn't mean you should make it easy for them. Auntie Nan's advice rings in my ears. I shrug, refusing to answer.

"If so, this is not the way to show your affection for her." Mrs. MacGregor sighs. "I don't want to have to do this, Brianna. You've been a model resident up until now. But the crime that was committed tonight doesn't mean we throw the rules out the window. If anything, you need to be more conscientious. So. I'm going to have to give you a written warning that you have seriously violated the rules and I am also going to have to confine you to your room for the evening."

"Serious?" I know I shouldn't say anything, but this is too ridiculous for words. All this cause I spent a minute in the kitchen.

Ms. Carter sighs. "You did lie to Mrs. MacGregor," she says softly. "That made it worse, Brianna."

"Precisely," Mrs. MacGregor says. She takes a paper out of a folder. She doesn't have to print it or anything, so obviously she decided she was going to punish me before I was ever called in here.

The paper says just what she said it would say, plus a warning that this is my first strike and if I get three I'm being taken in front of the board for an expulsion hearing.

Expelled. Sent to real juvie. My second chance gone.

Mrs. MacGregor takes a pen out of a cup on her desk. "Signing this doesn't mean you agree you're guilty," she says. "It just means you understand what we're telling you."

I squeeze the pen tight between two fingers, but I sign. There's no point in not. For all I know, it'll trigger that expulsion hearing right away.

No sooner have I signed than Security shows up to take me to my room for the night. I put my hands behind my back as I stand, but Ms. Carter says, "No need to stand at attention."

She glances at Mrs. MacGregor. Mrs. MacGregor's eyes are narrow, but she says, quietly, "Correct. We will trust you to cooperate with being escorted to your room. Please don't make me regret it."

My head is buzzing. I keep my hands behind my back the whole way to my room even though I don't have to cause I'm not convinced this isn't some kind of trick.

Locking me in is easy. Security lets me into the room by typing a code on the keypad outside the door and making me go in and close the door. I hear a few beeps and then the only thing I can do is rattle the doorknob cause I'm locked in.

I pace my room, feeling more and more like I'm back in one of the cells I was held in after my arrest. The room's not much of anything. A mattress and box springs in one corner, a desk and chair across from it. They gave me a laptop, too, but it's connected to their system, which means 99% of websites are banned and the ones left over are heavily monitored — any time I go online I have to click a thing saying I'm being watched, so the only site safe to access is the educational portal to do school online.

I pick up the photo from my desk and stare at it. It's my family's yearly Christmas photo, taken about a month before I was arrested. My arm's around Vicki and my other around her brother, Ken, who towers over all of us cause he's got a tall gene from somewhere the rest of us missed. Auntie Nan's behind us with her hands on our shoulders and Mom's on one side of her while Uncle Kevin's on the other. I'm smiling just as widely as the rest of them, but there's no light in my eyes and I can't help wondering if anyone else picked up on how miserable Natalie was making me.

I put the photo back, not wanting to think about that right now. I can't. I gotta figure out my next move. They locked me in here to waste my time, jailing me for the night cause I looked in the kitchen. What is it they're afraid I found there?

I grab a little notepad I was given for keeping track of school assignments and begin writing quickly, trying to remember everything I learned in the kitchen so my punishment will be worth it.

Let's see. Someone washed up in a hurry... there was still oil on the spoon... Ashley walked away to help Elizabeth with the salt... Molly watched the pot... Lisa making salad but wanted salt... Patrice came running in at the end and knocked Elizabeth down but Ashley helped her up...

I stare at my notes. Ashley's being framed, isn't she? She had to leave her area to help Elizabeth with the salt, and again when Patrice knocked Elizabeth down. So did someone use Elizabeth to get her away from the pot? Who? And did they poison the potatoes while her back was turned?

Elizabeth. She has to be scared to death, alone in the day room or maybe being interrogated, not knowing where I am or why I abandoned her.

I blink back tears. No time for that — I gotta come up with a plan, and quick.

I still have my copy of the written warning on me. I start to crumple it up, then stop. Something tells me I need this.

I bend over it, reading it again. And that's when it hits me:

This was all planned. Whoever went right before me snitched about the kitchen and that's why I was called in next.

I got the message loud and clear even though I can't remember who the snitch is. Back off, or we'll get you expelled.

I won't back off. I can't.

But I need a backup plan, people I can trust to keep things going if I'm locked up like this again. Even if the worst happens and I'm expelled. I could get through freaking juvie if I knew people were still trying their best over here to find out who did this to Tasha.

So... who do I ask? Molly rides with Lisa — at least, that's how it seems — and I don't trust either of them. Vanessa's a loudmouth and a bully. Ashley's already given up. And I don't know any of the other girls my age in our cohort well enough to bring this to them.

No, it's got to be Elizabeth and Simone. They may be the smallest girls here, but the three of us were all dragged off in cuffs for someone else's crimes.

Simone. She said she's being framed too.

And I'm locked up til morning now, so I can't help her.

If they find whatever it is that was planted to prove she was involved, sweet little Simone's gone, sent somewhere where she can't possibly survive.

I can't let that happen.

I gotta get out of here, but how?

The chair's attached to a slider on the floor so I can pull it out to sit but I can't lift it, not that it matters. The windows are high up and probably made of shatterproof glass so I'm not getting out that way. The only way out's through the door, which is just as locked as it was when Security put me in here.

I kick the bedframe with all my might. If this was a movie, a key would come flying out, but this is real life, so all I get is a sore foot and Security warning me over the intercom to cut it out.

They designed these rooms to hold people indefinitely. The only way I get free is if they let me out.

My foot's throbbing now, and for what?

I sink into my bed, but only for long enough to ease the pain. It's not broken, and anyway, it's my own fault, kicking the bed cause I got mad. I grab my paper and write at the top: *No losing control. No self-pity.*

I'm in a war now. Truth and justice vs. lies and violence. I never had much use for those superhero movies, but I wish I'd watched them now, cause I could use a crash course in how to become one.

Across the hall, soft footsteps sound and I hear a voice say, tearfully, "I didn't do anything, I swear." Then Security, a male one, says, "Just get in the room, kid. Mrs. MacGregor said you have to stay there all night, so that's how it is."

I stiffen. They got Ashley. Please tell me it's not cause of anything I said.

Wait... that's not her, is it? Nah, couldn't be. She was taken for questioning before me. No way they're first getting around to punishing her now.

Whatever. Whether that's Ashley or not, we're in this together, locked up for something we didn't do just like when I was arrested. I wish our rooms were connected by a vent so I could tell her to hold on cause I got her back.

Elizabeth pops into my mind all of a sudden, taking the gloves before we snoop around. Girl is SMART in a way people don't expect. That makes her the perfect one to take on this investigation.

Except... except the only reason she was in that kitchen is cause she would have gone into a full–blown tantrum if I didn't let her, and that would have ruined everything.

But maybe that was more calculated than I thought. Maybe she's as determined as me to find the truth and if I wasn't gonna let her help, she was gonna force her way in.

I jump up and write something on my notepad, quick, and then pull off the paper and stuff it in my jeans pocket. No... better get in pajamas, cause when they let me out in the morning if they see me in yesterday's clothes I'm cooked.

Gotta play the game, or at least make them think I'm going along. Gotta stay free as long as possible even though I know sooner or later, they'll lock me up again cause I'm getting too close to truths they don't want exposed.

I hurry to change into my program-issued Tiger Cohort t-shirt and plaid pajama pants and put my clothes in the laundry hamper even though I feel like throwing them on the floor.

Then I grab the note I just wrote for Elizabeth and put it in my pajama pants.

The next morning, I jerk awake when Security knocks on doors all along my hall, yelling, "Wake-up call! Up and at 'em!" The back of my neck's throbbing, making my head hurt, which means I barely slept last night. I used to get headaches like this all the time when I was first sent here, so I know exactly what they mean.

I rub the spot where my neck turns into my head to try to soothe the pain. Hopefully there's hot water when I get called for my shower, not that I'll be allowed to stay in it for any too long.

I get my things together anyway, checking to make sure I didn't lose that note for Elizabeth.

There's a knock on the door, but it's not Security — it's Ms. Carter.

I freeze as she calls, "Brianna? Are you awake?" I don't know if this is better or worse than Security coming to let me out.

"Y-yes, ma'am," I say, shoving my hands in my pockets to feel for the note. Each word makes my head feel worse and my cheeks tighten like I'm gonna puke.

No. I can't afford to be sick. I breathe in hard to keep the nausea at bay.

"Come on out then," Ms. Carter says. "I've re-activated your door lock."

I do as I'm told. Ms. Carter's face is drawn and tight and there is weariness in her eyes. Guess I'm not the only one who was up most the night. She gives me a sad smile as I slide out of the room.

"You need to search me or something?" I ask, then wish I hadn't. I don't need to put ideas in her head when I got that note on me.

Ms. Carter shakes her head slightly. "I think you've learned your lesson." She lowers her voice slightly and says, "Be smart. Don't get caught again."

I stare at her. It sounds to me like she's telling me to go behind Mrs. MacGregor's back to do what I need to do, but that can't be right.

She's on their side, not mine. What kind of trick is this?

"You all find who poisoned Tasha?" I ask, careful to keep my voice neutral.

"Not yet." Ms. Carter sighs. "I'm glad you stood up for your friends last night. I'd hate to see someone innocent get blamed.

My head shoots up straighter, making the pain worse. I rub the spot on the back of my neck hard. "So you know Ashley..."

"I do not believe it's her, no." Ms. Carter keeps her voice low. "But I stand by what I said. I don't care how you feel about Ashley, but you cannot afford to act without thinking, no matter how badly you want to help her." She pats my shoulder. "Go take your shower while I tell Mrs. MacGregor I spoke with you and confirmed you understand what you did wrong."

My head pounds twice as bad as she walks down the hall. I don't believe for a second Ashley's off the hook. And no way is she any more okay with me liking another girl than she was last night.

No, this was a warning. Stop stepping out of line or we'll pin it on Ashley... or maybe on you.

Yet that doesn't feel right.

It's like... a warning... but... somehow it feels like she wants me to do better at not getting caught so I can do her job for her and get the real poisoner.

But why would she risk her job to encourage me to keep breaking the rules? That can't be. She's staff, and that means she's looking for ways to control me... doesn't it?

My head's killing me. No way I can figure this out now.

I run to the bathroom, praying the pain doesn't get so bad it makes me puke.

The bathroom's empty for once, so I got my pick of shower stalls. Four of them when we got 20 girls in Tiger Cohort alone, so usually there's a line and some people everyone's scared not to let cut ahead.

I could go for the one closest to the door but that's got the most risk of someone seeing me without anything on when I step in or out, and I know the other girls are coming. I go to the furthest one so I can have a little crumb of privacy.

I'm quick but careful as I undress, putting my pajama bottoms furthest from the shower so that note can't get wet. I'd hoped to slip it under Elizabeth's door before I got started but Ms. Carter distracted me so now I gotta live with the risk.

The shower's too loud. Stepping in is like standing in the ocean with water roaring in your ears. Most days I can take it but today it's just making me sicker, canceling out any good the hot water's doing for my head. The water's only lukewarm at best, too. It's better than ice cold, but still.

Girls' voices fill the room but the sound of the water muffles them. Better hurry up and get out so I can dress with my back to them and get that note on its way while everyone's in here.

The other showers turn on, making my head pound even worse. Two voices come from far away, too quiet for me to make out much of what's being said. They're whispering, don't want to be heard.

I turn off the water but don't get out yet even though as soon as it's off, cold air hits my bare skin. I reach for my towel and close the door again, hugging myself while I try to listen.

"Some leader." It sounds like Ashley's voice.

"[muffle muffle]... switching sides." It's one of the white girls. Maybe Molly, maybe Lisa.

"[muffle]... to tell you..."

"[muffle]...cut...[muffle]"

Someone whimpers, I think, but I can't be sure.

By the time I step out, Ashley's standing by herself by the sink. She's staring at the floor, blinking back tears.

I hurry to get dressed. I can already hear the rumors starting about me trying to get her to see what I got under my towel.

My pajama shirt is damp cause it's too close to the shower, but whatever. The wetness isn't too bad, and I'm about to change into my day clothes anyway.

"Ashley?" I whisper. I want to ask her what's wrong. I want to hold her like I held Simone yesterday. But when she looks up, her cheeks darkening, I can't make myself do it. I'm frozen with fear of what she'd say and what would happen to me if someone's spying from one of the other shower stalls.

I say only, "Shower's free. Go ahead and take it."

Ashley gives me a watery smile. "Thanks." As she moves toward the shower she says, "Hey, Bri?"

I turn back toward her. "What's up?"

"Thanks for believing in me. Keep doing it no matter what you hear, alright?"

Her eyes are almost as wide as Natalie's were when she was all messed up on cocaine. I let my breath out slowly. Ashley's sober, of course. Can't get drugs in here, just like I can't get Natalie in here.

"Course," I say softly. "I know who you are."

My heart pounds. Has she heard my silent *I love you*?

My chest aches for her as she gives me a sad smile and mumbles, "You don't, but it's a nice thought."

She pushes past me before I can ask her what that's supposed to mean. I glance her way, then away. She's getting undressed and I can't let myself see her naked backside.

Ashley slips into the shower and slams the door closed. I stare at the closed stall.

I still don't think she did it, but it's obvious my girl's in trouble, and I can't promise I can fix it before it's too late.

After I'm ready to meet the day, I line up for breakfast with everyone else, but the door to the dining room is locked when we get there.

Elizabeth pushes through the crowd to get to me while someone tries the door. She throws herself at me, hugging me tight. "The rumors were false," she says. "Everyone said you were arrested last night."

"Nah." I try to keep it casual even though my stomach does flip-flops at the thought of what the administration could do to me if I'm not careful. I lower my voice. "You get my note?"

Elizabeth nods. "I didn't understand what you meant about the game still being on," she whispers. "You mean like chess?"

Crap. I forgot how literal minded she can be. "I meant it as a figure of speech," I whisper back. I can feel Vanessa's eyes on my back; I put my hand on Elizabeth's shoulder and steer her away a little in the hopes that it discourages Vanessa spying on us, and beckon to Simone to join us.

Simone comes over slowly. "W-we should stay lined up. This might be a test."

I shrug. "I'm not caring about their tests anymore. Listen, both of you." I hesitate, trying to find the exact right words. I pretend I'm talking to Vicki — please, God, let her never find herself in a place like this no matter what stupid thing she does — so I can figure out what to say. My head aches worse than ever and all I can get out is, "The people in charge of this place don't care who really hurt Tasha. They want to punish someone, that's all."

Simone gulps but says nothing.

I turn toward her. " You're gonna need to tell me what the real poisoner has on you," I tell her, "and if not me, tell Elizabeth."

Simone blinks back tears. "I don't want to go to real prison."

“I'm trying to keep you out of it, don't you get that?"

Simone flinches. I rub the back of my neck, feeling bad. I didn't raise my voice that much, did I? "Look, did you tell your lawyer everything when you were arrested?"

"I did," Elizabeth says, even though I wasn't talking to her, "and she said I should come here instead of regular juvie and my parents thought it was a great idea." She scuffs her shoes on the tiled floor.

"They were sold a lie," I tell her. "My mom too, even though I got a lawyer for an aunt who could have pushed harder for me than she did." The heaviness in my chest is so crushing I have to grab onto something to stop myself doubling over. I breathe through it, praying it's not my heart giving out. "Point is, you tell a lawyer everything and they have to keep it to themselves. Think of me that way, Simone." I rub my temples. Am I making sense? I can't tell.

"Okay," Simone says, her voice very quiet. Her eyes dart around the room, then back to me, and she lowers her voice to a whisper. "I-I saw someone take Tasha's Epi-Pen and I didn't tell. That makes me an accomplice." She looks down at her feet as she takes a step back, hugging herself.

"Nah." I rub my neck again. Something isn't adding up, but I can't think. "You can still fix it. Who did you see do it?"

Simone's eyes dart around again. Instead of answering, she makes a bunch of signs with her fingers, lightning fast. Between her speed and the way my head's killing me, all I get is that she made the same first sign yesterday.

"You should go to the nurse," Elizabeth says as I rub the back of my neck again. "You're sick."

Simone's eyes widen at the word 'nurse.' What's that about?

"Just a headache," I say. I turn slowly toward Simone, testing how it affects my head. I feel slightly nauseous, but it passes. "Something happened when you went there, though, right?"

Simone nods. She starts to sign again, but I grab her hand. "I can't understand that. Use words."

Simone freezes. She pulls away and says, "Can't. They're watching." She makes that same sign she did last night, for a third time.

I look around. There are girls all over the place, so I don't know who she means. Has to be Vanessa, right? That girl is always staring at me.

But when I ask her, Simone shakes her head slightly. She makes a thumb and finger that even I can understand.

L? For Lisa?

Lisa's not anywhere nearby. She's all the way over on the other side of the room talking to some girl from a different cohort. She turns as I glance at her. Her eyes are a piercing, unnatural shade of blue that doesn't go with her dark hair properly. One or the other is fake.

My head hurts worse than ever. I rub my neck as the dining room door creaks open.

Everyone starts pushing to get in the room at once. Mrs. MacGregor blocks the door, her hands on her hips. "This is not how we enter a room," she says firmly. "Anyone who is not lined up with their cohort will not get breakfast until they correct their behavior."

All the whispering stops as suddenly as if someone flipped a switch to make the room soundproof.

Simone shrinks back as Lisa and Molly push their way into line in front of us. "T-told you," she says under her breath as she lines up behind Elizabeth.

I put my hands behind my back, standing at attention like I'm supposed to while I wait for permission to come in, but I can't help glaring at the butterfly tattoo on the back of Lisa's neck. Mom would be disgusted by how much I hate this girl — she's big on never using that word — but everything about Lisa makes me want to shove her into the girl in front of her.

"Tiger Cohort may enter," Mrs. MacGregor says, interrupting my angry thoughts.

As we come in, another woman stands behind her, watching. The stranger is a white woman with long, reddish-brown hair. She's young, not much older than me, I'd guess. She smiles at us and says, "Hello."

"Girls, this is Inspector Goodwin," Mrs. MacGregor says. "She is observing us from the Department of Health."

Department of Health. Shit.

My stomach does flip-flops. One time they closed the coffee shop next to my old high school cause there were roaches in the kitchen area.

That's what these people do, right? Close things down?

"Go ahead and do what you normally do," Inspector Goodwin says. "Pretend I'm not here."

Nope. Can't do that. I need to talk to her. There's something she knows that I need to know, except I can't get exactly what it is cause my head's pounding. Besides, I can't approach her with Mrs. MacGregor standing right there. I don't need to burn through my written warnings in record time.

I hurry to wash my hands and go to my spot for breakfast.

Everyone has a to-go box at their space at the table with their name on it. The box is white but it's got a stripe with blue and yellow lettering.

Pancakes'N'More! Excitement shoots through me for a second, but then my stomach sinks. This isn't like when the whole family would pile into the car to go for Sunday breakfast and the hostess would make sure to get us a table in a quieter room with lower lights so Vicki could tolerate being there. I was able to get whatever I wanted then, but here, no one even asked me before they went ahead and ordered for us. Bet everyone has the same thing.

Besides, if they're ordering food in on a school day, it's gotta be cause that health person up there already shuttered the kitchen.

"No school today, girls," Ms. Carter says, as if she's read my mind.

"After breakfast, everyone's got to do their part to clean up and then you girls will do online lessons while we continue talking to some of you about what happened last night."

Simone gulps. "D-do you think they checked the nurse's records yet?" she whispers as she opens her to-go box. The sweet smell of pancakes makes my stomach growl, but it also makes my head ache worse.

"What are you afraid they'll find?" I ask her.

Simone looks away. "It wasn't me. They signed my name." She picks up her carton of chocolate milk, but her little fingers are shaking too much to open it.

I get the carton for her and hand it back to her. "Signed it to what?" I whisper.

Ms. Carter clears her throat. "Too much whispering on that side of the table. Brianna, come sit up here by me, please."

Elizabeth's head jerks up. "But Brianna is supposed to sit next to me!"

Ms. Carter sighs. "I know it's hard for you to accept change, Elizabeth," she says quietly, "but Brianna needs to sit wherever I tell her to sit, and today, I need her next to me."

Elizabeth's face trembles. "Brianna's seat is next to mine."

Morgan and Patrice snicker. I put my hand on Elizabeth's shoulder and whisper, "You'd better start counting your breaths or something. I need you free to help me investigate, not locked in your room for something this dumb."

"I'm not stupid," Elizabeth says, blinking hard.

"I know that. I'm saying — "

"Brianna," Ms. Carter interrupts. "I asked you to come here. Please do not make me repeat myself."

Damn it. Elizabeth needs me, but if I don't walk away now, it's game over. I don't need a second written warning any more than she needs the first, so I pat her shoulder and say, "Eat up," before I get to my feet.

My ears are ringing and I'm not dizzy exactly, but I'm a little more than lightheaded, and the fact that Morgan and Patrice's laughter is loud enough to hear all the way across the dining room doesn't help.

Vanessa glares at the two of them and they cut it out.

What?

Okay, I must be hallucinating cause of my headache, cause there's no way Vanessa just stood up for Elizabeth.

I throw myself into my seat next to Ms. Carter, feeling so sick I can't even enjoy being next to Ashley. She makes it worse, in fact, cause knowing she's nearby makes me break into a sweat.

"This is not a smart way to investigate," Ms. Carter says under her breath. "You need to..." She frowns. "Are you feeling all right?"

I shake my head. "Bad headache," I mumble, praying the tears stay in my eyes. All I need is Vanessa and them seeing me crying over a little headache.

Ms. Carter puts her hand on my forehead. "Not warm." she says. "But nevertheless, I'll get Dr. Osborne so I can take you to the nurse."

"I don't need — "

"Yes, you do," Ms. Carter says firmly. "You're clearly ill." She takes out her walkie talkie.

I slump forward in my seat. The only good thing about going to the nurse is I can find out what Simone was talking about. Maybe.

I wish I was faking to get in to investigate, though. Ashley's eyes are on my back and I can't stop thinking she sees me as weak.

Tears pop into my eyes that I know better than to let fall.

Dr. Osborne comes over and touches my head too. "Eh," she says. "Maybe slightly feverish."

"I don't have a fever," I say. "You all need to stop babying me." I look away, realizing too late I could get told off or worse for my disrespect. Maybe they'll chalk it up to me being sick. Please?

Sure enough, Ms. Carter says to Dr. Osborne, quietly, "Let it go. She's unwell, of course she's not at her best." She helps me to my feet. "Come, Brianna."

Dr. Osborne gives me a slight smile that is totally fake. "Feel better, soon, Brianna."

Like she actually cares.

As long as I'm up, I might as well try to catch the inspector's attention. I don't know what I'm going to say, but it's probably my only chance to say it so I'd better figure it out. I take a step in her direction.

"This way, Brianna," Ms. Carter says, putting her arm around me and gently steering me the other way.

I have to let her. I don't have the energy to pull away.

I turn my head over my shoulder, trying to get Elizabeth's attention. I know I'm not being arrested again, but it sure feels like it and she needs to know to take over.

six

NURSE WILKINS DOESN'T DO MUCH. She takes my temperature with an ear thermometer and asks me where the head pain is worst. "Your teeth hurt too?" she asks. "Any sore throat?"

She makes me tilt my head back so she can shove a q-tip up my nose to check for COVID.

As if. I get these headaches when I don't sleep enough. It's like clockwork. Less than six hours, I wake up with an unwanted visitor.

I try to tell her that, but she says, "We have to check. It's a health risk."

Translation: If that health inspector comes in here I want to be able to say I'm more careful about COVID than I really am.

It's all BS, but that doesn't mean I can breathe easy the whole 15 minutes I'm waiting for the test to come up negative. I've never once caught COVID even though Natalie used to make me take off my N-95 around her cause she said it was dumb to be scared. But in here we're not allowed masks unless we're already sick so I could have picked up anything.

"Not COVID, and not flu either," Nurse Wilkins says when the timer finally beeps. "Your temperature's normal. Maybe a cold, maybe a sinus infection..."

"Or maybe lack of sleep," I say, annoyed. How many times do I have to say it? "And if you think it's a sinus infection, why aren't I getting antibiotics?"

"We'd have to get you to the doctor for that," Nurse Wilkins says. "Let's try ibuprofen and some more rest first — if we can take care of this in-house, that saves everyone trouble."

So the thing I said I needed in the first place. Good thing I'm not actually sick if this is how they do things. I watch the nurse unlock the medicine cabinet, annoyed they lock up ibuprofen when you can get it over the counter in the outside world.

"That where you keep Epi-Pens too?" I ask, rubbing my temples.

Nurse Wilkins freezes. "Why are you asking about Epi-Pens?" She glances down at my chart on her tablet. "You don't have any allergies as far as I can see."

"I don't." I wince as a wave of head pain hits me. "Some girls are saying Ashley dagged her feet getting one from Tasha, but not me." My heart pounds. This convo isn't private regardless of confidentiality laws. 10 to 1 she snitches to Ms. Carter word-for-word when they've already made it clear me crushing on Ashley is against their rules.

Nurse Wilkins pushes her hair behind her ear. "So that's why you really came in here. I'm sorry, Brianna, but I can't really explain this. The program lawyer has advised me it's best to leave it alone."

Lawyer. So the program's already covering its behind. "Tasha's suing?"

"We hope not. That's what we're trying to prevent." The nurse pats my hand. "You're already sick. You don't need to make yourself worse worrying about this. If we all play our cards right, this program will stay open." She opens the bottle of ibuprofen and puts two pills in a little cup. "You'll need a second dose at dinnertime. I'll make sure someone gives it to you then. Sign the medication log and I'll give you this, okay?"

She signed my name.

I stiffen. Simone was talking about this log.

Nurse Wilkins opens a binder. There's a thick paper clipped to it that has a slit in it over a blank entry in the log. I try to slide it up to see what Simone supposedly signed for, but Nurse Wilkins puts her hand over the clip and says, "I can't let you do that. It's a violation of someone else's medical privacy."

Like they care about privacy. It's a violation of their desire not to get sued, nothing less. My head pounds and it takes everything not to be sick right here all over the log.

I breathe in sharply and let it go before I sign. "Do I come back here for a second dose later?"

"I'll send a note to your case manager to get it and give it to you. It's just ibuprofen." Nurse Wilkins hands me my pills and a cup of water. "Here you go."

"Case manager?" That's Ms. Carter, who I don't want involved in my medical care any more than she has to be. I take the pills. "Can't a friend do it?"

Nurse Wilkins frowns. "We're not really supposed to..."

"Like you said, it's just ibuprofen." I cross my arms, trying to decide whether to level with her or not. "Look," I say under my breath, my heart pounding so hard I think I might faint. "I have reason to believe someone signed out an Epi-Pen and used my friend's name."

Nurse Wilkins' eyes widen but she says, "That didn't happen."

"Maybe not, but if she comes gets my meds and there are two signatures — "

"Sorry to interrupt you, Brianna, but that's impossible. We don't just hand out Epi-Pens. We check IDs."

I stare at her. "The night nurse too?"

Nurse Wilkins fiddles with a lock of hair. "Of course," she says, smiling nervously. "She knows the rules. Now do me a favor and keep this crackpot theory to yourself before you start rumors that get us shut down." She snaps the log closed. "I never told you this, but ibuprofen isn't like an Epi-Pen. It's over the counter. Any girl who comes in with mild pain can get some, no questions asked unless there's some medical reason she can't tolerate it."

"Got it," I say flatly. My head's starting to clear, but it's not all the way there yet, and my brain still feels like it's wrapped in gauze. Is the nurse helping me or setting up some new trap?

"Here." Nurse Wilkins hands me a mask. I'm glad it at least looks like an N-95. I wouldn't trust this place not to stick to those paper masks that are worse than useless to save money. "In case you're contagious," she says. "Wear it except for meals."

I'm not contagious but N-95s are like gold to me. I put the mask on, wishing I could ask Mom if it's safe to wear more than once. I used to change mine out twice a day at school.

Nurse Wilkins watches to make sure I put the mask on before she sends me to get Ms. Carter. As I turn toward the door, I notice a disposal box mounted on the wall, white with a slot in it for getting rid of needles and stuff and a sticker on it warning it's got biohazards in it.

I put my eye up against the slot, trying to see inside.

There's a needle that's been disposed of with the cap still on tight. Wait... that's the missing Epi-Pen, right? It's gotta be cause what else would someone trash without bothering to uncap it? Besides, the one the medics used on Tasha looked like that, as far as I remember.

So you're telling me someone signed out the Epi-Pen and tossed it not more than a few feet away and the night nurse didn't scc a thing?

Nurse Wilkins says, "I asked you to step out and get Ms. Carter. Are you going to do what you're told or do I have to get Security in here to get you to move?"

Message received loud and clear: stop sticking your nose in this or you're going down.

"No, I'm going," I say. "I just — "

"Go, then," the nurse says firmly. "Final warning."

I hurry out of the room, my heart pounding.

I'm onto something major. But the biggest question is whether Nurse Wilkins is only covering her ass cause of possible lawsuits or cause she's part of something she shouldn't be.

Ms. Carter takes half a second to ask how I'm feeling before she goes to see Nurse Wilkins. Supposedly the nurse is updating her on my treatment plan, but who do they think they're kidding? She's snitching, no doubt about it.

Sure enough, when Ms. Carter comes out, she says quietly, "Nurse Wilkins cannot talk to you about the Epi-Pen, and you should not have asked."

She gestures with her head for me to follow her back toward the dining room. I resist the temptation to put my hands behind my back as

I walk. As much as I hated Tasha before her poisoning, now I think she got one thing right: all this standing at attention and acting like prisoners just gives the staff power over us they don't deserve.

As we walk down the hall, Ms. Carter continues to speak so low I have to strain my ears to hear her. "You have to understand, Brianna," she says, "that if you go too far, I won't be able to protect you. Mrs. MacGregor agrees with me that it would be a travesty of justice for you to go to juvenile detention. But this situation has put the program under a microscope, and if you become a liability for us, she will have no choice."

My throat tightens. "So she'll just throw me away?"

Ms. Carter sighs. "No, Brianna, but if you go about this the wrong way you will throw away your own future. Look, Mrs. MacGregor likes you. So do I. But if we're shut down, every girl in here goes to juvenile detention, at least temporarily until another placement can be found. So one girl locked up versus every girl in the program..."

I swallow hard. How can Ms. Carter stand here and tell me that it's not how I think and then in the next breath confess Mrs. MacGregor would have me locked up over nothing and tell herself it's for the good of the program? She doesn't give a damn about me. Nobody in this stupid program does. All they care about is covering their asses so they don't get sued, and if sending me to juvie when they know damn well I never did what I was arrested for in the first place does the trick, so be it. "So I'm expendable," I say, trying to keep the tears out my voice. "Got it."

"No. You are not. But you have to tread very lightly because of the politics involved. Now why were you asking her for Simone to — "

Elizabeth comes flying out of the dining room. "Good, you're back," she says.

Ms. Carter says, quietly, "Elizabeth. You're interrupting."

"It's an emergency!" Elizabeth says. "Simone is missing!"

seven

MS. CARTER STIFFENS but I don't trust it. Don't try to tell me she cares about Simone when we all know it's how this looks to the health inspector that's bothering her.

I turn toward Elizabeth, not wanting to look that ugly woman in the eyes another second. "Where'd you last see her?"

Elizabeth rocks back and forth, hugging herself. "Dr. Osborne sent her to get a rag and spray for our table and she never came back. And when Dr. Osborne asked if anyone knew why she's taking so long, Lisa said she saw her go in the bathroom. Dr. Osborne thinks she's taking long cause it's her period, but Lisa's lying. I know it."

"Calm down, Elizabeth," Ms. Carter says softly. "Lisa might be right. I'll go check the bathroom and make sure Simone isn't sick." She turns and walks away.

I put my hands on Elizabeth's shoulders. "I'll go check the closet. You wait for me in the dining room, all right?"

Elizabeth starts to follow me, but I say firmly, "I said wait here. If Simone's hurt she doesn't need a big audience."

Elizabeth's face crumples but she mumbles, "Okay."

No time to feel bad for hurting her feelings. I take off running in the direction of the supply closet.

Vanessa's squatting by the closet door. She turns as I come down the hall. "You better know this code," she says, gesturing toward the keypad. "Your little one is locked inside."

I stiffen. What did she do to Simone?

"I don't," I say. "Only staff." I turn toward the door. "Simone? Don't panic, alright?"

"B-brianna?" Simone sniffs.

"I'm right here," I tell her. "I just gotta figure out how to get this door open." I stare at the keypad. It's the same as the one for my room, which has nine numbers and a four digit code. I can't remember how you calculate how many possible combinations there are, but I'm sure it's a crazy big number that would keep us guessing for days unless we get real lucky.

I have an idea, though. I take my resident ID card out and touch it against the scanner by the keypad. But it flashes red and buzzes.

Damn it. You probably need to be a staff member to override the keypad.

"I thought of the same thing," Vanessa says. "Mine wasn't accepted either." She frowns as she stares at the keypad. "Wait...," she says, and takes a hairpin out of her hair and sticks it in a little hole on the bottom of the keypad.

I stare at her as she jiggles it. I'm about 99 percent sure she's not allowed to have hairpins. Pretty much anything sharp is banned, though we're allowed to use scissors at the art table in the day room.

"Careful," I say under my breath. "If Ms. Carter catches you with that..."

Vanessa laughs. "You think I care what any of those bitches say the rules are?" She jiggles the hairpin again. The lock suddenly flashes green.

"There," she says, and turns the doorknob.

It takes a sec for the automatic lights in the supply closet to turn on, but when they do, there's Simone, pressed against a shelf, hugging her knees to her chest.

"It's alright, *hermanita*," Vanessa says. "Come out."

Simone blinks. I hold my hand out and she takes it and lets me pull her up.

Ms. Carter comes down the hall. "Bathroom's empty," she tells me. "I hope —" She freezes. "Simone? What happened?"

"She was locked in here is what!" I say.

Simone sniffs. "It was an accident," she whispers. "I must have kicked the doorstop without realizing it and the door slammed shut behind me."

My eyes dart toward Vanessa's. She nods slightly.

She's not buying this either.

"I see," Ms. Carter says. "And you girls knew the code to get it open?"

I bite my lip. Vanessa gets away with way too much. But she used her powers for good for once. Besides, I'm no snitch and never have been.

"We made a lucky guess," I say. "I thought we were gonna be here til this time tomorrow."

Ms. Carter turns toward Vanessa who says, "Brianna should buy a lottery ticket next time we go to the gas station. She struck lightning with the code."

I hold my breath. If Ms. Carter asks me to repeat the digits I used, we're cooked. But she just says, "That is very lucky for everyone. Be more careful, please, Simone. And all of you, take a moment to center yourselves, but then I need you back in the dining room, okay?"

Simone nods. Ms. Carter walks off and then I say under my breath, "That was no accident, was it?"

Simone shakes her head. "I had to lie," she said, "cause otherwise it'll be worse."

Vanessa and I exchange glances. Again.

Simone says, quickly, "It wasn't her." She swallows hard. "A bad girl whispered, 'This is what you get for not keeping your mouth shut' and then she slammed the door closed."

Vanessa's jaw tightens. "Who? Tell me so I can beat them up."

Simone swallows hard. "I-I can't."

Vanessa squats. "Listen to me. No one will hurt you if they have to go through me."

Simone sighs deeply. She makes one of her signs again, but I can't see her hand cause Vanessa's in my way. It's gotta be one she's made before, though. L for Lisa? Or one of the signs I can't recognize?

Vanessa nods. "Come, little one," she says. "Walk with your head held high, show your enemy that you are not afraid."

Something ugly burns through me. I should be the one to tell Simone how to protect herself, not Vanessa. Simone doesn't need to learn how to act like someone who belongs behind bars.

I push that aside. I don't have time to be jealous right now. Besides, Vanessa's right. Simone can't afford to show fear, and doing the opposite will piss off whoever hurt her so they show themselves.

As we walk back, I say to Vanessa under my breath, "You mean it about protecting her?"

"Si," Vanessa says. "If you are willing to pay for my help." She smirks.

I cross my arms. "Serious? So if I don't do what you want you'll let Simone — "

Vanessa sighs deeply. "I wish it was different. But nothing is free in this world, and the sooner you learn this, the less danger you're in." She blinks hard, like she's near tears. But I gotta be imagining that. Vanessa doesn't cry.

Sure enough, her jaw is tight when I look again and she says, "I'll tell you later how you can pay for my services for your little one."

She flips her hair over her shoulder and walks off, making it clear she doesn't want to be seen with me and Simone.

My stomach does flip flops. What the hell have I gotten myself into?

Vanessa keeps me on tenterhooks all morning. I catch her shooting sly little glances at me while I'm eating the cold pancakes I didn't get to have when they were warm and fresh and after while I'm sweeping the floor.

Simone won't leave my side, either. She keeps following me around and half-heartedly wiping down the tables when I tell her to, but more often than not I catch her staring into space and twisting her rag.

My eyes keep darting from her to the adults. Simone needs something I can't give, but if they catch her not doing her part, they won't get that she's scared to death. They'll punish her, and maybe me too for not making her work harder.

"Simone," I whisper. "You gotta put getting stuck in the closet aside. It's over."

Simone shakes her head. "It's never over," she says flatly.

I pretend to be handing her the broom so I can take her hands. "It will be soon," I say firmly. "When you get me my pills from the nurse — "

Simone's gasps. "The nurse? But..."

"Listen to me," I whisper. I squeeze her hands. "Soon as you get those pills, they got two signatures. The fake one and the real. It'll prove you didn't sign anything last night."

Simone nods, but I can tell from how wide her eyes are she doesn't believe me. My eyes dart to Vanessa, then away. I know without a doubt that whatever she's gonna make me do, I'm gonna have to do it. I can't let Simone go on like this. "I got something else in the works to make sure you don't get hurt again."

Simone bites her lip. "What?"

I sigh. "Let's just say I'm about to make a deal with the devil."

"Oh, no," Simone says. "What are — "

"Simone and Brianna," Ms. Carter interrupts. "More working, less talking, please."

I hand Simone the broom for real. "Sweep up for me, okay? I gotta do something real quick."

I hurry across the room, praying she doesn't follow me.

Vanessa's standing over Morgan, who is wiping down another table, and watching with her arms crossed. "You'd better put more elbow grease in it," she says. "This little wipe does nothing."

I clear my throat. "Sorry to interrupt. Um, can we talk?"

Vanessa's eyes narrow. "If you want this one, you can have her. She's going to drag us all down being so lazy."

Morgan's eyes narrow and she clenches her rag tightly while Vanessa gestures with her head for me to follow her to an empty corner.

"You're sure hard on Morgan," I say, ignoring my heart pounding.

"That one," Vanessa says, "is on punishment with me."

I raise my eyebrows. "Why?"

"Crew business," Vanessa says, "which means it is not yours, but I will say that trying to be loyal to two sides at once is a recipe for disaster." She crosses her arms. "If you came here to defend Morgan, it is a waste of both our times. You want to settle your debt from earlier?"

I nod. "Simone's terrified," I say under my breath. "She's clinging to me like she's in kindergarten, and I can't have that. So, whatever it is I gotta do to get your protection for her, I'm in."

"No questions asked?" Vanessa says. "Good." She lowers her voice. "Continued protection, that's a big ask, and that means a big payment. It's not just one thing you have to do to settle this debt. Uh uh. From now on, you're my girl. That means you do what I say, always, and not half-assed like Morgan over there."

I gulp. "Forever?"

"That's what from now on means, doesn't it?" Vanessa takes a step forward. "You need to do something for me before I will agree to protect your little one."

I bite my lip, not liking this one bit. But I'm stuck, aren't I? I can't protect Simone by myself and whoever is after her is breaking her.

"What is it?" I say flatly.

Vanessa says, quietly, "I hate to be the bearer of bad news, but every sign points to your girl Ashley being the one who poisoned Tasha. I want proof so I can punish her properly. Find me some."

eight

I GLARE AT Vanessa so hard my headache starts to come back. Does she even believe what's coming out her mouth? Or is she messing with me cause she knows I'm crushing and wants to humiliate me over it?

"Ashley didn't!" I hiss, my jaw clenched tight.

"I tried to tell you, you're too good for her." Vanessa's voice is soft, almost like she cares she's breaking my heart. But then it gets hard again and she says, "Who is it matters more to you? Ashley or Simone? Because if you choose your girl over the truth, then whatever happens to the little one is on you."

I swallow hard. She's got me and she knows it. I hold my hands out. "All right, all right. I'll do what you want. But if I find proof it's someone else..."

Vanessa smirks. "You think I would punish a girl for the sake of it? If by a miracle someone else did this to Tasha, Ashley will get my full protection. But it won't happen. You don't want to see who Ashley really is, but my eyes are clear." She crosses her arms. "I know things about her that you don't, things that add up to why she wanted Tasha dead. She has to answer for it."

My throat tightens with anger. Vanessa's wrong. Ashley didn't do it.

But the way she shrank into herself around Tasha... the terrified look on her face... the way she didn't react when Tasha bumped her on purpose...

That's fear. That's a motive to kill.

"W-what things?" I stammer, trying to push away the tiny crumb of doubt in the back of my mind. I know Ashley's heart. I know it. "Tasha did to her like you're doing to me right now, that's what you're saying?"

Vanessa shrugs. "Make a deal, you mean? There are aspects of crew business you haven't earned the trust yet to know. But yes, Ashley was paying Tasha for something. If you want to know more, get it out of her along with the confession of her attempt on Tasha's life."

I start to ask something else, but Vanessa turns her back and says, "We can't be seen talking for so long. People will ask questions. Now go."

My stomach feels so tight I'm afraid I'm gonna puke up those pancakes, but I shuffle over to the other side of the room. I got no choice. Vanessa's right: Simone's safety is more important than anything else.

Ashley's over in a corner by herself, shoving empty to-go boxes into the trash. The closer I get to her, the more I hate myself for what I'm about to do. Everyone else is paired up, but she's alone. Probably no one wanted to work with her cause they all believe she poisoned Tasha. And if I do what Vanessa wants, I'll make it even worse. I'm the only one on Ashley's side. How can I take that away from her? How do I crush her spirit the same way she's crushing those boxes?

I can't.

I have to protect her. She's as fragile as Simone, even if Vanessa doesn't see it that way.

Wait... protect.

Vanessa promised she would protect Ashley if Ashley is proven innocent.

That's it. That's how I win this game.

I force myself to hold my head as high as it'll go as I walk over to her.

Ashley turns her head slightly as I approach. Her eyes have no sparkle in them, but they're still gorgeous, almost like I can see the ghost of the light that used to hit them all the time.

. "Oh," she says, her shoulders relaxing while I trace their curves with my eyes. "I thought for a minute someone was about to shove me into the trash bin."

"Never," I say. "Wouldn't let it happen." I lower my voice. "Listen, we gotta talk."

Ashley stiffens. "Y-you heard I'm going to be arrested soon, didn't you?"

Fear shoots through me. Ashley's been arrested before, just like me, so it wouldn't be the first time she was taken away in cuffs when she shouldn't have been, but still. The idea of her being taken from me hurts worse than my head has all morning long and I gotta blink hard to stop the tears.

"Not if I can help it," I reassure her. "Vanessa's another story." I glance over my shoulder to see how closely I'm being watched. Vanessa's inspecting the table Morgan is supposed to be cleaning, but I have no doubt she's keeping an eye on me too. Lowering my voice even more, I say, "She's got something on me and she ordered me to get her proof against you, but I won't."

Believe me. Please believe me. I won't betray you, not now, not ever.

Ashley's face falls. Crap.

"Y-you're brave, crossing Vanessa," she says quietly. "I wish I..." She looks away.

"Ashley," I say gently. "I know Tasha was doing the same to you. You wanna tell me about it?"

Ashley stares down at the to-go box in her hands. "I didn't take her out. You see how much a coward I am. You really think I'd have the balls to do it? Besides, why would I poison my own dish? That would be dumb."

She's not a coward. That's me. Cause whatever secret she has, I'd probably do the same if Tasha or Vanessa threatened to out me if I didn't. Besides, aren't I doing the same to protect Simone?

"I-I believe you." I cross my arms. "Anything you can tell me that can help me pin it on someone else?"

"You wouldn't be pinning. It would be the truth for once." Ashley is so close to tears it takes everything for me not to reach out and caress her cheek. "T-the only thing I can tell you is there's a war and we're in the middle of it. T-tasha forced me to be on her side and there was nothing anyone could do to help me." She throws the to-go box out, hard. "I can't tell you anything more, okay?"

I frown. "Who is it who has all this power? Simone won't tell me what she knows either."

Ashley freezes halfway to reaching for another to-go box. But then she shakes her head, making her curls bounce in a way that gets me breathing harder. "Listen, you gotta do what you gotta do. So go ahead and tell Vanessa I admitted I had the motive, means, and opportunity, and you're just working on getting the final confession out of me."

I swallow hard. Betraying Ashley's the one thing I'll never do, and it hurts that she can't get that. "No, Ashley. I — "

"Save yourself," she says. "Look, once you're on Vanessa and Tasha's bad side, you're dead. Right now the best I can hope for is I get put behind bars before Vanessa straight out kills me for what she thinks I did. But you can save yourself, Bri. You can get the target off your back if you just do what you're told. So let her think you're getting something out of me. It's okay."

I blink back tears. "I won't betray you like that. Come on!"

Ashley shakes her head. "Why not? Everyone else does." She throws a to-go box in the trash so hard her muscles bulge under her sweatshirt. "I'm done here. Excuse me."

She shoves her way past me before I can say another word, but I grab her arm. My fingers hit something bumpy and raised, like a scab.

"Ashley, please," I whisper. "Let me help. I know I can."

Ashley's face trembles, but she pulls away. "You can't! Just leave me alone!" She runs as fast as she can across the room, leaving me to stare at my empty hand.

My eyes dart around the room. If anyone saw that, I just put a bigger target on my back for nothing, cause now I've scared Ashley so bad she'll probably never talk to me again.

The thought hits me as hard as if Vanessa punched me in the stomach and I almost collapse into the wall, but I catch myself.

No matter how many times my brain remembers there's no time for self-pity, my body tries it anyway. But crying over Ashley's not gonna get me the truth.

Finding out who really poisoned Tasha will, and maybe then Ashley will finally see I've been on her side this whole time and stop fighting letting me into her world.

I push myself off the wall, breathing hard. Where are Molly and Lisa? Those two are always whispering and they're gonna tell me why.

There they are, by the conveyor belt, putting plastic utensils in to be washed.

I walk over as fast as I can.

"Hey," I say to Molly. "I don't know if you saw that, but Ashley's real upset."

Molly doesn't look up from the forks she's collecting. "Yeah. She's been messed up since the poisoning. Maybe even before." She glances at Lisa, then away.

I cross my arms. "I heard she's your best friend. Think you could care a little more?"

Molly scowls. "I do care!" she insists. "But —"

Lisa interrupts, "You're better off without her, Mol. I'm not sure if that bitch is a rat or a mouse, but either one adds up to a bad friend." She laughs to herself. "She's so scared all the time."

"It's not funny!" Molly snaps. Lisa looks up, slowly, and Molly takes a step back. "W-we were all friends before Tasha interfered."

Lisa shrugs. "Some of us were fakers."

I don't know what that means, but I can't afford to get sidetracked. "You guys were in the kitchen when she was cooking. See anything?"

Molly swallows hard. "Um," she says, pushing a strand of hair behind her ear. "It wouldn't have happened if Ashley hadn't stepped away. She should have watched her pot."

I raise my eyebrows. "You were next to her. Didn't you watch it for her?"

Molly's eyes dart to Lisa, then back to me. "Yeah, I mean, as much as I could. But I had to cook too. I couldn't..." She laughs nervously. "All I know is I didn't do it."

"Me either " Lisa says, "though neither of us is sorry about Tasha. She was going to get targeted sooner or later, strutting around like she owns this place. " Her voice holds a bitter note. "But like Molly said, we didn't do it. Sorry to say, it had to be Ashley. She was desperate to get Tasha off her back and she made the potatoes so..."

Something feels wrong, but I can't tell what it is. Is someone lying? Or is just I don't like the way they're talking?

"You're Ashley's ride-or-die," I say to Molly. "So if anyone knows anything about what Tasha was doing to her, it's you."

Molly swallows hard. "I promised I wouldn't tell." She glances at Lisa again, then away. "If it wasn't Ashley, it had to be someone who cared about her. Everyone saw what Tasha was doing, so..."

"Yeah," Lisa says. She locks eyes with me. "Everyone knows you're crushing on that bitch. You do something to save her?"

I stiffen. Shit. Everyone knows and no one likes it, but I wasn't expecting this level of hate. "Excuse me?" I say coldly. "You guys are the ones who knew Tasha was blackmailing her. So start talking. What dio you know about what Tasha had on Ashley?"

"Nothing," Lisa says, "but you're acting awfully suspicious. I'd be careful if I were you."

I stare at her. She's threatening me, and innocent people don't do that, but what reason would Lisa have to mess with Tasha?

Ms Carter comes over before I can say another word.

"Excuse me," she says. "Brianna, you seem to be floating around from table to table with no job to do."

"Yeah," Lisa says. "Stop being lazy."

I stand frozen, my arms crossed, til Ms. Carter tells me a second time to hurry up and go. I can't tell if she has my back or she's trying to mess me up with Lisa by making it look like I get special treatment.

Ms. Carter glances at her. "I didn't ask for your help, did I?" She turns back toward me. "I think we have enough coverage here. Go to the study room and get started on your math lesson." She nods at Lisa. "Stop staring and get finished so you can start yours too."

Vanessa locks eyes with me as I walk past and mouths, "Talk in a minute."

Great. I nod slightly and keep walking.

Inspector Goodwin is coming down the stairs as I head that way. What the heck? There's nothing up there but the library and the study rooms. What's that got to do with whether the kitchen's safe?

I look over my shoulder to double check that Mrs. MacGregor isn't around and adjust my N-95 so it's tight over my face. I don't need the damn health inspector complaining I'm not wearing it right.

"Can I ask you something?" I say, coming over to her.

Inspector Goodwin flinches. "Oh. I didn't see you standing there. What can I do for you?"

"For one thing, how come you were looking at the library?"

"I'm doing a general tour of the whole facility. My job is to make sure that there aren't any violations of the health code anywhere, not just in the kitchen." Inspector Goodwin glances at my mask, then away. "I hope you're not sick."

"Sleep deprived is all, but they gave me a mask at the nurse anyway."

"Is that what they usually do when someone has concerning symptoms?"

"I guess." I feel a cough coming on. I breathe in hard, hoping to hold it back til I'm done with this conversation. "Um, did you find anything about how Tasha got poisoned?"

Inspector Goodwin's jaw tightens. "I can't talk to you about that," she says. "I'd lose my job." She lowers her voice. "Just between us, the only thing Tasha ate before she got sick was the potatoes."

Great. So she's confirmed what we all knew already.

"K," I say. "I guess I'd better..."

"Wait a sec." Inspector Goodwin takes a card out of her pocket. "I can't talk freely here and I'm guessing you can't either. But if you want to continue this conversation, I'm open."

I glance down at the card. There's a green stripe on top and her full name, phone number, and email.

"I wish," I say quietly, "but this place is juvie without the bars. I can't call out except my approved list and they monitor email."

Inspector Goodwin's eyes narrow. "I'll find a way," she says quietly. "Keep your nose clean in the meantime." She steps aside so I can get up the stairs.

I drag my feet. I want to believe this lady's actually on my side, but I know better.

The study room is empty. Good. I don't need anyone staring at me cause I'm masked. At home I hated being the only one who still acted like COVID was a thing, but this place is next level. Here, masks aren't freely chosen cause you want to be cautious. They mark you as diseased and people stay far away while whispering and shooting suspicious looks your way.

Ms. Vargas, the study room manager, is typing away behind her desk when I come up to her. "Your lessons are in your educational portal," she says, not looking up. "Log into the computer and follow the instructions."

"K," I say. Under my mask, I'm biting my lip while I argue with myself about whether to say anything about Inspector Goodwin. I don't want to attract the wrong kind of attention, but I gotta know.

"You need something else?" Ms. Vargas asks.

"Yeah, actually," I say. "I was wondering... what was up with the health inspector being up here?"

Ms. Vargas stops typing. She lifts her head slowly and looks me in my eyes. I can see the row of computers reflected in her black-rimmed glasses. "I don't think that's any of your concern," she says coldly.

She wants me to look away, but I refuse to give her the satisfaction. I hold her gaze and say, quietly, "I just want to know what we're up against. I heard she could shut us down."

"The health department could, yes," Ms. Vargas says, "but that isn't something you need to worry about. Everyone is cooperating fully, as we should. We have nothing to hide, and we are not doing anything wrong. Now go do your lesson." Her voice is flat, robotic, almost like she's repeating a rehearsed speech she was given in case anyone asked her about the inspection.

I stand still, staring at her in the hopes she'll break and tell me the truth, but she doesn't. Instead, she says, "If you have questions about the educational material, you can click the icon on the portal and I'll do what I can. Otherwise, I'm busy and you should be too." She goes back to her typing.

I take my seat. There's no point to anything else since it's clear she's not about to talk.

I can't concentrate on my math lesson cause my mind's on what's up with the inspection on top of how to prove Ashley's innocent, the fact that Vanessa wants to talk to me, and how heavy this damn mask feels on my face. I click on a video hard, trying to will myself to focus on it. Some teacher drones on and on about sequences of numbers. The only thing that catches my attention is when he says that pattern recognition is all about thinking outside the box cause the connection isn't as obvious as it seems.

That's exactly what I need to do to crack this wide open. I pretend to pay attention, but instead of writing a sequence of numbers on my scrap paper, I write facts about the case:

The peanut oil was in the potatoes. Ashley cooked them, but she's too obvious. Ashley has motive — she was blackmailed by Tasha, but about what?

Someone signed Simone's name to an Epi-Pen after she saw someone else take Tasha's. Simone locked in closet. Vanessa making me do what I'm told to get Simone protection.

Health inspector up here. Nurse won't talk because she's afraid of being sued but someone threw away the spare Epi-Pen. Ms. Vargas told me to butt out. Ms. Carter friendly but keeps warning me to back off.

That's three lines of facts that seem like they're connected, but I'm obviously missing something.

The pattern between the first: Ashley's being framed. I kind of knew that already. Elizabeth said that it was too obvious, like someone wanted us to find clues Ashley did it, and Ashley more or less confirmed it. It's not a coincidence Tasha went down minutes after Ashley showed how scared she was of her, or on the night Ashley made the dish that got poisoned.

And the second line? Someone's framing Simone too, or trying to. I thought they were threatening her to keep her quiet, but what if it's a backup plan? If they can't make charges stick to Ashley, they'll do it to sweet, scared Simone.

Ashley and Simone are the same even though Simone's a tiny little thing and Ashley's only a year younger than me, maybe two. But they're equally terrified, which makes them equally easy to control.

Which means...

...whoever poisoned Tasha is someone who loves to prey on smaller, weaker girls who are easy to scare.

And there's one person I know like that. Vanessa. I mean, look what she's doing to me just cause she can.

Except she's got no motive to hurt Tasha. Those two are tight.

Still... it all adds up. Doesn't it?

Someone taps my shoulder, hard. I didn't hear her come up behind me cause I had my headphones on to make it look like I was doing my schoolwork, but I know without a doubt it's Vanessa.

I scramble to turn over my scrap paper before she can see her name on it before I peel off the headphones and turn toward her.

"Report time," Vanessa says quietly. "What'd the little bitch say?"

I let my breath out slowly. My instinct's to tell her to fuck off, but that's not gonna do me a bit of good, or Simone either. "Not much," I say carefully. "She admitted she's got motive and she was in the kitchen, but it's not like she signed a confession."

"So nothing new, then." Vanessa's voice is hard. She sits down backward on the chair next to me. "You can't let your heart get in the way. Unless you are seducing her for information, forget how you feel and focus on the truth."

I grab tight to the edge of the desk, breathing hard. Nothing about this convo should be turning me on, but the idea of me being a superspy seducing Ashley for intel's making me need to go to my room and take care of myself. "T-the truth is I still don't think she did it," I stammer. "Look, how's someone too scared to stand up to Tasha all this time gonna find the balls to poison her?"

Vanessa's eyes narrow. "You don't think that's exactly why she did it? She couldn't get her off her back the normal way and was desperate? I tried to tell Tasha that this one might not be built for being pushed as far as we needed, but she refused to listen. She is stubborn to her core, same as you, only in her case it nearly killed her." Her voice is softer than usual, almost wistful. It's like she's attracted to stubbornness. But she can't be. She's straight... isn't she?

Can't worry about that cause her words tell me something else:

Tasha refusing to listen to her plus her claiming Ashley got desperate enough to kill cause she couldn't get what she wanted any other way... is that projection? A confession pinned on someone else?

"I'm telling you, that's not Ashley," I say.

Vanessa raises her eyebrows. "You want my help with your little one or not? I will not do it for a girl who keeps falling for fakers who get her in trouble."

I freeze, my heart pounding. She knows about Natalie. How? Group, I guess. What we say in there's supposed to stay there, but Vanessa doesn't play by the rules. I knew that going in... why did I let my guard down? When?

Doesn't matter. Ashley's not Natalie no matter what Vanessa thinks, and I'm not about to be blackmailed into helping frame her.

But how do I fight back when I can't protect Simone on my own? I couldn't even get her free of that damn closet without Vanessa and the hairpins only she's allowed.

I hear myself say, "Lisa threatened me."

Vanessa scowls. "Threatened how?"

"I tried to ask her what she knew about the beef between Tasha and Ashley and she said if I didn't stop asking questions people would start thinking I was the one who did it." I hold my hands up. "I wasn't, case you were wondering."

"I know you aren't capable of it," Vanessa says. "Anyway, Lisa is talking out of the wrong side of her mouth because she knows exactly why Ashley wanted to kill Tasha, but she doesn't dare say it openly."

"Really." I keep my voice neutral even though I'm sure this is more BS. "Want to let me in on the secret?"

Vanessa hesitates. "Some things are not for me to tell. But I will say this. Whenever Ashley spoke to Lisa recently, she was a puppet being controlled by Tasha, all to hurt Lisa."

I raise my eyebrows. "They were enemies? So Lisa has a motive too?"

Vanessa's eyes widen. "Ashley is more likely. Her cowardice when it came to Tasha cost her everything, including the friendship Lisa thought they had."

I stare at her. "What exactly did Ashley do to her?"

Vanessa shakes her head. "You wouldn't believe it. You think that your girl is pure sweetness and light, but all Tasha had to do was push the right button and she had a weapon against Lisa." She crosses her arms. "Since you can't get a confession, we will have to do this a different way. After lunch you will come with me."

I look her in her eyes. "Come with you where?" I say coldly. She's not going to kidnap me any more than she's going to blackmail me. Not without a fight.

"To the hospital, of course," Vanessa says lightly, as if sneaking out's totally normal. "I know secrets I can't tell, but Tasha can, and she will tell us everything we need to know to nail Ashley for this."

nine

I STARE AT VANESSA. Girl's obviously lost her damn mind. "I can't do that and you know it," I say. "I'm already on my first written warning. What do you think'll happen to me if we get caught?"

"We can't get caught, then." Vanessa flips her hair over her shoulder. "This is the price for my protection. Is it yes or no?"

I swallow hard, remembering Simone's wide eyes and the way she tried to stick close after me and Vanessa got her out of that closet. I can't let her get hurt, but how am I supposed to pull this one off?

"How about a video chat?" I say. I don't know how I'll make that happen either, but it feels safer than sneaking out. "Mrs. MacGregor said she'd arrange them."

Vanessa snorts. "Like we can trust a word out of that bitch's mouth. She still hasn't done a thing about your girl messing with Tasha, has she?"

ASHLEY. IS. INNOCENT. I make myself breathe deep. Can't let Vanessa get me off my game. "So we'll arrange it ourselves. There's gotta be a way."

"There's not." Vanessa crosses her arms. "But fine. Since you're so determined to do things your way, I'll give you a chance. Get it set up before dinner tonight or be ready to go out the window after." She turns away from me and puts headphones on. Conversation over.

I stare at my reflection in the computer screen, barely recognizing the girl who stares back at me. Wide-eyed, scared. In too deep. There's no way I can pull this off. None. The admin has to authorize video chats and they're not gonna listen to me.

But I have to try. I bite my lip as I slide out of my seat and tiptoe out of the room.

Ms. Carter's not in her office when I get downstairs. Damn it. The one time I need to talk to an adult, there she's not.

I hear voices coming from Mrs. MacGregor's office as I walk past. I stop and listen to see if one of them's Ms. Carter.

"I doubt it's going to end with this health inspection," Mrs. MacGregor says. "Next will be a full investigation by the State Oversight Board, and God knows what these girls will say when questioned. Some of them will undoubtedly make things up without being aware that they're signing their own arrest warrants by helping get this place shut down."

"We need a contingency plan," Ms. Carter says.

"Like what, Loretta? The state has the power to shut us down, and then what becomes of these girls? Juvenile detention? That will destroy some of them, and certainly ends any chance for any of them to reclaim a future unencumbered by a criminal record."

"Like I'm not aware!" Ms. Carter snaps. "I'm telling you, some girls should be recommended for early release. The vulnerable ones especially. Simone Richards. Elizabeth Waters. Brianna Hunter."

What? I make myself flat against a wall, unable to believe my ears. Ms. Carter thinks I should be allowed to go home?

"We're not at that point yet," Mrs. MacGregor says. "These girls could still use our help."

Help. Right. Cause we're helped by being in fake juvie.

"Be that as it may, the situation is dire," Ms. Carter replies. "Unless... I'm telling you, you should let Brianna help us catch the poisoner. We do something about the girl who did this and a lot of this goes away."

Mrs. MacGregor is quiet for a second. Then she says, "I'll think about it. But I don't like it. Any state inspector who learns we're using residents instead of summoning the police... they won't understand that these girls have been traumatized by law enforcement. They'll see it as us exploiting a vulnerable resident. And Brianna has already gotten herself in trouble trying to help. If they see her disciplinary record..."

That's only cause you wrote me up over nothing. You said it yourself. I'd never been in trouble before now.

I know I should walk away, but I can't get myself to act right. Before I know it, I've knocked on the office door.

The talking stops as quickly as if someone hit the off button. Ms. Carter opens the door a crack. Her eyes widen but her jaw gets tight, making her face look square, and her eyes dart to Mrs. MacGregor, then back to me. "Brianna. Please tell me this is an emergency and not you searching for reasons to get out of your schoolwork."

My heart pounds. I shouldn't have knocked til I had a clear idea what to say when Ms. Carter opened the door. "Um... I guess it is. I-I mean, it was big enough for me to come down here, wasn't it? Can you let me in for a minute?"

Ms. Carter's eyes dart to Mrs. MacGregor again before she nods and opens the door.

I come in, slowly. I'm shaking so bad I feel like I might fall over and have to grab onto the edge of the desk instead of standing at attention like I've been taught to do around adults in the program.

Mrs. MacGregor pales visibly when she sees me like that. "Sit down, Brianna," she says gently. "Tell us what's wrong."

I sink into a seat and grab onto the arm rests. "I-I don't know how to... Vanessa..."

The adults exchange glances again. "Vanessa what?" Ms. Carter hands me a bottle of water. "Here. Drink. Breathe. You're safe."

I gulp the water while telling myself to chill out. I gotta get ahold of myself. And snitching isn't the answer, either. She'll know it's me and she'll take it out on Simone.

But I started this, so I gotta finish it. I say, slowly, "You have to authorize a video chat with Tasha cause Vanessa's losing it."

Ms. Carter frowns. "She's threatening you, is that what you're saying?"

"Not me," I say quickly. Liar! But it's not like these two would punish Vanessa if they knew she was blackmailing me into being her partner in crime, so telling the truth would only make everything worse. "Herself." I let my breath out slowly. "You didn't hear it from me, but she's planning on running away to visit Tasha."

Mrs. MacGregor crosses her arms. "What's her plan?"

"I don't know. I only overheard." God, the lies are flowing as easily as they did when I was messing around with Natalie. This time it's out of necessity, but that doesn't mean I like myself any better for it. "But you know she's serious, and if she gets away with it, won't they want to shut us down cause you let someone escape?"

Mrs. MacGregor sits up straighter, her lips pressed tightly together. "We," she says, "did not do anything. And we are not going to be threatened by a 16-year-old who imagines she has power that she does not have, either. We'll call Vanessa in for a little chat."

"No! You can't do that." I look away, realizing too late I'm talking myself into another write-up. "She'll know I'm the one who told. You think anyone around here will put up with me being a snitch?" I lean forward. "Don't you see? If you let her talk to Tasha she'll stay put. Plus maybe Tasha'll let slip to her something that leads to whoever poisoned her. So it's a win-win."

Ms. Carter says, quietly, "Brianna has a point."

Mrs. MacGregor says, quietly, "I do not like this child calling the shots. I never have. We are supposed to be in charge and regardless of Vanessa's situation..."

"You know why that is." Ms. Carter glances at me, then away. What in the world?

Mrs. MacGregor mouths something to her. Aloud, she says, "I don't know that Vanessa will calm down if we allow this. I don't want her to escalate."

Shit. Looks like I'm going to have to get ready to go out that window after all.

"We did promise..." Ms. Carter turns toward me. "Mrs. MacGregor and I need to check with the hospital about Tasha's condition and discuss among ourselves whether this is a good idea. Please go tell Vanessa to hold her fire until we've made a decision."

I stand. "Please don't take too long," I say. "She's gonna make her move tonight. I'm sure of it."

"We understand," Mrs. MacGregor says. "Thank you for bringing this to our attention."

They're not going to do shit. I know it and Vanessa will too.

Now what?

ten

I HURRY BACK to the study room to try to break the news to Vanessa without her flipping, but the seat next to me is empty.

I look around as I sink into my chair. No Vanessa anywhere. But what I do see is Morgan leaning over and saying something to Simone. Simone's eyes widen and she slowly stands.

Crap. Whatever Morgan's doing to her, Vanessa's purposely letting it happen.

I'm about to go over there to stand up for Simone when she comes running over to me. "Brianna! Brianna!" she says, her voice too loud. "M-morgan's stuck with her math. S-she says only you can help." She stares at me.

"I'm coming," I say. I take Simone's hands in mine and say, very quietly, "She threatened you?"

Simone nods. "S-she knows..." She begins signing so fast that even if I was fluent in ASL I wouldn't be able to follow. But there's that sign again, a fist with her thumb tucked under her third finger.

It clicks all of a sudden. M. *Morgan*.

"Morgan knows you know about the Epi-Pen?" I whisper.

Simone swallows hard. "Me and Patrice were playing Ping Pong but Morgan made Patrice go with her a-and she did like this to me." She imitates the zipped-lip hand motion and then drags her finger against her throat.

So. Morgan told Simone to keep her mouth shut or else. That tracks. But it's not absolute proof she stole the Epi-Pen and anyway, why would she mess with it when she's one of Tasha's right hand girls?

"She stole it or she saw too?" I ask.

Simone looks away. "W-we have to get over there quick or Morgan will make me sorry."

I squeeze her hand. "Okay. But after this is over, you and me are gonna talk."

Simone gulps but says nothing.

I walk side by side with her back to her area, holding my head up as high as I can. I want Morgan to get that Simone's not alone and that I'm watching her back. But how can I pull it off when I can't even get out from under Vanessa's thumb?

Morgan looks up from her computer. "Good. You got my message." She pats the chair next to her. "Sit."

Who does this little girl think she is? She's not much bigger than Simone but she's throwing her weight around like she's Tasha.

Still, I need to find out what her game is, so I pull out the chair and sit down in it. "Let's get that math," I say, pretending I don't know that's just a cover.

Morgan snorts. "Like I care about uncovering what X stands for in a bunch of dumb equations. I ain't never gonna use this crap in real life." She nods at Simone. "Tell your little bitch to put her headphones on. This isn't for her ears."

Simone grabs her headset and hurries to get it on before I can tell her not to show any fear.

"Don't call names," I tell Morgan. "I can still walk away."

"Yeah, no," Morgan says. She lowers her voice. "Vanessa put me in charge while she's pissing."

Yeah, right. Vanessa put a ninth-grader in charge. I doubt it, just like I doubt she's really using the bathroom. Vanessa's extra-long bathroom breaks have always seemed like a cover for something but til now I've let it go cause whatever illegal thing she's doing sure isn't my business.

"Why you went to the office?" Morgan says, her voice hard.

Oh. So the little minion's going to interrogate me. I take a breath so

I don't do anything dumb and say, quietly, "How else am I gonna get Vanessa that video with Tasha? It's gotta go through them."

Morgan's eyes narrow and she frowns, confused. Guess she didn't know about that. But she recovers quick, crossing her arms."Or you were snitching." She glances at Simone. "You better remember what'll happen if you stab her in the back."

My throat tightens. Vanessa threatening Simone is bad enough, but having one of the littles do it? I say, quietly, "Happens I got them to agree to consider it. Now, how about you tell me something. You stole that Epi-Pen, didn't you?"

Morgan's eyes flash. "Not me," she says, giggling. "I can't believe you're so dumb as to believe that." She swirls her mouse around her screen to stop the screensaver from coming up.

I bite my lip, telling myself not to take the bait. "So you saw something, then?"

"Nope." Morgan giggles again. "Your bitch did but she's too much of a coward to ever tell." She raises her voice on the last words to make sure it gets through Simone's headset. "I'll tell you something, though. There were two of us on the couch watching TV with Tash. She was between me and... someone else, and she wasn't paying attention to anything but the screen. So if I was gonna take that Epi-Pen, that's the time I'd do it. But it ain't me who done it. So you do the math who."

Simone's shaking her head slightly. She heard that.

Is she telling me Morgan's lying?

I don't have time to worry about it now cause Morgan goes on, "Now, shut up about that. You have til lunch to get this done so you'd better get to work."

"She told me dinner," I say, a note of triumph creeping into my voice. Got her! She's not working for Vanessa... I don't think anyway.

Morgan smirks. "She changed her mind. So you gonna do it or..." She shoots an evil, narrow-eyed look Simone's way.

"I'm working on it," I say.

Morgan hugs herself. "I wonder what Simone would do if I yanked that headset right off her head," she says softly, almost to herself. "Would she scream like a little bitch or burst into tears like a baby?"

I go silent. Message received: do what you're told or else Simone gets it.

I feel eyes on my back as Morgan puts her headset on, ending the conversation. But when I look over my shoulder, no one is there.

I spend the next part of the morning trying to figure my way out of all this. I can't go directly back to Ms. Carter cause if I do, Vanessa will know and she'll have Morgan take it out on Simone. But there's no way to get her that video without convincing Ms. Carter to okay it.

Or is there?

I go back to the middle school area and crouch next to Elizabeth. Lowering my voice, I whisper, "You have any idea how to set up a video chat with the hospital without getting caught?"

Elizabeth bites her lip. "Why?"

I bite my lip. I want to tell Elizabeth the truth so bad my chest hurts, but there's no guarantee she'll agree to keep her mouth shut. She operates from a different set of rules than these wanna-be gangsters and there's no getting through to her if she doesn't want to do something their way.

"I need it for the investigation, that's all."

Elizabeth scowls. She doesn't like being left in the dark any more than I do. "Can't you even give me a little hint? Please?"

No choice now.

I lower my voice. "I want to question Tasha but I can't do that if I can't get her on video." Elizabeth starts to say something but I put my finger to my lips. "No one else can know. Now do you know how or not?"

Elizabeth swallows hard. She stares at her reflection in the computer screen, thinking. "Maybe if we could get a grown-up's log-in," she says slowly. "When we sign into the computer it knows we have restrictions, but I bet if Mrs. MacGregor signed in she could do whatever she wanted."

I glance over my shoulder at Ms. Vargas. She's holding a book level with the desk, trying to hide that she's reading.

"You think her?" I whisper.

Elizabeth tilts her head back, a weird half-frown on her face. "Maybe. What are you gonna do?"

"You'll see." I pat her shoulder before walking away.

I have no idea what I'm gonna say to Ms. Vargas to get her to give up that password. I gotta stop playing this by ear. It's only getting me in deeper trouble.

"Psst!" Vanessa hisses as I walk past.

I'm tempted to ignore her, but something tells me that's a bad idea. I turn toward her slowly, crossing my arms.

Careful, Brianna. You can't lose it in front of her.

But I hear myself say, "Back from the bathroom, huh? Or wherever you were?"

Vanessa's eyes narrow. I can almost see the brain cells firing under there, calculating how to deal with me.

I don't know what she's hiding, but she wasn't in that bathroom cause nature called.

"Run-in with the bitches who run this place?" she asks. "Or something else got you so wound up?"

"It's that dumbass Morgan." My jaw's clenched tight. "I don't wanna be a snitch, but she's messing with Simone and saying she's doing it in your name so maybe you should know about it."

Vanessa presses her lips tightly together. "You did good, bringing this to me." She pats the seat next to her. "Morgan will be dealt with but first I need to know you're doing what I asked of you."

Again with the wheeling and dealing. Doesn't she know any other way to relate to me? I let my breath out slowly. "They're... considering it, which means — "

"Christmas will come more quickly," Vanessa says. "They are not on our side. But you knew this, didn't you?"

I nod slightly. "I had to try that way first. But I have another idea." I lower my voice. "I don't know how to pull this off, but if we can get her password, we're in." I gesture toward Ms. Vargas. Vanessa frowns and I explain, "Staff probably has access to video chat and then we'd just have to find how to contact Tasha."

Vanessa grins. "Genius," she says. "I knew I could count on you. Okay. Leave the next step to me." She clicks a few buttons on her computer then calls, loudly, "Teacher? I can't get into my account. It logged out and won't let me back in."

Ms. Vargas frowns. She comes over and says, "Stop yelling across the room." She leans over and says, "Log in and show me what happens."

"I don't think so," Vanessa says. "Write your login and password for me."

Ms. Vargas crosses her arms. "Why would I do that?" She starts to walk away.

Vanessa says, "Cause anyone with eyes can see you trying to hide that book. I keep my mouth shut if you give me your login."

Ms. Vargas pales but she says, quietly, "Young lady, if you think you're going to blackmail a staff member..."

Vanessa turns toward me. "You saw her reading too, didn't you?"

I nod even though I don't want to. Better Ms. Vargas than me. Or at least that's what I tell myself.

"Fine," the study manager says. "I'll be right back." She walks off.

Vanessa smirks, but I feel sick to my stomach. She hasn't won. I'm sure of it.

Ms. Vargas takes forever before she comes back with a post-it. I try to meet her eyes. I want to tell her silently that I'm being forced just like her. But she won't look at me.

I look away, ashamed of what I'm about to do. I should never have joined forces with Vanessa. Not if she's gonna be like this.

"Type it," Vanessa hisses. "Hurry it up."

I begin typing. I know it's wrong but at the same time, when you're being held hostage you do what it takes to survive.

The door opens and Ms. Carter comes in, making a beeline for where Vanessa and I are sitting.

Shit.

I'm caught red-handed.

eleven

I HURRY TO stick the post-it under my desk as Ms. Carter approaches. Vanessa nods approvingly.

Ms. Carter's eyes dart from Vanessa to me. "A word, please, Brianna. There's been a complaint and I need to hear your side."

I stand, my heart pounding, and put my hands behind my back. Vanessa shakes her head slightly at me. I ignore her.

I'm not her. I can't carry myself however I want in this place.

Elizabeth jumps up as Ms. Carter gestures for me to follow her. "Wait!" she says. "Brianna didn't — "

"This is between me and Brianna," Ms. Carter says firmly. "Sit back down, Elizabeth." She turns toward Vanessa. "Sorry to interrupt your tutoring session, but this can't wait."

"Whatever you think she did is wrong," Vanessa says. "Brianna is as clean as they come."

My stomach sinks as it hits me: Vanessa's talking in code like she did with Ashley.

Behind my back, I squeeze my left wrist so hard it hurts. Nothing's adding up. Ms. Vargas snitched when she went to get her password. That much is obvious. But why did Ms. Carter come herself instead of sending Security to get me and Vanessa for trying to steal Ms. Vargas' password? And why am I the only one in trouble?

I've been set up, but I don't know why or exactly what I'm taking the fall for here.

Ms. Carter doesn't take me to the office, either, or even downstairs. Instead, she takes me down the hall to one of the therapy rooms and changes the sign to say DO NOT DISTURB.

"Sit wherever you'd like," she says, gesturing toward the couch.

"I'll stand, thanks." I cross my arms. "Want to tell me what's going on here?"

Ms. Carter raises her eyebrows. "I could ask you that, Brianna. Ms. Vargas says you and Vanessa tried to manipulate her into giving you her password for the computer. But I have a hard time believing that's the full story."

"It's not," I say cautiously. I get it now. This is a trap, her pretending she's on my side so I confess everything and then Security can swoop in and take me.

Still seems like a lot of trouble to go to when she could have just had Security get me in the first place, but what do I know?

Ms. Carter sighs. "You're not going to make this easy," she says, "but that's all right." She pats the couch across from her. "Sit and listen if you don't want to talk. I need to explain something to you."

I sink into the couch, my heart pounding. What in the world have I gotten myself into?

Ms. Carter says, carefully, "There are a lot of things you don't understand about the forces at play in this house, Brianna. I know you want to clear Ashley's name and expose the real poisoner, and that's a noble goal, but it isn't as simple as you think it is."

More code. "If you'd say what you mean, I might have a chance at understanding you," I say bitterly.

"It bugs you how indirect I'm being. I'm sorry about that." Ms. Carter crosses her arms. "I'm trying not to break several confidences I've been sworn to." She sighs. "Mrs. MacGregor and I have to walk a delicate tightrope every day. We have to answer political pressure in a way that will keep this program running and we have to protect every girl in here, including some who have secrets in their past that could put them in serious danger if they were to be exposed."

I swallow hard. "Like Ashley?" I say. "Tasha was holding something over her and she won't say what it is." I bite my lip, praying I haven't said too much. I know Ashley's not guilty, but Ms. Carter doesn't and the last thing I need is to hand her a motive on a silver platter.

"Yes, like her. And Vanessa too." Ms. Carter sighs. "I can't punish you for what just happened without punishing Vanessa, and right now that isn't worth it. But what I can do is guide you to think more carefully about how you are approaching situations. You got yourself into deeper trouble than you realized with your friend Natalie, didn't you? You were lucky you only caught a misdemeanor possession charge and not one that would have completely destroyed your future. So now, whether it's Ashley or Vanessa or anyone else, it's very important that you check yourself often, make sure you aren't blindly following someone down a path that leads nowhere good."

My head starts up again, just a little. I rub my temples, trying to ignore the high pitched ringing in my ears. "Can't get away from Natalie, can I?" I say. "I know I screwed up with her, but why's that got to follow me around the rest of my life?"

"It doesn't," Ms. Carter says calmly, "but until you get a handle on this, new versions of Natalie are gonna keep popping up in your life, tempting you to do wrong. And I don't want to see you get in any more trouble than you already have. You know where that leads."

I bite my lip. "I'm already locked up," I say nervously, "and Ashley's not leading me to getting arrested again and neither is Vanessa."

"You sure about that? You could have been expelled for what you just did to please her."

"It was me!" I snap. It's the dumbest thing I could have said. We both know that's a lie. "I wanted to know what Tasha knows about her poisoning so I told Vanessa we gotta get into the system on a staff account so we can video call her."

Ms. Carter looks me up and down. "Letting others drag you down and taking the blame when you get caught," she says quietly. "This is not good." She stands. "I want you to reflect on your choices and on why you keep following girls into trouble. Send me an email tonight explaining your behavior today and what you think was behind it." She looks me in my eyes. "I want it before lights out. Do you understand what I am telling you to do?"

I understand, all right. She wants a BS email throwing Vanessa under the bus. Can't do that without throwing Simone there too, so it's not happening. But I gotta play the game long enough to avoid losing what little freedom I've got so I mumble, "Yes, ma'am."

"Good," Ms. Carter says. "Go back to the study room, then." As I get up, she adds, "You can tell Vanessa she will get what she wants, but not exactly the way she wants it. And no, I'm not going to explain further, so don't bother asking me."

My mind's racing as I nod and walk off. Ms. Carter let me off easy, but less makes sense than before.

Only one thing's clear from everything that just went down: Vanessa's protected.

Even if she's the one who poisoned Tasha, she'll never go down for it.

That's dangerous.

But so am I. Ms. Carter was pushing me to back off before I expose something I don't understand, but all I got from it is twice as much determination to expose the rot in the walls of this place.

The closer I get to the study room, the more rage burns within me. Ms. Carter's words about how lucky I am I didn't get in worse trouble won't stop echoing in my ears. Lucky when I'm locked up here, forced to deal with Vanessa on the daily, forced into a world full of bullies and blackmail that makes the things kids used to say about me at my old school seem like a walk in the park?

But yeah, I am lucky, cause the stuff I did with Natalie... I could be in juvie til next year and then real prison for the next 20.

Does she think I don't know that? Does she think that wasn't running through my head while I was stuck in holding that night, unable to sleep cause I didn't know what the judge was gonna do with me the next morning?

Mom was so disappointed in me that night when I called to tell her I'd been arrested and the next morning when she had to come to court early to sit with me and the public defender. I'll never forget the weariness in her voice when she told me there was nothing she could do til morning or the dark circles under her eyes like she hadn't slept any more than me. But what hurts worse than all of that is knowing that I did so much other crap that she doesn't even know about.

Mom doesn't know, or Auntie Nan either, that me giving Natalie money for drugs was only the start. She started demanding rides and I did that too. She doesn't know all the times I sat double parked on some street I had no business being on, not sure if I was more afraid of the cops pulling up or some random with a gun who wanted to take my car or worse.

And she doesn't know... she doesn't know that if I tried to say No to giving her money or rides, Nat would promise that as soon as she was good and high we could fool around on her bed.

Yeah. I didn't just give her money for drugs. I paid her for sex.

And Ms. Carter thinks I don't know I'm lucky I only got caught with the drugs that were part of that whole scheme?

I let my breath out slowly, trying to tell myself to leave all that in the past while a voice in the back of my head whispers I'd better not tell anyone that, ever, because if my family knew, I'd be done.

Gotta get it together. Can't let the other girls see me cry.

I pull the study room door open.

Morgan's in my seat. "Bet she snitched," she says loudly.

"Better learn some respect," Vanessa says while my hands curl into fists without me planning them to. "And scram. You're in her spot."

Morgan scowls but she gets up. I throw myself into my seat.

Vanessa says, quietly, "Don't let that bitch get to you." Does she mean Morgan or Ms. Carter? Does it matter?

I shrug, grabbing my headset and turning it over in my hands, breathing in time with feeling its weight to try to get back in control.

Vanessa frowns. "Carter was hard on you but you can be harder."

"It's not that," I say flatly. "She made me sit through some therapy BS that got me all stirred up." I bite my lip. "Won't get to me for long though. Listen. She gave me some cryptic message for you."

Vanessa's eyes widen. "Did she, now?" she says, her tone neutral.

I nod, hoping I can remember now that I brought it up. "Something about how you won't get what you want but you will." I rub the back of my neck. "I forget the exact wording. Sorry."

Vanessa's jaw tightens, but she says nothing.

"There's something else," I whisper. Gotta get back on her good side before it's too late. I can't live with myself if Simone gets hurts cause of me. "Morgan stole Tasha's Epi-Pen that night."

Vanessa clenches her jaw even harder. "I knew she was a traitor," she says, almost to herself. Aloud, she says, "How do you know this?"

My heart pounds. If I tell, do I make things worse for Simone or better? "Two witnesses," I whisper. "She threatened them into silence."

Vanessa's eyes widen. "You'd better spill everything," she says. "You know I can't take it only on your word, but if it is true, all involved will answer to me."

My eyes dart around the room. Patrice is grinning at someone, looking to all the world like the child she is. How can I throw her to the wolves, or Simone either?

The PA chimes ring, warning that the system's about to come on. The sharp sound makes me flinch, and across the room Elizabeth slumps down in her seat, pressing her headset against her ears like she's trying to block out the sound.

"Attention Tiger Cohort," Ms. Carter says. "Could everyone please line up and come to the conference room for a special announcement?"

Now what? I stand up slowly, ignoring the buzz of 20 different conversations echoing in my ears. Everyone wants to know what the hell this is about and whether we need to prep for some crazy punishment for everyone cause of what one person did.

I drag my feet to the line and slip in behind Ashley. Just knowing she's nearby calms me. I breathe in her perfume, letting it wash over me, and try not to think about how it would feel to kiss her.

Ms. Vargas puts her hand on my shoulder. "You. Get to the back of the line."

My eyes narrow. "Why? What did I do?"

"You know what," she says. "And maybe Ms. Carter thinks you're too sweet and innocent to punish for it, but I don't. Now go, and pray that I forgive you by the next time I see you."

I swallow hard. Being separated from Ashley's the worst punishment I can think of. I did it to myself, though, and if I don't cooperate I'll get my second write-up and be one step closer to expulsion.

I walk slowly to the back of the line. Everyone's silent all of a sudden, staring at me as I shuffle past them, my head bowed slightly and my hands behind my back. Morgan snickers as I walk past and I tell myself Vanessa's putting her in her place over it, but I know I'm lying to myself.

Simone turns her head around as I slide in behind her. "I'm glad you're next to me even though you shouldn't have got in trouble," she whispers.

"Face forward, please, everyone," Ms Vargas says sharply and Simone hurries to turn back around.

I blink back tears. The study manager mocked me by calling me sweet and innocent, but you know who is? Simone, that's who.

I can't let this place change her.

I concentrate on putting one foot in front of the other as we all head toward the stairs.

twelve

THE CONFERENCE ROOM is so bright that my eyes hurt. I've only ever been in here for Restorative Justice Circle — when someone does something minorly bad, like trip another girl in the dining room or take too long in the shower so the hot water gets used up, we have a BS meeting where the girl who got hurt gets to explain how the other one made her feel.

I've heard that girls sit here on trial with Mrs. MacGregor right before they're expelled, though. I look around, memorizing every aspect of the place so I won't be thrown off if that turns out to be me.

The room's got too much white in it. The walls and table are painted the same bright shade and there's white papers in front of each seat, which thankfully is made from some fuzzy black fabric. The only other color in the room comes from a big screen in the wall in front of where Mrs. MacGregor is working on a laptop, which looks like a flat-screen TV.

I start to pull a chair out. Mrs. MacGregor looks up and says, sharply, "Find the paper with your name on it, Brianna. Don't sit in someone else's seat."

The papers are all identical, but there's no point in arguing. I walk around the table. Mine's at the far end, as far from Ashley as you can get, and I'm sandwiched between Molly and Lisa. Yuck.

At least Elizabeth's on Molly's other side, so I can lean over if she needs me.

I throw myself into my chair, fantasizing about magically switching Ashley's paper with Lisa's so she ends up next to me.

Elizabeth leans over Molly. "Patrice said they have security footage of the poisoning," she says. "I don't believe her. Do you?"

I shake my head slightly. There's no way they'd let us all see something like that. They'd just call whoever was on that tape to the office and deal with them privately.

"I did not say that," Patrice says from Lisa's other side. "I said — "

"Ew," Lisa says. "Stop breathing on me before I catch something."

Patrice's pale, white cheeks turn overripe-tomato red.

"Lisa," Ms. Carter says quietly, but Mrs. MacGregor is already flashing the lights on and off so she doesn't go on.

"All right, ladies," Mrs. MacGregor says. "We called you all in here today because we have a surprise for you. Tasha is well enough to speak with all of you for a few minutes. So, we are going to connect with her via video and then we will give each of you girls a few minutes to talk with her."

Vanessa spins her seat back and forth. "In front of everyone? No privacy?"

So that's what Ms. Carter's message meant. I stare at Vanessa, trying to gauge if she's really pissed or play acting. My money's on this being real cause of how her eyes are spitting fire.

"What we want and what is possible are sometimes two different things, Vanessa," Mrs. MacGregor says. "This is the way we are doing it. Now, we need to go over the ground rules. We've printed out a sheet for each girl who wants to talk to Tasha to sign, but we're going to explain first."

Vanessa leans back in her chair, pressing her arms tight against her chest. Her eyes are narrow like she's pissed, but I see something else in her.

She's calculating, figuring out her next move.

What is she planning?

I bend over my paper, ignoring her, and read the rules without really listening:

The conversation will be public, but only one person will be speaking to Tasha at a time. When it is your turn, you may have up to 10 minutes with her.

You are not to talk about:

- Illegal activity (gangs, drugs, etc)

My head shoots up. I'm not dumb; I know shit like what I was arrested for goes down in jails and probably here too, but this cohort's so tiny that the idea of any kind of gang almost makes me laugh.

But if Tasha was involved in something, that's a motive to kill.

I read the next part:

- Rumors and speculation about who poisoned her
- What she knows about that night.

What? So the admin's kneecapping the investigation, making it against the rules to talk to her about anything useful. Why? What they got to hide?

Talking about forbidden topics will result in forfeiting the rest of your allotted time.

Not if I do it right. Tasha probably has nothing to say to me anyway, but if I can get her talking without the admin catching on, I'm golden.

I look around the room to see how everyone else is taking this. Molly is fidgeting. Vanessa's rolling her eyes.

And Simone...

Simone's staring down at the paper and hugging herself like she wishes she could disappear into it.

I whisper to Elizabeth, "You know what's wrong with Simone?"

Elizabeth nods. "Simone doesn't want to talk to Tasha."

Ashley somehow hears from all the way on the other side of the table, cause she pushes her paper away and says, "Do we have to? I'm not interested."

"Why?" Lisa says. "Afraid she'll tell the whole world what you did to her?"

Ashley's eyes narrow. "I didn't," she says flatly.

"Don't engage," Ms. Carter tells her. "And Lisa, that is inappropriate. You just forfeited your opportunity to talk to Tasha."

"Like I wanted to," Lisa says under her breath.

I turn toward Molly to ask her what's up with that. Her eyes are darting back and forth, nervously.

Why is she so anxious?

"You okay?" I whisper.

Molly nods. "J-just the idea of seeing Tasha..." She fidgets. "Bet being stuck in the hospital's making her even more aggravated with everyone than usual."

"Did you sign your papers, girls?" Ms. Carter interrupts.

I hurry to sign mine. Even though it's probably useless, I have to get my time with Tasha. It's my only chance of finding out anything about what she knows.

Ms. Carter collects the signed papers "Those who have elected not to speak need to sit quietly while the conversation is going on," she says.

Ashley bites her lip. I don't blame her for being upset, not one bit. Why should she be forced to listen to Tasha after the way that girl treated her?

Mrs. MacGregor does something with a laptop plugged into a projector at the front of the table. Her screen is on the far wall, where we can all see it. She clicks on the video chat icon. After a minute, Tasha's face comes on the screen.

I stiffen as I stare at it. Tasha's lying in her hospital bed. She's got one of those tubes in her nose to help her breathe — I can't remember the name even though Mom's told me a million times — and an IV in her arm. There's all kinds of monitors behind her, checking her breathing and heart rate and all that.

She looks... small. Her hair is straight down instead of in braids and is lying limply across the pillow, and she doesn't have nearly as much color in her brown cheeks as usual. Her eyes don't have much light in them either.

I remember all of a sudden how she looked when the EMTs laid her out on the floor. She was like a ghost then, like she knew she was dying.

She doesn't look much different now.

"About half of the girls want to talk to you," Mrs. MacGregor says, "and the rest are silently hoping you get well soon."

"Right," Tasha says, and laughs. Same old Tasha, but her voice is raspy and even that one word's left her gasping for breath. "What about... um... the girl... in... the... dining... room... who couldn't... take... joke... when I... stole... her... fork? She brave... enough... to... show... her... face?"

What the hell is this? Why is she calling me out?

I stand anyway. Can't show weakness. Besides, I wanted to talk to her, didn't I? "I'm here, Tasha."

"Good," Tasha says. "I... want... to... talk... to... you... first."

Mrs. MacGregor nods. "Go ahead, Brianna." She pats the chair where I'm supposed to sit to talk to Tasha.

I come up, slowly, my heart pounding, and sit down in the chair.

Don't show any fear. I let my breath out slowly and say, "How you feeling, Tasha?"

"Getting... there..." Tasha has to stop to catch her breath. "Who-ever... did... this... needs... to... know... I'm... coming... back... stronger... than... ever."

She's staring at someone in this room, or she would be if she could sit up.

Who is that message meant for?

"Listen...," Tasha says before I can say a word. "That... day... in... the... dining... room... was... a... test. You... passed." She grins.

A test? What? "Um, thanks?" I say uncertainly.

Tasha laughs, which makes her cough. After it passes, she says, "You... didn't... let... me... mess... with... your... little... You... sent... her... away... and... faced... me... your... self. Mad... respect." She gasps for breath, then holds up her finger. A second later, the chat thing dings and displays on the screen:

Your loyalty ain't misplaced. None of your friends is a problem & we got a common enemy.

Mrs. MacGregor's jaw tightens as she reads it. "Let's not go there, please, Tasha," she says. She glances at me. "Anything else you want to say before we move on?"

She wants me to shut up before Tasha says something I'm not supposed to hear. I won't do it. "One more thing," I say.

"Make... it... quick...," Tasha says.

"Right. I won't keep you long, but listen. There's all sorts of rumors flying around here about that night and some girls are getting beat up on the regular. Think you can tell anyone who needs to hear to back off?"

Tasha nods. She types on the screen: *I know you all can read, so don't pretend you didn't see this. Hold your fire til you know who did what or pay the price.*

"Maybe we should let you rest now, Tasha," Mrs. MacGregor says.

Tasha shakes her head. "I... have... business... where's... Ashley?"

Ashley gasps as everyone turns toward her. "No," she whispers. "Please."

Vanessa stands. "I'll take her time if she doesn't want it."

"There's... my... boo," Tasha says. "Grab... Ashley... for... me."

"Tasha," Ms. Carter says quietly.

"You'd better do it," Lisa says. "Face your accuser."

Ashley's eyes flash. She turns toward Ms. Carter. "I-is she allowed to..."

Ms. Carter says, "No, and Tasha, if you are inappropriate this conversation will end."

Tasha grins. "I'm... always... appropriate."

Ashley stands. *Brave girl*, I think as she takes a few steps forward, slowly. I can't tell if my heart's pounding cause this makes me love her even more or cause I'm scared for her.

"All right," she says. "I'm here." Her voice is hard and tough, but I catch a slight shake.

"Good." Tasha grins. "Don't... worry. I... kept... my... promise."

Ashley's eyes narrow. I can hear her breathing coming harder. "Now...," Tasha says. "Repeat... after... me. 'I'm... too... soft... to... kill. Tasha... knows... I... didn't... hurt... her.'

Ashley swallows hard. Her eyes dart everywhere, but she does what she's told, whispering it so low I can barely hear her.

"Louder," Tasha orders.

"No," Ms. Carter says, stepping in. "You made your point, Tasha. Ashley, go ahead and sit down. Sick or not, Tasha is not allowed to bully you." She puts her arm around Ashley and leads her away.

Tasha laughs. "They... missed... the... point... Ness."

"I got it," Vanessa says. She crosses her arms. "You know for sure she didn't?"

Mrs. MacGregor clears her throat, but I already know that's the extent of her enforcing this rule. Good. I want to hear the answer too.

Tasha nods. "They... weren't... after... me. They... wanted... her." Her breath comes in gasps and wheezes, almost as bad as when she got poisoned. She holds up her finger, then begins typing:

Ness... get who really did this to me. Please.

Mrs. MacGregor walks in front of the screen, blocking the message. It reflects off her white sweater, making it impossible to read. "I think we need to let Tasha rest," she says. "Anyone else who wanted to talk to her will have another chance when she's a little stronger."

"On three," Ms. Carter adds, "let's all tell Tasha 'Get well soon.'"

Half of us just mouth it but she lets that go, then tells Tasha they'll be in touch when they're ready for another session.

Mrs. MacGregor disconnects. I stare at the screen, which now says SIGNAL LOST against a green background.

There isn't gonna be any next time. This was it.

At least Tasha cleared Ashley. Now Vanessa's gonna have to admit I was right.

My stomach sinks even though I'm happy for Ashley. She's cleared, but I didn't do it, not really. Plus...

...there's still a poisoner sitting in this room and I don't know who it is.

thirteen

MRS. MACGREGOR DISMISSES us for lunch as if Tasha didn't just turn the world upside down. I get up slowly as the full weight of her words hit me:

They weren't after me. They wanted her.

"Her" being Ashley.

Someone hated Ashley enough they were willing to try to kill someone else just to frame her. Who in here could be that cold?

My eyes dart around the room. Almost everybody's at the door. Most of the girls are jostling each other, using their elbows to try to get a space in line they aren't entitled to. Simone's hanging back, staying out of the fray, but I know it's not her who hurt Tasha, so that doesn't help me.

Only one still sitting's Ashley.

She's frozen, staring into space while she runs one finger up and down her arm, blinking hard.

"Ashley?" I say, taking a step toward her. "What's wrong?"

Ashley shakes her head but says nothing. I long to scoop her up in my arms, but instead I just take another step, intending to sit with her.

Ms. Carter's voice cuts through the air. "Brianna. In line, please, so we can go. You too, Ashley."

Ashley sighs so deeply her whole body shakes and her chair scratches the floor hard as she gets up.

I can feel the weight of everyone's eyes on her, so she's gotta, too. Maybe that's why she walks slow and hunched over as an 80-year-old grandma.

I slip in behind her but before I can even ask if she's okay, she says, "I'm coping. Leave me alone."

She's not, and I don't want to, but I gotta respect her space. I turn my head forward, staring at Ashley's back as Ms. Carter goes down the line checking us off on her list to make sure no one's missing.

I tell myself I wouldn't even begin to know what to say, but my heart won't stop breaking for Ashley anyway.

The smell of fresh rolls hits my nose soon as I slip through the dining room door. Bread from Gold's Bakery — the most famous place in downtown Cedarwood, ten minutes by car from the little apartment Mom and I share — should be a treat, but today it makes my cheeks feel tight with nausea and my head start throbbing all over again. When it's my turn at the sandwich bar, I stand frozen, unable to decide if I want a pretzel roll or poppy seeds, while behind us, Ms. Carter gives us some dumb lecture about how Leo Gold used to be in a program like us but now he's co-owner of one of the most successful small businesses in town.

Yeah, yeah, yeah. None of us in here have a dad willing to put us in the family business in order to bankroll our second chance.

And while we're on the subject of money, how long before the budget for buying food from local businesses runs out and they start shipping us off to juvie cause they can't afford to feed us?

We all know if that happens, I'll be the first put behind bars so whatever secrets these walls hold stay hidden. I'd better crack this mystery fast.

"Move, bitch!" Lisa says. "The rest of us need to eat too."

The only thing that stops me punching the smirk off her ugly face is my knowledge that's a one-way ticket to juvie. I grab a poppy-seed roll, but I take my time about it, moving slow on purpose to show Lisa that I'm not about to let her win.

My headache's in full force by the time I hit the table with my buttered roll and two pieces of ham on the side. I throw myself in my seat and rub the back of my neck as I take my N-95 off, wishing I could get away with ditching this thing permanently.

"I didn't expect that, did you?" Elizabeth says excitedly. "I thought for sure Tasha would go along with framing Ashley. But now that's out of the way, and by the way, didn't I say it was too obvious and she was being framed?"

"Elizabeth," I say quietly. "Can you not? I'm not feeling it right now." I turn toward Simone. "I need headache meds. Do me a favor and run to the nurse for ibuprofen."

Simone's eyes narrow. "D-do I have to?" she stammers. "Can't Elizabeth — "

"She said you, *hermanita*," Vanessa says from behind us. I flinch as her gravelly voice cuts through the air — where'd she even come from? "She must have her reasons." Vanessa turns toward me and says under her breath. "What are they?"

"I"m sick and I need meds," I say. "Better stay away before you catch something."

Vanessa crosses her arms. "And here I thought you would gloat your girl's name was cleared. You are full of surprises." She lowers her voice. "Headache or not, I need the inside scoop. Why Simone?"

She's not going to leave this alone. Guess I gotta tell her. "So she can prove someone forged her name on the medication log when they signed out that spare Epi-Pen. Nurse wouldn't let me see earlier."

Vanessa's eyes widen. "Leave it to me," she says, patting my shoulder, then turns toward Simone "We go together, si? Get your *hermana* her meds so she stops biting off everyone's head?"

Hermana. Sister. How does Vanessa know how tight me and Simone are? She's like a comic book villain who magically knows all for the sake of the plot.

"We'll be back," Vanessa says. "Drink some water in the meanwhile. Dehydration makes it worse." She turns away from me before I can answer. "Come, Simone."

Simone gulps so loud I can hear it, but she follows Vanessa.

I slump in my seat. What have I done? The less time Simone spends around that bully, the better. But for the third time today , I have to ask myself if I had a choice. My battery's nearly dead from the pain. How can I be expected to fight Vanessa on this under the circumstances, especially when the admins made it clear that whatever she wants, she gets?

Vanessa's arm is wrapped around Simone in a sisterly way, but she's squeezing her tight enough to pin her arms to her sides. That's an abduction in plain sight if you ask me, and the worst part is, there's nothing I can do about it. I groan softly with pain as they disappear through the side door.

"You should eat," Elizabeth says. "I always feel sick when I don't."

I pick up my sandwich just to keep her quiet about it. When Elizabeth gets stuck on something, she won't stop repeating it, and my head can't take that right now.

The bread's got the perfect blend of sweet and salty to it. I gobble it down in five seconds and long for a second one even though I can hear Mom's voice saying, "That's not proper nutrition, Brianna. Bread is a side piece, not lunch." Sometimes having a doctor for a mom sucks cause she always knows too much.

After dinner one night, Mom puts me on dish-drying duty so she can talk to me. "Grades slipping, skipping school, ignoring curfew... this isn't you, Brianna."

I scoff, trying to hide my annoyance. "Course it is," I say. "I can't be anyone but me." My voice shakes.

Mom crosses her arms. "Brianna," she says softly. "I can see you're hurting, baby. What's that mean, you can't be anyone but you? You wish you could, I can see that. But why would such a smart, beautiful girl throw everything away to try to be something she's not?"

I swallow hard. Cause everyone hates me. Cause the only girlfriend I can get is mad heavy into drugs and the more I'm with her, the more I'm aware no one else would ever want me. "If you think my life is something to envy, you don't know anything about me," I say, my voice choked up.

Mom puts her hand on my shoulder. "Talk. to. me." I bite my lip, shaking my head slightly. I don't know how to tell her that I'm in over my head, drowning, really, and I don't know how to make it back to the surface. I can't say the words cause if she knew Natalie was having me take her to get drugs...

Mom says, "Tell me the truth, Brianna. I won't be mad and I won't punish you, I promise. But I need to know. Are you... have you started using drugs?"

My throat is so tight I can't breathe. How can she think that of me? All the times I've taken Natalie, I've never once been tempted to use myself. Still, it's too close to the truth. It's like I'm using without touching the stuff cause I'm not eating, not sleeping, not going to school...

I shake my head slightly. "You know me better than that, Mom," I say, my voice choked, and grab another plate from the rack, scrubbing my towel as hard as I can over it.

I bite my lip now. There's no reason to be thinking about this. None. So what if Mom was trying to help me? I didn't let her and now look what happened.

A chair scrapes against the floor. Ashley gets up and goes to the trash even though she's only taken about two bites of her sandwich.

"Ash?" I say as she walks past.

She keeps going. Either she doesn't hear me or she's pretending not to, and I cant tell which it is.

Simone and Vanessa aren't back by the time Ms. Carter tells us to clean up after ourselves so we can go to afternoon activities. I stand up slowly, hoping Vanessa didn't get Simone in trouble, and check my head. The pain's still there, but duller. I guess eating helped after all, though I feel like my body's twice as heavy as usual and my thinking's slowed way down.

"Where's Simone?" Ms. Carter asks me.

I flinch. "She went with Vanessa to get me my meds," I say carefully.

Ms. Carter lets her breath out slowly. "Good. I was afraid she got stuck in a closet again." She walks away before I can ask her what she means.

Did she... did she just admit that she knows Simone getting locked in that closet wasn't an accident?

Was that really only this morning? I rub the back of my neck, unable to believe it. It feels like 10 million years ago.

Ashley slips past me and out the door leading to the bathrooms. I glance over my shoulder to make sure Ms. Carter isn't watching before I follow her.

I shouldn't. She said she wanted space. But something tells me she needs me.

I feel like a damn stalker as I catch the bathroom door before it closes and tiptoe in behind her. I wasn't even this bad with Natalie.

Ashley goes over to the sink. She rolls up her sleeve and stares down at it.

I freeze. She's got all sorts of scars running down that arm, like a roadmap made of cuts.

Ashley reaches under the sink and pulls out something taped there.

A razor, the super sharp kind like men sometimes use to get their beards off.

She puts the razor against her skin.

I gasp involuntarily. Worst thing I can do cause if I startle her...

The razor clatters into the sink. Ashley turns toward me, her hands out. "Sorry you saw that," she says. "I-I wasn't gonna cut, I swear. I thought if I just touched the razor to it, it would be like doing it."

"K," I say flatly. I swallow hard. "All those scars... you did that to yourself?"

Ashley's cheeks darken. "It's not what you think, all right? You saw, now go away and forget it."

I freeze, suddenly remembering that Tasha was holding something over Ashley and Vanessa said something to her about the potatoes being sharp.

They knew. They fucking knew and they used it against her, to control her.

"I'm not gonna tell," I say. "Promise." I cross my arms. "But why now? Tasha cleared you so why do you need — "

"She humiliated me," Ashley says, "and she could take it all back just for fun." She stares at the scars, breathing hard. "You think I wanted you to know I do this to myself? You've been like, the only person on my side, and now you know I'm crazy."

Ashley's eyes are so wide and full of fear. I hate myself for wanting more than ever to kiss her cause of those eyes. She's in pain — what's wrong with me?

"You're not," I say, "not any more than me." I cross my arms. "I'm here cause I let some girl drag me to the pits of hell, took her to get drugs on the regular cause that was the price of her loving me. And I thought that was normal." I shake my head. "I was so far gone when the cops pulled me over part of me hoped I was getting arrested cause then it would be over. I wouldn't be able to tell myself I wasn't doing this anymore and then go right back to it."

Ashley swallows hard. "Least your foster parents didn't call the cops on you. Imagine this woman who promised this was your forever home blocking the door to make sure you stuck around til they came to get you." She swallows hard. "You're really telling me you never even touched cocaine or speed or anything?"

"Weed sometimes," I say. "I was stoned more often than not, but..." I let my breath out slowly. "Don't let Tasha win, all right? Don't do this to yourself."

"It's not as simple as all that." Ashley blinks hard. "Sometimes I can't help myself." She bites her lip. "Look, you've been great and all, but trying to save me's a waste of time. Don't bother anymore."

I take a step toward her. "You a waste of time? Please." My heart pounds. Do I tell her how I feel? She probably already knows, but going from an open secret to the truth... in this place, that's dangerous. "You're not a project," I say. "You're... I help you cause your smile lights up the room and lately it's been missing too much."

Ashley bites her lip. "You're too good for all this," she says. "I wish I was different but..." She sighs as footsteps sound. "Go do what you came here to do," she says, raising her voice. She hides the razor quick and slips into a stall.

I stare at the door as she slams and locks it. I'd wait all day for her to come out if I was allowed, but I'm not. Besides, she's making it clear she wants me to go and I gotta respect that.

I turn and walk slowly away, praying Simone's back with my meds, cause now my head's twice as bad again.

Ms. Carter's spraying a table with cleaner, but she turns her head as I come in. "Where were you?"

Something in me snaps. "I had to pee,"I say. "That against the rules too around here?"

Ms. Carter raises her eyebrows. She looks me up and down while I refuse to look away. Finally, she says, "Ask first next time, please. I'm not having people disappear without explanation on my watch." She gestures toward a small cup on the table. "Here. Take your headache med and then I need you to help Simone with the broom."

I shove the pill ino my mouth and swallow it down without any water or anything. It almost sticks in my throat and I catch myself wishing it would.

I freeze. What? No matter how bad things got, I never wanted to hurt myself. That's not me. That's Ashley.

I don't have to be her just cause I'm worried about her.

I let my breath out slowly, letting the thought wash over me. Guess that's what Ms. Carter means in group when she keeps saying that she's gonna help us learn where we end and other people begin.

I walk slowly over to Simone. I know it sounds crazy, but I feel this need to keep reminding myself, *I'm Brianna, not Ashley*.

"This broom is too big for me," Simone complains, breaking me out of the weird trance I'm in. "You sweep."

I look over my shoulder. I'm not supposed to be doing the littles' jobs for them. "

“Let me see it," I say. Simone hands me the broom and then I make her let me put her hands on it so I can see if it's really too big for her.

"Both hands together," I tell her, and gently move her right, which she has all the way down by the bristles, to where it belongs. As I hand her back the broom, I say under my breath, "What happened at the nurse?"

Simone squeezes the broom handle tight. "Um..." she says. "The nurse made a big deal of asking for my resident ID when it's only headache pills. She reminded me of that dumb cop that insisted I threw that egg. All he had to do was look in my bag and see the eggs I bought were closed but he put handcuffs on me instead." She leans her chin on the broom, staring into space.

"Probably the same one that got me for those drugs," I say flatly. "But that was a while back, right? Come back to now and tell me about the nurse. You showed her ID and then what?"

"She let me sign and then she made like a hmm sound and Vanessa made her say what that means." Simone twists the broom handle instead of sweeping. "The nurse said she had to talk to the night nurse about something when she comes in but she wouldn't answer me what." She makes a few halfhearted sweeping gestures.

"Maybe she wants to check your ID against what the night nurse took," I say. "If she took one at all."

"She did not," Vanessa says, coming up to us. She glances at Simone. "Go sweep, hermanita. Brianna and I need to talk in private."

"You found who signed my name?" Simone asks. "Was it Patrice?"

"No," Vanessa says, her jaw tight. "And private means you go over there and I talk to Brianna without you."

Simone's face falls but she does what she's told.

"I was too hard with the little one?" Vanessa asks me.

"Maybe," I say, careful to keep my tone neutral. "Simone's not usually like this. It's Elizabeth who has to be told ten times and doesn't accept being left out of something."

"I admire the spirit," Vanessa says, "but these littles need to learn to respect us. But that will come." She crosses her arms. "I did get something from the nurse," she says quietly. "I have ways to get information from her that Simone does not and I played this card because it was so important."

My heart pounds. I have no idea what any of that means, but I don't dare ask. "And?"

"And," Vanessa says quietly, "a certain traitor has been caught red-handed. It is on the camera if the administration bothers to look that Morgan signed out a second Epi-Pen using our hermanita's name."

fourteen

I STARE AT VANESSA. "So Morgan took two Epi-Pens?" I say, my voice hard. "First Tasha's, then a spare? What for?"

"It isn't obvious?" Vanessa crosses her arms. "She wanted Tasha to die."

I swallow hard. "You think? She's young, maybe she didn't know — "

"If she's big enough to steal every Epi-Pen in the house, she is big enough to know she is almost signing a death certificate for Tasha when she does this." Vanessa hits her palm with her fist. "But don't worry. She will be taken care of."

My heart pounds. "Now? I'm coming with you."

Vanessa's eyes narrow. "I appreciate you want to help," she says, "but some things are not for your eyes and ears."

My throat tightens. "Serious?" I say. "First of all, Morgan's sitting on info that could crack this thing wide open, and I'm the one who started looking into what happened to Tasha."

"And she asked me to finish the job," Vanessa says. "Besides, this is for your own good. You can't be pressured to snitch if you haven't seen anything."

"I don't snitch. Ever." I press my arms tight against my chest. "But maybe I should change that. See, I just saw Ashley in the bathroom, and

I know you know what she was doing there." I drag my finger over my arm.

Vanessa's eyes flash but she says, quietly, "You saw her cutting again?"

My throat tightens. I'm not sure I buy this caring act, not when Vanessa's known for months and done nothing. I nod anyway cause I started this so I have to finish it. "How could you and Tasha — "

"It is past history," Vanessa says, her voice hard, "and I had reasons that I cannot explain right now." She crosses her arms. "I was hoping she would learn her lesson after getting caught."

I stare at her. "Serious? You blackmailed her to get her to stop?"

"It was not me. It was Tasha. I only asked her... never mind." Vanessa sighs. "Are you calm enough to be useful when we confront Morgan or do you have more yelling to get out of your system?"

My cheeks darken. "I'm alright, I guess." I'm not, really, but Vanessa's the last person I ever want knowing how all over the place I am right now.

"Come, then," Vanessa says, her lips a thin line. "We will get the truth out of Morgan and then I will punish her."

I swallow hard. I know Morgan probably helped poison Tasha, but I can't help thinking that she's still a kid.

Morgan's sitting at a table by herself, twisting a rag and hitting it against the table instead of doing any work. I roll my eyes, wondering why I felt bad for her a second ago. Every time I try to extend a little grace her way, she disappoints me acting like an entitled brat.

We're almost there when Ms. Carter says, "Excuse me, girls. I'm doing my final checks now, but it looks like everything is adequately cleaned. Instead of hanging out here, I want you all to go to the day room."

I freeze.

"Let her go first," Vanessa whispers. "That way she stews in her fear about what I will do to her if the nurse told me what she did."

I bite my lip. This feels all wrong, just like the night I was arrested. Earlier that night, Natalie wanted a ride to "see a friend," which was code for taking her to meet her dealer. Something felt off in the air while I was sitting and waiting for her, like when you know it's getting ready to thunder but the sky's still clear. She made me double-park in front of some guy's apartment and I kept thinking someone was about to sneak up and carjack me, but nothing happened except me feeling dumb.

Not an hour later, I was in the back of a cop car headed for juvie after the cops caught me with cocaine in my glove box. Ten minutes after I dropped Natalie at home, they pulled me over with a BS excuse that I sped through a yellow. Soon as I opened up that compartment so I could get out my registration card, there it was: a little baggie of white powder that gave the cops everything they needed to cuff me up and throw me in a squad car. Didn't matter I had no record and no evidence I was high. I tried to tell them those weren't my drugs and I hadn't even known they were there, but they didn't care. They came at me with guns out like I didn't have my hands in plain sight so they would know I wasn't gonna try anything crazy, and the next thing I knew they had me facedown on the cold, dirty shoulder of the road, yelling at me to lie still so they could cuff me when I wasn't moving in the first place.

I squeeze my eyes shut, trying to block out the sound of their voices barking orders and the feeling of the cuffs snapping closed over my wrists.

I take another breath. Point is, that night my better angels warned me to stay home and if I'd listened, I wouldn't be here dealing with Morgan and her nonsense. I'd be home watching a movie with Mom, a big ol' bowl of popcorn between us.

I blink hard. The air feels like that again. Heavy. Electric. Dangerous.

But what choice do I have when I'm already in this deep?

It's my fault I'm trapped. I could have gone about my business if I hadn't thrown a tantrum about Vanessa going after Morgan alone.

I count silently to 4 in my head before letting my breath out like they teach us in group. *They can't arrest me when I'm already under arrest*, I tell myself, but I know that's BS. One wrong move and I'll be cuffed up all over again and thrown on a bus to juvie.

Two girls are huddled in the corner by the stairs as we pass by. I turn my head. Is that Ashley half hidden in shadows?

"Please," the girl says, her voice shaking. "You know I'm good for it."

Yep, that's Ashley, and she's up to something she shouldn't be.

I tap Vanessa to get her attention and gesture.

"Drug deal?" I whisper.

"Maybe." Vanessa's jaw is set. "Keep it moving, Bri."

"But..."

Vanessa sighs. "You know how it is here. To get in someone else's business like this, it screams snitch." She squeezes my shoulder. "Come," she says, and lowers her voice in a way that makes me shiver involuntarily even though I didn't think I was into her like that. "I will take care of your girl. Promise."

Yeah, right. This is the same girl that knew Ashley was cutting and used it to force her to do things she didn't want to do.

My shoulders slump as Vanessa throws her arm around me. I don't have any energy left to fight her.

I feel like she's dragging me away the same way the cops did after they put me in cuffs.

Morgan's over at the Ping Pong table with Simone and Patrice. Simone reaches for the ball, but misses. She throws her paddle down, then lets her breath out slowly. "Only a game," she says to herself, then turns to me. "I'm glad you're here. Morgan cheats and we don't want to play with her."

"Don't, then," I tell her. I'm not in the mood for this nonsense.

Simone gulps. "I wish," she says, looking away.

I put my hands on her shoulders. "Simone," I say under my breath. "We got proof that signature was forged, remember? You don't have to do what she wants any more. You're free."

Simone shrugs. She looks so tiny as she picks up her paddle. I wish she would listen to me, but trying to tell her anything more is just wasting my breath.

"We will take this problem off your hands. Don't worry, *hermania*," Vanessa says. She turns toward Morgan. "You. Paddle down. Come. We need to talk."

Morgan scowls. "I didn't do nothing," she says.

"Maybe wait til we accuse to start defending," Vanessa says. "Now are you coming or do I have to pull you by those cornrows you just put in?"

"I'm coming, I'm coming," Morgan mumbles. "I'm just telling you — " Vanessa gives her a stare so cold I get chills and she shuts up and throws her paddle on the table.

"I won, you lost," she says to Simone. "You owe me chips. Pay up on Friday."

Simone swallows hard.

"She's not paying you anything," Vanessa says. "Not one crumb from the bottom of the bag." She glances at Simone like she wants to say something else, then changes her mind. "You're in the hot seat," she tells Morgan, "so I would be careful before making demands of any of my girls."

Morgan's eyes widen. "She's yours? What?"

"I just said she was," Vanessa says, crossing her arms, "but we will not talk about it over here where anyone can listen." She glances over at the couch, where Lisa is curled up reading a book, and rolls her eyes.

Vanessa makes Morgan come with us to a corner of the room that has chairs set up. We use this area for meetings sometimes when it's not so serious we need the conference room. Morgan throws herself into an easy chair, scowling.

"Don't get too comfortable," Vanessa says. "You have questions to answer, and you can't afford any wrong ones." She hits her palm with her fist.

Morgan gulps, but she crosses her arms. "Bring it on. I'm not scared of you."

"Spoken like a guilty person," I say, crossing my arms. "My aunt's a lawyer, Morgan, I know all the tricks."

Morgan laughs nervously. "So?"

"So," I go on, "that's not all I know. Me and Vanessa, we both know you stole two Epi-Pens. One from Tasha herself and one from the nurse's office. What's up with that?"

Morgan's smile fades. She twists a cornrow, looking away. "Stop lying on me."

"You need to listen to yourself," Vanessa says. "You are the one lying.

We know you tried to help kill Tasha. The only question is what I should do with a girl who so easily betrays Tasha and then just as easily lies about it." She takes a step forward.

Morgan flinches. I say to Vanessa, "Remember what I said before. Maybe she didn't know better." I turn toward Morgan. "That what happened? Someone told you it was just a little joke?"

"No. I'm not dumb." Morgan squeezes her hands together, her eyes darting everywhere. "You don't understand. I had to."

More blackmail? Was there anyone who wasn't living with some kind of threat hanging over their head? "Who made you do it?"

Morgan shakes her head slightly. "All I can say is, there are some people in here you don't want to cross."

I glare at her so hard my eyes hurt. "You're telling us next to nothing," I say, annoyed. "Look, Morgan, we don't hate you, all right? But how am I supposed to help you if you won't tell me the truth?"

Morgan laughs "You help me? You got jokes, huh?" She swallows hard. "You think Simone getting locked up in that closet was bad? Keep pushing and see what happens."

I breathe in sharply, gasping aloud before I can stop myself.

"ENOUGH!" Vanessa says. "Didn't I tell you Simone was my girl and you'd better keep your hands off her?" Morgan shrugs. Vanessa squats so they're at eye-level. "You had a chance to talk and you threw it away. So now... there will be consequences. I can't tell you what they are or when they will happen, but what we sow we always reap sooner or later. I am not the only one who knows you are a coward who would rather poison a girl who looked out for her when she first came here than risk a secret being exposed. And once people realize this, they will know you are the perfect person to pick on because you are too afraid to fight back. Now get out of my sight."

Morgan's eyes flash. "All cause your precious Simone's name was in my mouth! She's not so innocent, you know. If I'm a coward, so's she, cause she saw what I did and she didn't say a word."

Vanessa glares at her. "This nonsensical response only proves your weakness. Go. I don't want to share the same space with you right now."

Morgan's jaw is set and she's got a scowl on like she doesn't care one bit what Vanessa thinks of her, but I can see in her eyes that she does, more than anything.

She turns and slinks away.

Vanessa stands still, tapping her fingers on her elbows while her nostrils flare and her eyes spit fire.

"You alright?" I say, realizing too late that's the wrong question. Vanessa's not ever gonna say anything but "yeah," cause to do otherwise could give me ammo against her.

Vanessa nods. "Thinking is all." Her jaw tightens, making her face more square. "Morgan is right," she says. "Simone kept quiet."

I stiffen. "That's not fair, Vanessa. You know as well as I do why. Look how small she is, and you're over here expecting her to stand up to someone making the kill sign at her."

"Smallness is no excuse. I was tinier than her when..." Vanessa swallows hard. "Never mind. The point is, if she lets her smallness be an excuse people will trample her. I have to toughen her for her own good." Her eyes dart everywhere.

I stare at her, torn between wanting to know what happened to her to make her this way and not knowing why I care. She's a bully. What else do I need to know?

"I told you before, staring at other girls is a bad idea," Vanessa says. The words are hard but her voice is soft. "Be useful and go get Simone. She needs to understand she did wrong."

"But — "

"You asked me to take care of her. This is part of it." Vanessa's voice is very quiet. She takes a step toward me. "Is she the only one I need to teach a lesson to?"

My throat tightens with anger. All sorts of smart-ass answers run through my head. But they stay there, unsaid, while I turn like the coward I am and drag my feet toward the other end of the room.

I hate myself for what I'm doing to Simone, but I don't see a way out.

Vanessa's Natalie 2.0 except she has me caught in a steel trap, one I can't get out of without Simone getting hurt.

I blink back tears, telling myself to get it together before Simone sees something's wrong.

fifteen

SIMONE GRINS AT me when I find her at the chess table, playing with Elizabeth. "Look!" she says. "I'm winning her for once."

A quick glance at the board tells me that's not the case. Elizabeth has her pieces lined up to take a pawn and checkmate the king all at once. "That's great," I say flatly, not willing to crush Simone's spirit altogether.

Simone's grin fades. "What's wrong?"

"Vanessa..." I swallow hard. "She wants to talk to you."

Simone's eyes widen with fear but Elizabeth pipes up, "So? She's not the boss of us."

Simone runs her fingertips over one of her braids like she's double-checking it doesn't need to be fixed. "I-it's okay," she says. "I know she's mad at me so I need to get it over with." She stands, sighing deeply. "She wouldn't walk back with me after the nurse. She said she had something to do but I knew what she wanted was to be away from me."

I put my hand on her shoulder. "I'm gonna be with you the whole time in case she goes too far. Promise. Come on."

Simone nods. Elizabeth stands too and says, "If you're going, I'm going too." She glares at me as she pushes her glasses closer to her face. "And I can't be talked out of it so don't bother."

"Your funeral, I guess," I say. "No telling what she'll do with an extra person there, though."

Elizabeth's eyes widen but she tosses her hair over one shoulder and says, "I don't care what she thinks."

She does, but I don't want to waste time arguing so I let her follow us.

Vanessa's eyes narrow as she turns. I say quickly, "Elizabeth insisted on coming too."

Vanessa shrugs. "This might be a good lesson for her too." She pats the seat across from her. "Sit, Simone."

Simone sinks into the seat. Elizabeth slides over and stands next to her, her arms crossed, while Simone puts her hands in her lap and stares down at them.

"I'm sorry I didn't get the Epi-Pen from the nurse," she says. "I tried cause I knew Morgan had the other one and I didn't want Tasha to get hurt but she got there first."

Vanessa freezes, her lips parted like she was about to say something. I can't say I'm any less shocked. That's the most shy little Simone has ever said at once, and to jump in with it before Vanessa can start in on her takes guts.

"It's good you tried this," Vanessa says, "but we need to talk about before that. You saw Morgan take the Epi-Pen, yes?"

Simone nods. "M-Morgan did like this to me," she stammers, and makes the same signs she showed me, earlier. "I was so scared I didn't even tell Brianna til she made me."

"This morning," I add quickly, "long after it was too late." My cheeks grow hot. I shouldn't have said it that way. I was trying to make sure Vanessa knew I didn't see Tasha in danger and do nothing, but it came out like throwing Simone under the bus.

Vanessa crosses her arms. "Morgan is nothing," she says. "She is all hot air and trying to be tough."

Simone gulps. "But what if she gets a knife from the kitchen and —"

"It will not happen." Vanessa's voice is firm. "You should have come to me, hermanita," she says softly. "Staying silent helped Morgan hurt Tasha. You understand this?"

Simone stares at the ground. "I tried at the nurse," she mumbles.

"Besides," Elizabeth interrupts. "She wasn't friends with you then so how was she supposed to know?"

I breathe in sharply. Elizabeth can't seem to help talking herself into trouble, not that I'm much better. I was polite and all with the cops, but Mom always says my acid tongue's about to get me into something I can't get out of and being here hasn't improved that much.

Vanessa's eyes narrow. I say, "She's got a point. Not an hour before this all went down, you and Tasha and Morgan were messing with me and Elizabeth in the dining room. Simone wasn't gonna risk it."

Vanessa's eyes dart. "I have never... I am not a bully."

"I didn't hear you standing up for us when Tasha and Morgan started," Elizabeth says.

Vanessa's eyes snap. "There were reasons for this."

"And there were reasons I didn't tell!" Simone says, her voice shaking. "Morgan said I was going to go to grown-up prison cause she signed my name in the medical log." Her voice cracks. "I'm sorry I didn't tell, all right?"

Vanessa lets out a long, slow breath. She squats by Simone and tilts her chin up. "Look at me," she says softly. "Maybe when you were arrested you were a child, but in here you cannot be. That is why I do this, not to make you cry but to help you become tough. At home your mama says eat your vegetables to grow big and strong. Well, in here I am the vegetables. I teach you strength." She pats Simone's shoulder. "Now dry those eyes. Tears solves nothing in here."

Simone wipes her eyes with the back of her sleeve. The judge must not have been in his right mind, sending such a little thing here with girls ten times as big who'll eat her up for lunch and spit out the bones.

"That's better," Vanessa says. "Now, it is unacceptable to give in to threats. If Morgan or anyone else tries to scare you like this, you tell me. Comprende?"

Simone swallows hard. "Yes, ma'am," she mumbles. My chest aches with annoyance. Vanessa's only three years older than her. What right does she have making Simone treat her like she's an adult? And what's wrong with Simone she keeps going along with it?

"That's better," Vanessa says. "Now I need a cool-down. Go sit at the art table." She crosses her arms. "You will not draw. Turn your chair to face the wall."

"O-okay," Simone mumbles. She gets up, blinking back tears.

.

"You can't do that!" Elizabeth says. "You're not — "

"Elizabeth," I say, my voice very quiet. "Don't."

I lock eyes with her. She stares right back in mine, hers blazing. After a minute, she mumbles, "Fine," and runs after Simone.

I freeze, looking at her, then back at Vanessa. Vanessa mumbles something to herself in Spanish. Then she says, quietly, "The fiery one has cojones, I will give her this. Let's hope she doesn't teach Simone a wrong lesson." She presses her arms against her chest. "I am walking this off. Go handle your little ones while I am gone."

She turns and walks away. Her footsteps are heavy and they echo in my ears long after she's gone.

I get myself together and go to the art table. Simone's sitting at the art table, staring into space, but she hasn't turned her chair to face the wall. Next to her, Elizabeth's opening and closing a drawer in the table, nervously. It's got scissors and rolls of ribbons in it. One of the scissors looks broken, like it's only half a pair, but I can't tell if that's for real or I just didn't see right.

"Is Vanessa still mad?" Simone asks as I come over.

I nod slightly. "She'll get over it. I think she's more upset Elizabeth came over here than anything else."

"It had to be done," Elizabeth says. She takes a roll of yellow ribbon out the drawer and plays with it, twisting the loose part between her fingers. "Where Simone goes, I go."

"Elizabeth's trying to distract me," Simone adds, blinking hard. "We were talking about the poisoning. We think someone told Morgan to steal the Epi-Pens."

"Yeah," Elizabeth adds, "and someone had to smuggle peanut oil in here. We think it happened at the last store run but we can't figure out how yet."

"Yeah, me either." I agree. Store runs happen on Fridays. When Mr. Lancaster stops to fuel up the house van, we're allowed to visit the convenience store. Ms. Smith makes a list and takes two at a time. She checks their receipts to make sure no one bought any contraband before she lets them back on the van and takes the next two. "No way she'd let anyone on with peanut oil," I say, "especially after what happened with Ashley."

"What happened?" Simone asks. "Morgan distracted me laughing about me buying a strawberry kiwi vitamin water."

I squint, trying to remember exactly. I remember sitting in the van looking out the window during Ashley's turn. I wasn't being creepy or anything, but watching her walk through the parking lot with Ms. Smith made me feel lighter inside. Not that I could see much through those damn tinted windows. But something happened cause I saw Ms. Smith shake her head and say something and Ashley argued back.

"She was mad when she came back on the van, but she wouldn't tell me why," I say. "You know how she is."

"It wasn't peanut oil," Elizabeth said. "That would have got her more than yelled at."

"M-maybe it was another peanut thing," Simone says. "Cause I heard Molly ask Ashley..." She swallows hard. "Maybe I should tell Vanessa."

"Tell me what?" Vanessa says, coming up to us. She crosses her arms. "Funny how we are all talking and not looking at the wall like we were told."

"This is more important," I say firmly. "We were trying to figure out how the peanut oil got in the house in the first place."

Vanessa's jaw tightens. "And?"

"And," Simone says, "Molly asked Ashley to buy her a snack and then Ashley got in trouble outside the van."

Vanessa's eyes get even more narrow. I say, "Tasha cleared her, remember?"

"Silencio. I am trying to think." Vanessa presses her arms tighter against her chest. "We know your girl did not poison the potatoes. But I am sure this incident was engineered on purpose. What I don't know yet is whether Ashley was used as a distraction or this was part of the attempt to frame her." She turns toward Simone. "Redeem yourself, hermanita. What did Molly ask Ashley to buy?"

Simone's eyes dart all over the place. "Those sandwich cookies that have peanut butter inside."

Vanessa nods. "Gracias. So that means — "

A shadow falls over us. Ms. Carter clears her throat.

"Sorry to interrupt, girls," she says. "I need to see you, Brianna. Come with me, please."

I stand, slowly. "What did I do?"

"Who says you did anything?" Ms. Carter's voice is calm, even. "I need to discuss something with you in private." She nods at Vanessa. "The younger girls are supposed to attend social and emotional skills training in 10 minutes. Please make sure they get to Therapy Room A on time."

"I will," Vanessa says, her eyes narrow.

"Is Brianna in trouble?" Simone asks.

"Yeah," Elizabeth says. "She's been with us the whole time, she didn't do anything wrong."

Ms. Carter's eyes soften. "I can't discuss with you why I need to see Brianna. She will be back. I promise." She pats my wrist. "Let's go to the conference room."

My heart pounds as I turn and follow her. A voice in my head screams that I should walk with my hands behind my back, but I refuse to give in. If they want that, they're gonna have to cuff me.

I pray that's not where this is headed.

sixteen

THE CLOSER WE get to the conference room, the more I feel as if I'm caught in quicksand, pushing with everything I've got not to be pulled under. I catch myself walking with my hands behind my back after all, more than once, and I keep hearing voices — not ones that aren't really there, just memories I'd rather forget.

"Take the plea, Ms. Hunter. Anything else is a waste of the taxpayers' time and money."

"But I didn't even know that stupid baggie was there! All my drug tests came back clean so why — "

"You know and I know you're clean but the law says that since that baggie of cocaine was found in your car, you're guilty of possession."

"Brianna, please." Mom's voice is heavy, like she hasn't slept any more than I have. "I'd rather you be home, but since that's not an option, this deal will at least give you a chance at a future."

I blink back tears as Ms. Carter hits the digits to unlock the conference room. I had wanted so bad to fight those charges. It wasn't fair for me to be locked up for drugs that weren't mine and I wanted my name cleared. But if I'd decided to keep fighting, I'd be fighting alone. Not even Mom was on my side, or Auntie Nan either, and she's supposed to be a criminal lawyer.

When the chips were down, they all abandoned me, threw me to this place to be someone else's problem and now here we are with me about to be in trouble for something and not even know what I did wrong this time.

This is a damn Kafka novel, and the worst part is, I shouldn't be here.

Ms. Carter gestures for me to go ahead in. I double check my mask to make sure it's over my nose and mouth properly before I do.

I take the seat on the far end of the table. Let Ms. Carter feel like royalty cause I'm all the way on the other end. I don't care.

"What are you doing all the way down there?" she says. "Come sit next to me; don't make me yell across the table."

I hate myself for obeying, even if I do drag my feet the whole way.

"I don't know what this is about," I say as I throw myself into the new seat, "but if it's that email I owe you, it's not lights out and I haven't had time yet to —"

"It's not," Ms. Carter says softly. "Relax, Brianna. I'm not looking for reasons to punish you. Though I do have to wonder what it is you think you've done that would warrant this level of panic."

I glare at her. "Doesn't matter if I've done anything or not. You want to punish me, you will."

"Ah, so this is about your arrest," Ms. Carter says. "I'm not going to beat a dead horse, but that situation is far more complicated than you're making it out to be and you know why."

I shrug. I don't want therapy. I want her to tell me what she wants with me now and get it over with.

"Anyway," Ms. Carter says, "the reason I asked to see you is that I received a copy of Inspector Goodwin's report via email, and your name came up. It seems you spoke with her."

"I-I just wanted to know if she had any intel on how that peanut oil got in Tasha," I stammer.

"And to find out what she was doing upstairs," Ms. Carter says, her voice even. "Fortunately, she sent the report to me to look over and forward to Mrs. MacGregor, so I can redact anything that points to you talking out of turn. I don't want you getting a second written warning, especially over something this inconsequential."

I raise my eyebrows. "Um, thanks, I guess." I cross my arms. "What kind of punishment are you handing down instead?"

"None. I just wanted to reiterate that you need to be careful. I also wanted to tell you something else." Ms. Carter leans forward.

My heart pounds. "D-did the report shed any light on what happened?"

Ms. Carter's eyes go up and to the right, like she's thinking hard about how to answer. She says, her tone far too neutral for my liking, "Nothing we didn't already know. It confirmed that Tasha ate peanut oil laced potatoes. It is a lucky thing no one from any other cohort asked for leftovers because the dish was infused with it, and Tasha isn't the only resident with a serious allergy."

I sit up straighter. "The potatoes were meant for our cohort, though," I say. "Someone targeted her, not that I thought otherwise."

"I suppose." Ms. Carter taps her pen against the table. She's as nervous as me, but why? "The reason I brought you down is that the statements you made to Inspector Goodwin, particularly your explanation of how your communications are monitored here, got the attention of the Juvenile Justice Project. Earlier today, a lawyer named Nicole Whitestone contacted us. Ms. Whitestone would like very much to speak with you about the conditions here."

I cross my arms. "All that just cause I said I'm not allowed to call out to just anyone?"

"Words have power, Brianna. That's why it's so important you watch what you say." Ms. Carter sighs deeply. "Especially right now, when we are under a microscope. A girl with the best of intentions could say the wrong thing and get us that much closer to being shut down by the State Oversight Board."

I gulp, thinking about what'll happen if we're sent to juvie. Maybe I could handle it. I don't know. But Elizabeth? Simone? Those babies would be crushed in a way that there's no coming back from.

"How do I make this right?" I ask. "I-I mean, you must have turned this lawyer down flat, right? Cause no way you're gonna unleash me to say more things that could mess things up for everyone."

"We didn't tell her anything yet," Ms. Carter says. "Mrs. MacGregor does not even know about it. But what I said is that we need time to think things over and discuss them with you and with our general counsel. I did speak to a lawyer affiliated with our program and she said that it's best to leave the decision up to you. Refusing to allow you to speak to Ms. Whitestone could be construed as us attempting to stop residents from speaking freely about the conditions in this program, which would trigger a larger investigation. However, if you do not feel comfortable, you cannot be forced to speak to her."

I bite my lip. "This Ms. Whitestone," I say slowly. "Is she like, a criminal lawyer? Could she get a second look at my case?"

"I don't believe so. But the Juvenile Justice Project does help children who they believe are being wrongfully incarcerated or too harshly punished. I happen to think that you are exactly where you need to be and that you have an opportunity to thrive here that you wouldn't in juvenile detention. But again, you must be free to speak your mind if you choose to speak to Ms. Whitestone or any other member of the Juvenile Justice Project. I ask only that if you do agree to this meeting, that you be honest, and not just about the things that have you upset."

I swallow hard. Ms. Carter is saying one thing but meaning the opposite. *Talk if you want, but don't snitch. Tell them only the part of your story that makes us look good so we don't get shut down.*

"I'm no snitch," I say. "I'm not about all that. So if I talk to her it's not to get the program in trouble. But I don't think my case is nearly as complicated as you do. Those weren't my drugs. I was locked up for them anyway. And even if you leave all that aside, the way the cops treated me... it's wrong and I want that lawyer to look me in my eyes and tell me I did right by making the deal to come here instead of fighting it."

Ms. Carter sighs. "If that's what you want, I can't stop you. But I still maintain that even if your arrest was unfair, you are where you are meant to be."

I glare at her. "You'd better not say this is God's will."

"I wouldn't impose my religious beliefs on you. But I do think..." Ms. Carter sighs. "Sit tight. Ms. Whitestone's office is only ten minutes away and she said she had cleared her schedule this afternoon so that she could be here at a moment's notice. So if you are sure..."

"I'm positive," I say, even though my heart's pounding. What if this makes things worse? The whole reason Auntie Nan said I should stay silent and let the cops make their case without my help is that they got all the power and they can come down twice as hard if they don't like me standing up for myself.

Isn't this the same thing? Aren't I painting a bigger target on my back?

But then I hear Vanessa's voice in my head saying it was cowardly to stay silent when Morgan took that Epi-Pen.

I don't want her voice there, at all, but I can't help agreeing with it.

I gotta be brave.

This might be my only shot at justice, and I have to take it no matter how scared I am.

seventeen

I'M STILL ARGUING with myself when Ms. Carter comes back with Ms. Whitestone ten minutes later. Ms. Whitestone's a white woman, with long blond hair that she has tied back into a bun behind her head. She shouldn't wear it like that cause it makes it too obvious her ears stick out like vase handles, not that I'd tell her that.

I try to tell myself she's my only hope, but my stomach's sinking fast. Maybe I'm too quick to judge, but nothing about this woman tells me she's up to the task of getting me justice. She looks like a middle-aged housewife, like the moms of some of the kids at my old school, the kind who think their kids are always right and won't believe they're the ones bullying girls like me.

Her firm handshake after Ms. Carter makes the introductions surprises me. I didn't think she had it in her. She sits down but doesn't say anything til Ms. Carter's gone and the door's closed.

"I don't know how much Ms. Carter told you about why I wanted to meet with you," Ms. Whitestone says. Her voice is annoyingly high and perky, like a high school cheerleader in an adult's body. "But the first thing I want you to know is that everything you say is completely confidential. Ms. Carter and Mrs. MacGregor can't make you repeat it and they can't punish you for talking to me. In fact, if anyone tries to, I want you to contact me right away."

Yeah, right. I lean back in my seat, my arms crossed so hard over my chest it hurts. "Like I told Inspector Goodwin, I can't make unapproved calls."

"My number will go through. They're not allowed to interfere with calls to legal counsel. And if worst comes to worst, you can fall back on your legal rights. Once you say that I'm your lawyer and you want to talk to me, they have to arrange it."

"Right." I swallow hard. "So, um, Ms. Carter didn't know if you're a criminal lawyer or what."

"I specialize in civil lawsuits. My expertise is in making sure that programs like this follow the laws that are designed to keep residents safe. And to that end — "

"Oh." My whole body feels heavy, but I tell myself to cut that out. It's not like I expected anything would actually come of talking to her. But for one little second, I had hope, and that makes it hurt twice as bad to know I'm stuck here for at least a year when I didn't do anything to deserve it. Letting my breath out slowly, I say, "Civil suits. So can you sue cops?"

"If it's warranted, we have people for that." Ms. Whitestone is staring at her notes. "Look, if you have questions about the arrest that led to you being incarcerated here, we have people we can get you in touch with. But I do have to tell you, Brianna, that we can't take every case. I wish we could, but with limited resources and a system that is incarcerating far too many children... we have to focus on the ones that are the most urgent."

"Right. I understand." My voice is flat. "The cops treated me like some super violent mob boss over a tiny little baggie of cocaine, but that doesn't count as injustice."

Ms. Whitestone looks up. "It's not that it doesn't count," she says softly. "Of course it does. It's just that if we help you first and a child who is being held with adults at Rikers dies in prison in the meantime... you wouldn't want that any more than I do."

Simone's face pops into my head, terror in her eyes. *"I can't tell or I'll go to real prison. With grown-ups."*

I blink back tears.

"That doesn't mean we won't try," Ms. Whitestone says, reaching over and patting my hand. "I'll pass your information onto my colleagues in the criminal appeal department as soon as we're finished here. But in the meantime, the best thing you can do is help me out, okay? My job is to make sure that you and everyone else here is safe, and if you're not... well, that *is* urgent and I will do what it takes to make sure that changes. So what do you say? Will you answer some questions for me?"

I bite my lip. "Mrs. MacGregor says if we get shut down we're all going to juvie."

"That was before you had a lawyer on your side. I'd rather Mrs. MacGregor correct any violations of the health and safety code than risk being shut down. But if the worst happens, I will make sure that the court understands what a proper placement looks like for every resident and fight for you to be sent to a different program, if not released altogether." Ms. Whitestone flips a page in her legal pad. "Any other questions before we begin?"

I don't want to talk to you anymore. But it's too late for that. I said I'd do this so I have to.

Ms. Whitestone says, gently, "I notice you're wearing an N-95 mask. Is that something any girl who wants can obtain?"

I tell her the same thing I told Inspector Goodwin about that. Ms. Whitestone takes notes and moves on to the next question. The things she wants to know aren't in any logical order as far as I can tell, jumping from hygiene and illness prevention to what books and websites we're allowed to whether I've ever been put in restraints or in solitary confinement.

"My room count?" I ask bitterly. "I got a BS written warning and they locked me in there til morning."

Ms. Whitestone frowns. "I hope you had access to a bathroom."

"Toilet only. Not the shower." My heart pounds. I'm sure I've said too much. "It wasn't as bad as when I was arrested," I add, "cause at least I was in the same place all night and Ms. Carter brought me a full meal from the dining room."

Ms. Whitestone writes that all down. I'm still in my mood, but I have to admit it feels good to get this all off my chest. She asks a few more questions and then wraps up with, "Do you feel safe here, Brianna?" Her voice is soft enough to make me think for a fraction of a second she actually gives a damn before I remember she doesn't think my case is urgent enough to fight for.

"I guess." I look down at the ground. "Not like when I was arrested," I say, purposely trying to make a point. "You know the cops had half a dozen guns pointed right at my heart even though I was fully cooperating? I kept my hands up and came out slow like they said but they snapped at me to get down on the ground anyway." I shake my head. "I managed to survive that, so anything here is peaches and cream."

"I'm sorry that happened to you. I know the cops can be overzealous, especially with certain..." Ms. Whitestone sighs. "Anyway, that shouldn't have happened. But since it did and you're here, I need to know... is there anything here that makes you feel unsafe?"

I bite my lip. "Besides knowing someone poisoned Tasha, you mean?" It's not exactly a lie. That does scare me more than anything. But if I was gonna be 100% honest, I'd tell her how many girls are being blackmailed while the administration either doesn't know or doesn't care. But saying so feels too much like crossing a line into snitching, and the last thing I need is to be labeled as one.

"That is unnerving," Ms. Whitestone agrees, "especially since there's reason to suspect it's a gang hit. Speaking of which — "

"Gang hit?" I repeat, and laugh bitterly. "What gang? There's 20 girls to a cohort. When Tasha was here she had maybe two or three with her all the time." I hope my face is hiding that my mind's going a mile a minute. Calling it a gang's dumb, but that's what Vanessa's crew looks like to some people, I guess. Tasha said the attack wasn't about her and I thought she meant Ashley, but what if she meant Vanessa?

No. That couldn't possibly make sense. Hurting Tasha wouldn't get to Vanessa in any significant way. She's more likely to be involved than to be the target.

"So to be clear, you don't think there's gang activity here?" Ms. Whitestone says.

I shake my head slightly. "Not exactly." I say, keeping my tone as even as possible. The word "gang" is rubbing me the wrong way, but I'm sure she won't understand that. "There's some girls that like to boss people around, that's all."

"I see," Ms. Whitestone says. "And which side of those girls are you on? The good side or the bad?"

What the hell is this? Is she even really from the Juvenile Justice Program or is she working for the cops?

"I'm friends with one of them," I say carefully. "Not close or anything. Just enough she leaves me and my friends alone." I swallow hard. Every time I open my mouth, the wrong thing comes out, making everything worse.

"Perfect," Ms. Whitestone says, She leans forward, her blue eyes sparkling. "I'll level with you, Brianna. I had an ulterior motive coming here today."

"You lied?" I feel like I should be mad, but I can't seem to summon up enough outrage to mean anything.

"Not exactly. I do plan to pursue litigation to ensure that the law is followed. But I also need the help of someone on the inside. And I think that person could be you."

I stare at her. "You want me to be a snitch."

"No, nothing like that. I don't want you to spy on people and report back or any of that stuff you see on TV. But I do need eyes and ears. So all I'm saying is, if you should happen to see something that feels wrong, like you have this sense something's not being done the right way and it bothers you, I'd appreciate it if you'd let me know."

"And if I don't you'll ignore me if I call you for help."

Ms. Whitestone gasps "Oh, honey, no. Of course not. This isn't a quid pro quo. This is just an additional way to keep you and everyone else safe." She takes a card out of a small holder and hands it to me. "This is my contact info. Like I told you before, they can't stop you reaching out to me. So I'm not going to pressure you or threaten to withdraw as your counsel or conveniently forget to pass your name on to my colleagues in the appeals department if I don't hear from you within a certain time frame. I promise. But if you should see something and you want to say something, I'm here for you."

"Got it." My voice is still flat, but I make myself smile. "Thanks."

"No problem." Ms. Whitestone stands. "I really do hope everything works out for you. The story you told me about how the cops treated you breaks my heart and I wish I could do more for you. But who knows? Maybe my number will be more of a lifeline than you think. In the meantime, you take care, all right?"

She holds out her hand. I shake it even though I don't want to. Then I sit in the conference room a minute, staring at her card and trying to decide what my next move is.

I don't know what'll happen if I refuse to snitch to Ms. Whitestone about the program, other than her suddenly being too busy to take my call if Mrs. MacGregor has me sent back to juvie over some BS meant to silence me. But I already know that's my answer. Getting this place shut down isn't gonna help anyone. Sweet little Simone will get sent to juvie, and Elizabeth too. Besides, if Vanessa finds out I'm a professional snitch...

I don't even want to think about what she'd do to me.

No, I'm not risking that.

What I am gonna do is finish putting the pieces together about the poisoning. At least two of the little girls are involved. Patrice and Morgan. And someone's blackmailing them.

Bet it's not just them either. With all the blackmail being tossed around here, the rot goes deep. There's gotta be girl after girl involved, all too scared to stand up for themselves, and at least one person pulling the strings.

If I can untangle this, every girl involved in hurting Tasha will be gone and then maybe there's a chance I'll have won enough respect from Tasha and Vanessa that they'll leave the rest of us alone.

Ha! Who am I kidding? Bullies gonna bully.

Still, exposing the truth my way is way better than risking my life for a damn promise that *maybe* someone will take a second look at my case so I can go home.

I push my chair out and leave, holding my head up high as I make my way back to the day room.

The whole way back, I feel like Ms. Whitestone's eyes are on my back. I know that's crazy. She's a lawyer, not some supervillain, but my pounding heart won't let the feeling go even though my brain knows it's nonsense.

I move faster, feeling like I did once when some guy followed me out the city bus after church choir and I ducked into a 7-11 in case he planned to rob me or something.

No one's in the halls, making me feel even more creeped out. By the time I get to the day room, I'm breathing hard and gotta stand against the wall catching my breath a minute.

"You okay?" Security calls as she passes.

I nod, but she's already gone.

I let my breath out slowly and walk into the day room, looking around for Elizabeth.

No. Not her. The one I gotta talk to is Vanessa

She waves from the hot seat corner. "Your littles are in their assigned group," she says. "We should be too, but I wanted to talk to you while it is quiet." She pats the chair next to her while I wonder how it is she can get away with not going to group. "What did they want with you in the office?"

I sink into the chair, aware I'm the one on the hot seat now. Doesn't matter. I was gonna tell her anyway. She deserves to know some people are going around calling her a gang leader.

"It was crazy," I say, carefully. "Some lawyer from the Juvenile Justice Project wanted me." I lower my voice. "They tried every which way to get me to snitch on the program, but they failed. I'm not trading my integrity for a pile of maybes they're dangling like a carrot in front of me."

Vanessa's eyes narrow and her jaw tightens. For a second, I think I see fear. "Snitch on the program and not on the people in it? This is crazy."

"Yeah. She wants to take this place DOWN. The crazy things she asked me."

"You told her nothing, I hope," Vanessa says. "Our last conversation should have impressed on you the only one you ever snitch to is me."

"Course," I say, smiling nervously. "Only thing I said was — "

"THERE YOU ARE!" another voice says, bouncing off the walls like an actor in a Broadway play. It takes me a sec to realize it's Ashley cause her voice is as slurred as it is booming, and I almost can't understand what she's saying.

She runs clumsily toward me. Her arms out like she's gonna hug me... or try to fly away. "I was looking everywhere," she says, her words tumbling over each other. "You've been fighting so — wait, don't hate me, I'm just trying... whoops." She almost trips, then giggles. "Anyway, I love... I know it's dangerous to say so don't be... the thing is..."

Her words slur together into rambling nonsense while she reaches for the buttons on her sweater, mumbling that she's too hot.

I look her in her eyes. Her pupils are as big as when the eye doctor puts drops in.

Fuck. She's high.

eighteen

I STARE AT ASHLEY. She giggles again and pushes a curl away from her face. "Help me... sweater," she says, her voice so slurred that it almost sticks in her throat.

I lay on a mattress in the abandoned warehouse we used to hang out in, waiting for Natalie to be high enough to come to me. Something felt wrong, bad, like I didn't really want this. I stared at the ceiling, telling myself that this is what it meant to have a girlfriend and trying to get myself good and turned on for her cause I already knew once that cocaine hit her brain, she would be insatiable.

"L-let's get you to your room," I stammer, then my cheeks get hot. That's the worst thing I could have said right now.

Ashley giggles again. "I like how you think," she says. "I want... yeah, let's do it... are you... you know, first time? I'm not. One of my foster homes... but we don't talk about that." She laughs but it's not funny.

She just told me someone abused her. But is that true or is that cocaine brain nonsense?

"I meant so you can sleep this off," I say firmly. "You can't be seen like this in here, don't you get that? If staff or Security sees you..."

Ashley stiffens. "You won't tell, right?" She glances at Vanessa. "Lose the snitch."

Vanessa's eyes widen.

"Ignore her," I tell Vanessa. "She doesn't know what she's saying, don't hold it against her."

"I'm aware," Vanessa says, her voice hard and her jaw clenched.

"Come on," I tell Ashley. "I don't want you to get in trouble."

"Don't tell. Please." Ashley sighs deeply. "They called the cops," she says, her voice shaking. "Can't... wasn't forever..." She smiles suddenly. "You... can be... use cuffs on me... ooh yes."

I turn my head over my shoulder. "Help me get her out," I say under my breath to Vanessa.

"Not a bedroom," Vanessa says. "Take her to the garden. I can watch her there until she comes down."

"No!" Ashley says. "Please! It's too open and the trees are watching." She tries to pull away from me, shaking with fear.

"Do it," Vanessa says. "If she starts to OD I know what to do."

Fear shoots through me. OD? I'd never even considered...

Natalie collapsed once in front of me and I froze, not knowing what to do. I wanted to call 911 but I was scared I'd get arrested cause I knew she was high and probably had drugs in the warehouse, too. While I was fighting myself, her brown eyes popped open and she mumbled, "What happened?"

Still, can I trust Vanessa? Her idea of help comes with a price, and Ashley's suffered enough.

"Fine," I say at last, "but I'm staying too." I put my arm around Ashley. "Come on. Let's go to the garden."

"Ooh, sex in flowers...," Ashley says. "You'll stay?"

I ignore her. My heart's pounding so hard I feel like I might be the one to fall out even though I haven't touched shit, and part of me shivers with desire at touching her.

No! What's wrong with me? She's too messed up to know what she's doing. What's wrong with me, thinking for even half a second that it would be okay to take advantage of her?

"Come," I say softly, and steer her toward the garden, glad that Vanessa is following behind so that I can't do anything I can't take back.

But going into the hall is a huge mistake.

The therapy groups have just got out and a bunch of littles are headed this way. Ashley shrinks back, cowering in fear. She giggles suddenly as I pull her back toward the day room.

"Cover my mouth," she mumbles. "Super sexy."

Before I can get her out of sight, Patrice points. "WHOA!" she says. "LOOK AT THAT!" She laughs.

Ashley pulls against me so hard she almost knocks me over. "Hurry," she whispers.

Shit. Shit shit shit.

Vanessa slips between Ashley and Patrice, but it's too late. Security is pushing through the crowd.

"All right, ladies," Security says. "What have we got here?" She glances at Ashley, then freezes and slowly takes out her walkie-talkie. "Don't move, any of you," she orders, and says into the walkie-talkie, "We have a situation here. Possible 10-50."

10-50. That's the code the cops said in the radio when they called for backup on me.

They know.

And now we're both in trouble, probably. Ashley for getting high and me for trying to get her somewhere safe.

It's the night of my arrest all over again, with Security surrounding us.

I put my hands up.

nineteen

SECURITY GLANCES FROM me to Ashley. Vanessa's in front of us but their eyes slide right over her like she's a ghost.

One of them takes out a little flashlight and shines it in Ashley's eyes first, then mine. I squint and look away, but no matter how hard I blink I still see white circles of light.

"This one's normal," Security says. She nods at me. "You can put your hands down, hon."

My arms are aching something fierce as I slowly lower them and put them behind my back. Meanwhile, Security helps Ashley turn around. "We're going to restrain you for your safety," she tells Ashley.

Ashley struggles. "Bri... help!" she says. She frowns suddenly. "You told?"

I breathe in sharply.

Even Natalie never accused me. She'd check the locks fifteen times and flinch if a siren blared in the distance, but she always thought it was the rest of the world out to get her. Never me.

Ashley doesn't mean it. It's the drugs.

Still, the fact she could think for a second I'd ever turn her in... that hurts so bad I can barely catch my breath.

"I'd never, don't you know that?" I say softly. "I'll speak up for you in the office, alright? I swear I will." I leave out that I have no idea what I can say. They caught Ashley red-handed. There's no question she's high, and almost no way she's not getting expelled for it.

Ashley struggles and cries as Security pulls her arms behind her back and wraps those plastic cuffs around her wrists. "Ssh." Security looks over Ashley's head at me. "What's her name?"

How long they been here and they can't keep track of 80 girls' names when they probably see only a fraction of us? "Ashley," I say flatly. There's no point in keeping it to myself.

"Ashley," Security repeats. "We're not here to hurt you, all right? We're here to make sure you and everyone else here is safe."

"I didn't..." Ashley mumbles. She struggles but Security puts an arm around her, hugging her. I shouldn't wish that was me but I do anyway.

I look away.

Security nods at another guard. "Take the two girls who were with her to the office. Staff needs to understand what happened here." Then she looks me in my eyes and adds, "I'm sure these two will behave themselves on the way. No need for restraints."

Message received. Cooperate and we won't cuff you.

"Let's go, girls," another guard tells me and Vanessa, while the first one and her partner take Ashley in the other direction.

Security lets us walk together, but we're mostly silent. Vanessa doesn't hold her hands behind her back like I do — she keeps them at her sides — but she's strangely compliant. I guess even she's not that untouchable.

Her being so quiet scares me more than anything.

I want to lay into her about we could have stopped this before it started if she'd let me interfere with that drug deal I saw Ashley making by the stairs. But there's no way to do that without Security hearing and reporting back to Mrs. MacGregor, so I keep my mouth shut.

We're not even alone when Security deposits us on the wooden bench outside the office. One of them stands guarding us while the other goes to talk to Mrs. MacGregor.

"Psst..." I whisper anyway.

Vanessa turns toward me, but puts her finger on her lips. Security says to her, "Do me a favor and slide over to the other end of the bench. We can't have you girls telling each other what to say in there."

"We would not dream," Vanessa says, but she slides over. She puts her hands in her lap, but her eyes are narrow and I can see her calculating her next move. "She is heartbroken her *amiga* is in trouble. But Ashley will be all right, si?" She's looking right at Security and I can't shake the feeling she's sending a message, but that doesn't make any sense.

Maybe Vanessa has some sort of power in the dining room and the day room, but no way does a 15-year-old have the means to tell Security what to do. Not even her.

Security says, "She's under a doctor's care. She won't OD, not on our watch."

That's something, anyway. "Is she going to juvie?" I ask, my voice hoarse.

"Not up to us," Security says. "But I can tell you that so far, no one's called the cops."

I nod, but I can't stop remembering the way Ashley pleaded with me to help her as they pulled her arms behind her back. I didn't betray her the way she thought, but I failed her. I should have done everything in my power to stop her getting that coke in her system and I did nothing.

No, the voice in my head whispers. *There was nothing you could do.*

It's true. Even if I'd stopped her today, she'd just get her coke another day. Didn't I live through my relationship with Natalie? Addicts gonna use. Only thing I can do is not make it easy for them like I did with her.

I didn't give Ashley the money or the drugs. That's something, right? Way better than how I was with Natalie, anyway.

Mrs. MacGregor's office door opens. "Vanessa first, please," she says.

Vanessa pats my shoulder and whispers in my ear, "Admit nothing." Then she disappears inside, leaving me to stew.

Of course I'm not gonna admit a thing. I'm not dumb. But that doesn't tell me how to get Ashley out of trouble, or myself either.

Vanessa's in there a long time, too, way too long for someone who's not saying a word.

She's not following her own advice, is she?

Finally, the door creaks open and she walks out with her head high. "I survived," she says hoarsely. "When you are finished we will compare notes in the day room." She disappears before I can answer.

"Come, Brianna," Mrs. MacGregor says. "We have some important things to discuss."

My body's so stiff from sitting on that stupid bench I need Security to help me up. I walk slowly in, staring at my feet like I'm on my way to the execution chamber.

Might as well be, far as I'm concerned, cause I'm sure they're gonna try to use the threat of juvie to get me to turn against Ashley, and I'm not about to play that game.

Mrs. MacGregor's office is so small I can barely breathe. As it is, every time I walk in here I have this sinking sense like I've been sent to the school principal.

I sink into the seat across from her. "Is Ashley..." I begin, my mouth dry.

Mrs. MacGregor nods, her lips a thin line. "She is under medical supervision right now. We paged the on-site doctor and it was determined she can detox safely without going to the hospital. But we could have had a very different, very tragic outcome." She leans forward. "Were you aware that there was a possibility she could overdose?"

I cross my arms tight against my chest. Vanessa said to admit nothing, but how can I do that when silence is the same as a confession? "Why do you think I was taking her to the garden?" I say, struggling to keep my voice even. "I thought Fresh air would do something for her."

Mrs. MacGregor raises her eyebrows. "Really. So you weren't looking for a secluded area for your own purposes?"

"My own... what? No! That's gross."

"Brianna." Mrs. MacGregor's voice is soft but firm. "We've talked about this before, about how you allow your... affection for Ashley to dominate your thinking. I can imagine that if she was willing, which the drugs certainly made her, that you would find it difficult to resist temptation."

My throat tightens. Bet she wouldn't be saying any such thing if Ashley was a boy. But can I really fight her on it when those thoughts did flash through my mind, even if I didn't act on them? "All I wanted was a safe place for her to come down," I say quietly. "I didn't want her dragged off in cuffs like happened."

"You may not approve, but the way Security handled the situation likely saved her life. Ashley has been clean for eight or nine months now. When a person who has not used in a long time returns to it, they're at significant risk because their body is no longer used to the amount they used to take. Perhaps you thought you were helping, but if Ashley had overdosed and no one but you knew where she was..." She shakes her head. "That would have been a tragedy."

"For Ashley or for the program?" Acid tongue strikes again, but I can't help it. She doesn't give a damn about Ashley, or about Tasha, or any of us. She just cares how it looks to the State Oversight Board.

Mrs. MacGregor leans back in her chair, looking me up and down. "Were you aware that Ashley was on the edge of relapse?" she says quietly.

I shake my head. "She seemed down after the meet with Tasha, but it didn't make sense. Her name's clear now, so..."

"Sometimes it happens that way. Relapses are unpredictable." Mrs. MacGregor sighs. "I did hope that Ashley would be able to help us identify and cut off the source of the drug trade in this facility. But clearly she was more fragile than we thought."

I stare at her. Is she saying what I think she's saying? "Ashley was a snitch?"

"Did I say that?" Mrs. MacGregor's voice is hard. She lets her breath out slowly. "We are talking about your relationship with Ashley and what you knew about the cocaine she got her hands on tonight." She crosses her arms. "You have maintained that the similar drugs you were arrested for were not yours, and I believe you. But tell me, did this friend of yours have contacts on the inside?"

"If she did, she didn't tell me." My voice is flat and I'm only half paying attention to what I'm saying cause my brain is echoing this thought about Ashley being a snitch.

If she was... and someone knew it... that could be what Tasha was talking about when she said Ashley was the real target.

Whoever was dealing knew that Ashley knew so they had to get rid of her. Framing her for something as serious as poisoning Tasha would do it. Only so far, it hasn't worked.

So did someone convince her to get those drugs as Plan B for removing her? Maybe. But why Tasha? Yeah, Ashley had beef with her, but wouldn't it have been easier to go after Ashley directly?

"You're sure there's nothing you can tell us about the drug trade in here?" Mrs. MacGregor says.

I glare at her. "I don't use and I don't sell. I don't know what more you want from me."

Mrs. MacGregor nods. "That's all I wanted to know. She flips a page and I'm sure another written warning is coming, but she just says, "All's well that ends well, I suppose. We try to teach Patrice not to gossip, but this time it drew attention where it needed to be. Ashley is safe and we will make sure she continues to be. So I don't see a need for additional punishment at this time. But Brianna... if you ever see another resident doing something so dangerous, don't try to hide her. Get her help before it's too late."

That pulse starts up behind my eye, the one I get whenever I've been pushed too far. *You mean like the way you let Tasha blackmail her for months?* But saying that would be snitching and Vanessa'll give me hell for it, so I only say, "Yes, ma'am, I understand." and wait for her to dismiss me before I go.

I'm not in the mood for Vanessa at all, but avoiding her's probably worse. What I really want is to hide under my covers in my room and not come out for a week or when I hear good news about Ashley, whichever comes first, but going to your room during daylight hours isn't allowed unless you're sick enough to have to stay in bed, and the little headache I had earlier doesn't count.

I walk quickly toward the day room so I can get this over with. Elizabeth gets up from the chess table and runs up to me. "Brianna! Patrice said Ashley was super high and you and her got arrested together."

I take the deepest breath I ever breathed. It won't do to spit fire at Elizabeth; she won't understand it's nothing personal. "I'm here, aren't I?" I say, my voice choked.

"But Ashley isn't," Elizabeth says sadly. "She was my favorite big girl besides you."

She tilts her face up toward me. Her eyes are wide and full of tears she's finally learning not to shed in here, and the way she's looking at me is so earnest. She 100% believes I have the answers to why shit like this goes down. I love her for that but I hate she's put her faith in me when I'm not the one who can do what she needs done. "Yeah," I say. "It sucks." I let my breath out slowly again. "And it's Patrice's fault so she'd better stop telling stories." I ball my hands into fists.

Elizabeth shrinks back. "Don't punch her," she says, a pleading note in her voice.

"I won't. But I'm about to give her the verbal bitch slap she's deserved a while. First Tasha, then Ashley. She's gotta start keeping that mouth shut."

Elizabeth scowls. "You sound like Vanessa."

I freeze. Is it true? Am I turning into Vanessa just like I turned into Natalie when I was with her?

No. That can't be. I'm not a damn chameleon. Like I told my mom that time, I'm always me, even if it's not the part of me anyone wants to see.

"I'll go easy on her," I say weakly. "I just can't let this go. Sorry."

Elizabeth's lower lip quivers. I turn and walk away quick, before her tears can get to me. It's like I'm split in half, like Bri wants to listen to Elizabeth and not do something dumb that'll get her expelled but Anna is in charge right now and she wants to beat it into Patrice that she has to keep her mouth shut from now on.

And no matter how much I tell myself to stop, I can't.

I storm over to the corner where Patrice is playing Ping Pong with some other little whose name I can't even remember right now cause she's not one of mine. "YOU BITCH!" I say. "What'd you think you were playing at, pointing Ashley out to Security like that?"

Footsteps sound behind me, but no one's there when I glance over my shoulder. Looks like my luck hasn't run out yet. Good.

Patrice's eyes widen. "It wasn't on purpose, I swear! It's just like when Tasha was poisoned! I had to do it or else."

I glare at her. "Or else what?"

Patrice whimpers. "I have a little side hustle, okay? And if it's exposed, I'll be expelled so I have to do what I'm told."

I take a step toward her. "You sell drugs? You sold the ones that got Ashley in trouble?"

Patrice puts her hands over her face, protecting herself from me. "No! No! Not drugs! Please, you have to believe me, all I did was point at her, I didn't..."

"Cause you'd rather she be expelled than you! YOU COWARD!" I lunge toward Patrice...

And suddenly someone grabs me from behind, holding me so tight I can't move.

I struggle but Vanessa's voice is loud enough to cut through the noise coming from inside my head. "Stop, Brianna! This is not the way to handle this."

"Ashley's gone," I say, my voice shaking. "They wouldn't even tell me where..."

"I know," Vanessa says quietly. "Get yourself together, I got more information from the bitch in charge than you did." She's bear hugging me and I gotta admit it feels good even though that thought feels like cheating on Ashley.

I breathe and let it go. The more my anger goes down, the hotter my cheeks get. Vanessa's the last person I needed to see me losing it like this, and for her to have to restrain me...

I hang my head in shame.

"Lift that head," Vanessa snaps. "We do not do pity here." She waits until I do and then lets me go. "Walk with me," she says in the same no-nonsense voice my mom used to use when kindergarten-age Brianna acted up.

Vanessa nods at Patrice. "You are not off the hook for making sure Security caught Ashley. But you will be punished my way, not Brianna's. Enjoy your game while you still can." She puts her arm around me, pinning mine to my sides as she walks me off.

All of a sudden I remember the cops ordering me out of the car with my hands up and all those guns.

They were wrong that night but if they'd seen how I acted right now they'd say they were justified in what they did to me.

I swallow hard. I gotta do better.

Vanessa takes me to the hot seat again. She stands in front of me, her arms crossed. "You want to tell me what that was about?"

I sare at my clasped hands in my lap. "Mrs. MacGregor pushed me one step too far, I guess. When I saw that girl playing Ping Pong like she didn't just get Ashley sent away, I lost it."

Vanessa nods, but she says, her voice very quiet, "The lecture I gave the littles earlier wasn't just for them. You are one of my girls now. When a little bitch like Patrice hurts one of us, she hurts all of us, and it is for me to take care of, not you, especially not if you are going to make fireworks without knowing the right way to fight."

What's she gonna do, send me to the art table for timeout? I manage to keep that disrespectful thought to myself for once, saying instead, "I'm just so MAD. If she hadn't run her mouth..."

"I know," Vanessa says, "but it seems there is a reason for this that you can't get out of her with your fists." She sits across from me and whispers, "Ashley has not been expelled. I kept my word to you and made sure of it."

I stare at her. How on Earth does she have this power?

All of a sudden, something clicks.

Vanessa is always untouchable. Security and staff do what she wants.

Ms. Carter told Mrs. MacGregor there was a reason for that.

She knows things she's not supposed to know, like the details of how Natalie got me in trouble.

She's always in the right place at the right time and the way she held me back reminded me of the cops.

"Ashley's not the snitch," I say weakly. "That thing she said when she was high... she knew that you..."

Vanessa presses her hand over my mouth, not hard enough to hurt but hard enough to shut me up. I stare at her, breathing hard, scared and turned on all at once even though I'd rather it be Ashley pushing me around like this.

"Do not finish that thought," Vanessa hisses. "If anyone else puts it together, there will be another attack and this time it will succeed. *Comprende*?"

I nod and she takes her hand off my mouth. I try to remember the little bit of Spanish I learned freshman year. "*Es verdad?*" I whisper.

"Si," Vanessa says, and adds in English, "but not exactly how you think. You have not earned the trust for the full story but it will come one day."

"Okay," I say. "But tell me one thing. When you said Tasha blackmailed Ashley, was that the truth or was she supposed to help you with this?"

Vanessa stares into space. "Both," she says, her voice so quiet I can barely hear her. "Tasha had her own ideas. But Ashley came here with a drug problem so when she got caught in Tasha's net I realized I could use it to my advantage. So yes, she was being made to trap the dealer."

I swallow hard. "Tasha doesn't know?"

Vanessa shakes her head. "She was not the target. And that is all I can say. There are too many eyes and ears in this room." She pats my shoulder. "Go play chess with the red-haired one. You will need to sharpen those skills for the battle ahead." She walks away, making it clear this conversation is over whether or not I do what I'm told.

Simone grins when I come to the chess table. "Come play on my side," she says. "Elizabeth keeps kicking my butt."

"I don't know chess is supposed to be a team sport," I say, "but if it's all right with Elizabeth, I guess so." I pull up an extra chair and sink into it, wondering what Elizabeth told Simone about my little outburst earlier. Probably nothing, cause if Simone knew she'd be terrified of me.

I sink into the chair. Gotta concentrate before I lose Simone the game.

"Let's start over," Simone says.

"Flip your king then," Elizabeth says. "We can't start again unless you resign."

Simone looks at me and I nod. She flips the king over. Elizabeth grabs two pawns off the board, a silver and a gold, and hides them behind her back to randomize which side we play.

"Y-you're sure you want to play two against one?" I stammer.

Elizabeth nods. "Simone could learn to be a grandmaster from you. You're that good."

"I'm not nearly tournament level, but nice you think so," I say.

Elizabeth holds out her fists for me to choose one. We get silver. Elizabeth turns the board around and I help Simone set up. She's breathing a little hard and she mixes up where to put her queen and king even though I know she knows better.

"Queen on her color," I remind her.

Her cheeks darken. "I hate when I do that," she says. "Some people think I don't know how to play." She slams the pieces down as she switches them.

"You sure that's what's bothering you?" I ask her, putting my hand on her shoulder. "It's not like you to get so mad over something so little."

Simone looks away. "Patrice knocked over our board on purpose before," she says, "but you didn't hear it from me." She glares at her pieces. "She said you'd better leave her alone or me and Elizabeth will pay the price."

"Yeah," Elizabeth says. "She turned into a bully again. Sometimes she acts like a friend but other times..." She punches her palm with her fist. "If you weren't gonna get in trouble, I wouldn't care if you punched her so hard she never got back up again."

I breathe in sharply. Elizabeth sounds like Vanessa, but I can't blame her for it. I was the one who had to be held back from throwing Patrice to the ground before.

And now she and Simone are paying for what I did. I gotta be more careful cause whatever I do ripples out to them.

"None of that," I tell Elizabeth. "We tell Vanessa soon as this game's over, that's all."

"Why?" Elizabeth says. "She acts like the boss but she's not any better than us."

Simone wriggles. "Can we just play? You all are making me super nervous."

I squeeze her shoulder. "Let's table this for now," I agree, "but later we'll pick it back up and decide what to do."

Elizabeth makes the first move and I show Simone the French defense for our opening. We don't get very far before a shadow falls over us.

It's an adult, but one I don't recognize — a tall woman with jet black hair and skin that is somewhere between white and tan.

"Hi, Dr. Balsam!" Elizabeth says.

"Hi, Elizabeth," Dr. Balsam smiles. She turns toward me. "You must be Brianna."

I swallow hard. "How did you get my name?"

"I could pretend I have psychic powers. That would be cool, right? But it would also be lying. Ms. Carter showed me your picture."

My heart pounds. "Why?" I ask, then turn back to the board. "Move that pawn first, Simone."

"Because," Dr. Balsam says, "I'm working with Ashley and she asked me to give you a message. Would it be okay with you to take a break from your game to talk privately with me?"

I don't really feel like going anywhere with Dr. Balsam, but I've been around long enough to know adults don't really mean it when they act like you got a choice, so I let her take me into one of the therapy rooms. She lets me choose my seat, too. That's how this game is played — let you think you got some control over something small so you won't flip out about all the things they're choosing for you that make you want to break something.

I sink down into one of the couches. Dr. Balsam takes a chair and pulls it up close to me. She doesn't have a notepad or anything but you can bet she's evaluating me.

"I know you care a great deal for Ashley," she begins, "and I want you to know she cares about you too. That won't make what I have to tell you any easier, but I think it's important you know that."

I stiffen. If she knows I like Ashley that way, God only knows what she'll do with that info. "Just tell me this," I say. "Why did she relapse right when things were getting better for her?"

Dr. Balsam sighs. "It breaks your heart to see Ashley spiral downward back into drug use," she comments. "I wish I had a definitive answer for you as to why. But addiction is very complicated, Brianna, and there's not usually any one reason. I can't comment on what Ashley was feeling — that's private. But I can tell you that sometimes, when someone has gone through something rough and they get through it, it's the first time they let themselves feel all the fear and anger and pain they've been dealing with. And when those feelings come flooding back, it can feel like you're drowning. Have you ever felt like that?"

Yeah. Half an hour ago when I went off on Patrice. But I'm not telling this woman that, even if she is doing a better job of being understanding than most. Like Vanessa said earlier, admit nothing so they can't hurt you.

"I thought you had a message for me from Ashley," I say thickly.

"That's fair." Dr. Balsam sighs. "I did want to give you the opportunity to talk. I know you're going through a lot too, and have been since you were arrested and sent here."

I shrug, but say nothing.

Dr. Balsam says, her voice soft and gentle, "First of all, Ashley has given me permission to tell you that I am treating her in the Water Bear wing."

I gulp. "The locked cohort? So, like juvie within the house?"

"It's not juvie." Dr. Balsam's voice is still too soft. "It's isolated for the residents' protection. These are girls who have been struggling with severe trauma, and they need a small group, lots of structure, and a safe place to begin healing. But she won't be held behind locked doors all day every day. She'll be doing plenty of things outdoors and in the kitchen, just not when all the other girls are in those spaces."

I bite my lip. "So it's like a psych ward?"

"I suppose you can say that. It's a soft place for her to land until she's ready to get back on her feet." Dr. Balsam crosses her arms. "She will have visitors eventually but Brianna — and this is the part I think might be really hard for you to hear — she doesn't want to see you right now."

I blink back tears, remembering Ashley accusing me of betraying her. "S-she knows I didn't call Security on her, right? I was trying to help her, not..."

"She does know that. It isn't anything you did, Brianna. It's... well, Ashley thinks the world of you, and right now she's carrying too much shame on her shoulders to feel comfortable. The idea of you judging her is too terrifying."

"I would never..."

"I know. And I promise with treatment and time, this will change. But right now, it's very important for her recovery that she be allowed to make choices about who she spends time with, so we need to respect her boundary."

"Right." My voice is flat, pressing down hard on all the things I want to say but can't. No one's respected my feelings or boundaries since the moment the cops pulled me over. Not even after I was transferred from jail to here, where supposedly I get more freedom. I still gotta go to school when and where they say, do the chores I'm told to do, eat the food I'm told to eat. I'm not even allowed out in the garden without permission and one false move gets me sent back to juvie. And now they're playing this game where Ashley gets to call the shots? Please. We both know Dr. Balsam decided I'm as toxic for her as Natalie was for me and forbid us hanging anymore.

Dr. Balsam crosses her arms. "I can see the devastation in your eyes," she says softly. "I'm here if you want to talk."

"I don't," I say, my voice hard.

"That's okay too. Is it all right with you if I sit with you while you process your thoughts? You don't have to speak if you don't want to, but for the next half hour I'd like to be there in case you change your mind."

Yeah, right. Bet if I told her to fuck off she wouldn't do it.

I test my theory, saying bitterly, "I want to be alone."

"That's fine," Dr. Balsam says. "Ms. Carter has my contact info, so if you ever decide you want to talk, she can arrange it." She pats my shoulder. "I know Ashley's breaking your heart right now," she says softly. "I wish I had the words to make it better." She lets that hang in the air a minute — obviously, she's testing me to see if I'll ask her to stay after all. When I don't, she sighs deeply and walks away.

For the first time since my arrest, I'm really, truly alone, not counting when I've been locked in my room as punishment.

My chest aches, and I hunger for Ashley in a way I can't put into words. I try my hardest to hold the sobs back in case Dr. Balsam is listening outside the door or something, but I can't do it.

The sobs come fast and furious, so much so I'm afraid I'll fall over if I try to stand so I can get a tissue. It's not just Ashley. It's everything. But losing her feels like the last straw.

I fought so hard to clear her name, only for her to get arrested for something dumb, and now I can't see her and probably won't ever be allowed again.

I'm so angry at her for getting in trouble that I want to kick over the chair Dr. Balsam left here, but for once the sane part of me's in control and I don't do that. I just throw myself on the couch and kick at the arm rest, my cheeks growing hot cause I'm way too old to throw tantrums and I know it.

I squeeze my eyes shut tight, imagining I got to go to the garden with Ashley after all, imagining holding her, telling her it's okay. Imagining her being sober and saying she loves me...

My breathing slows and I stop kicking the armrest.

The next thing I know, I'm waking up from a nap on that couch. It takes me a minute to remember where I am, but when I do, I jump straight up. How long have I been in here? If anyone thinks I'm hiding from my responsibilities...

And Elizabeth and Simone are waiting for me, too.

There's a soft knock at the door and Ms. Carter comes in.

"I'm up, I'm up," I say. "I didn't mean to hide in here, I swear."

"It's all right," Ms. Carter says softly. "Dr. Balsam said you needed some space. But I do need your help. Mrs. MacGregor asked me to have a girl help me with kitchen inventory while the younger girls are setting the table for dinner. Do you feel up to doing that for me?"

I stare at her. What's wrong with her that she's talking so gently to me? Does she think I'm gonna shatter into a billion pieces or something?

"K," I say. I blink hard. "How long before Ashley comes back to our cohort?"

Ms. Carter's eyes dart up to the side. "I really don't know," she says softly. "I am sure she will work hard with Dr. Balsam, and hopefully in a few months she will be ready to rejoin us. But in the meantime, I want you to keep putting one foot in front of the other. There is life beyond your relationship with Ashley, or with anyone. I want you to start to realize that."

I stare at her. I'm not selfish enough to think she had Ashley removed cause she thinks she's toxic for me but her words aren't convincing me otherwise.

"Come on," Ms. Carter says, and puts her hand on my shoulder. I let my breath out slowly and smooth down my shirt so no one will ask questions.

twenty

MS. CARTER TAKES me to the pantry in the kitchen, the same one that Elizabeth got the gloves out of when we searched the room after the poisoning. It's the first time I've been allowed in since. The room feels smaller than I remember, and there's not much space between the stove and the counter next to it. Molly and Ashley were practically working on top of each other.

My eyes burn when I think of Ashley.

I stare at the stove. Molly was so close... she had to be the poisoner. But she couldn't be. It's too cruel, thinking she would frame Ashley, who's supposed to be her best friend.

But... if she was the one dealing drugs...

No. Seems to me she's more likely to get high herself than to sell. It takes a certain type to deal, and a girl who's always nervous isn't it.

"You still with me, Brianna?" Ms. Carter says, making me flinch. Crap. She's been instructing me what she wants done all this time and I haven't heard a word.

"Sorry," I say. "I, um... are you sure all the report said was that the peanut oil was in the potatoes?" My voice shakes for no reason.

Ms. Carter stiffens. "They aren't finished," she says gently. "They are running additional tests to confirm when it was placed in the dish." She lets her breath out slowly. "Anyway, the Department of Health is concerned about what it says is meager supplies on hand for feeding all of you girls. Mrs. MacGregor can't quite believe that is true, so she is asking us to inventory the pantry. She will re-order anything needed. If you could take one item at a time and let me know how many there are, that would be a big help."

"Yes, ma'am." This doesn't sound too bad, though something is whirling around in the back of my head that I can't quite catch.

I start with the shelf closest to me and find three cans of vegetable soup and three clam chowder.

Ms. Carter frowns. "Only three of each? I'm certain we got a case-load last week."

I freeze as it hits me what's bothering me. Patrice.

She had a side hustle that was supposedly harmless.

She's been stealing cans of food and selling them, hasn't she?

"I-I'll check under the shelves in case something fell," I say, my heart pounding. If I tell Ms. Carter what I'm thinking, that makes me a snitch. But if I don't, Patrice is gonna get us shut down, stealing food that's meant for all of us. Not to mention if a new order doesn't come in time, we'll starve.

Ms. Carter nods. I kneel by the bottom shelf and put my hand under it, feeling for cans I know aren't there. My hand hits something plastic and small... what is that?

It would be easier if I got on my stomach and tried to see under the shelf, but the thought of doing that makes my stomach do flip-flops. I'm not getting down on the floor. Not ever again after the cops made me.

"You got a flashlight?" I ask, breathing hard. "There's something..."

"Here." Ms. Carter takes her phone out. I stare at it longingly. The cops confiscated my phone when I was arrested and I haven't seen it since.

Focus, Brianna.

I let my breath out slowly as Ms. Carter shines her light under the shelf. I still can't see. I'm gonna have to get down on the floor.

GET DOWN ON THE GROUND! NOW! SPREAD YOUR ARMS AND LEGS! LIE STILL!

I force my breath out. This is different. This time I'm getting down by choice, not cause I've got a bunch of guns pointed my way.

I get down, keeping my head up just enough to see. There it is, wedged between the shelf and the thing holding the shelf up.

A tiny bottle.

I know what this is before I get my fingers around it. I grab it, pull it out...

And it's a discarded bottle of vanilla extract, empty.

I sniff it to be sure, but there's no peanut smell. It smells like Ashley's perfume, making me tear up all over again.

Are you kidding me? I got down on the ground and deep in my memories for nothing but trash?

I slide back out and get back on my feet. "Someone couldn't bother to walk ten feet to the trash," I say, annoyed.

"Hmm." Ms. Carter frowns. "I have to say, that doesn't make much sense. Vanilla is kept in the spice cabinet — not here."

I shrug. "Guess someone carried it with them to here and let it drop." My voice is even. Calm.

But my thoughts are racing.

That vanilla didn't belong here. Someone planted it.

This was a test. If they can get away with this, next time they'll plant something incriminating — maybe even the peanut oil.

With Ashley out of the picture, they need a new scapegoat. The only question is, they targeting me... or one of my littles?

twenty-one

I WANT TO check the rest of the kitchen for anything I missed the first time. Maybe something else is out of place. If that vanilla's here, I bet the peanut oil bottle is hidden in the spice rack. But Ms. Carter won't let me. She tells me the program's still not out of the woods and she doesn't want to have to explain to some surprise inspector why she's letting residents poke around the kitchen. I'm pretty sure that's BS, but I don't argue.

"Go check on Elizabeth and Simone," she says. "They are supposed to be on table duty and I don't know if anyone ever made them stop playing chess and attend to their chores."

I go into the dining room and they're right where they're supposed to be, with Vanessa watching. Elizabeth automatically puts a plate in Ashley's spot and Vanessa doesn't correct her.

Vanessa calls me over and whispers to me that she knows Patrice is trying to retaliate. "This is why you leave the fighting to me," she says firmly. "I do not have it in me to punish you immediately after the loss of your girl, but you are on thin ice after making so much more work for me."

I gulp, wondering if she's the one who planted that vanilla bottle as a warning.

"Won't happen again," I say quickly. "Listen, I got ammo against her."

Vanessa crosses her arms, but she says, "I'm listening."

I explain about the cans and how I think Patrice is stealing food to sell. Vanessa agrees it's likely but tells me to leave it to her, warning me, "Not a word to the littles. Your misadventure put a target on their backs already, and we don't need it to grow."

I don't think anything can change that, but I go along with what she wants... for now. It doesn't matter anyway cause Mrs. MacGregor makes me move to Ashley's old seat on the other side of the table. She doesn't explain why Ashley's not here and nobody asks. I don't know if that's cause everyone's afraid of the answer or they already know.

The next couple days are way too quiet for my liking. Normally, after something like Ashley getting arrested for drugs, there'd be rumors flying all over the place about what she did and with who, and since Mrs. MacGregor thinks I wanted to get Ashley alone so I could take advantage of her condition, there should be dirty looks thrown my way and whispers just loud enough for me to hear about me being perverted and maybe gay, which too many girls think are synonyms to begin with. I don't mind them keeping their hate to themselves, but it's weird. It's like the gossip channels have been shut all the way down, at the house and at school, too.

Even Vanessa can't put that much of the fear of God into Patrice. That loudmouth is plotting something. I'm sure of it.

It's getting so I'm looking over my shoulder all the time, thinking I'm being followed. It's worse than when I was with Natalie. I had to keep an eye open whenever we were on our damn drug runs cause if the cops were around or someone looked sketch, Natalie would have me drive through a maze of streets to lose them.

Thursday night, Elizabeth and Simone ask me to help them with homework in the library after dinner, and I got this sinking feeling that it's a cover for something really bad.

Sure enough, Elizabeth says, "Yesterday my math workbook disappeared and today I found it under the seat in English and Language Arts."

I raise my eyebrows. "Better be more careful."

"Noooo," Simone says. "Someone stole it and gave it back. Show her, Elizabeth."

Elizabeth's hands shake as she opens the book. On the back page, someone's scrawled right over the answer key, drawing a crude caricature of Elizabeth and Simone in a jail cell.

"What do you think they're gonna do?" Simone asks, playing with a braid nervously.

I shake my head. "I've had a feeling someone might try to frame you now that Ashley's gone," I whisper. "We'll all keep an eye out tomorrow. But I'm curious, how come you went to me and not Vanessa?"

Simone says, slowly, "I wanted to but Elizabeth didn't. She said you look out for us more."

I bite my lip. If Vanessa finds out we're keeping something this big from her...

Someone's watching us. I can feel it.

I gulp, praying it's not Vanessa. When I look, no one's there, just Lisa headed toward the bookshelves with Molly.

"Anyway," Elizabeth says, "Patrice or whoever drew this is stupid. We should talk about something else." She claps her hands. "I know! We haven't talked about the investigation in DAYS. It's like we forgot all about it when Ashley was arrested."

A lump forms in my throat, but not as big as usual. Am I getting over Ashley being gone already? I hope not. She's too important for me to move on in less than a week.

"Yeah," Simone says. "What should we do next?"

The littles are both staring at me like they expect me to have some genius move up my sleeve. I push my hair behind my ear. "Tomorrow's Friday," I say. "Maybe we can use the store run to get intel. If someone bought peanut oil, maybe the manager'll remember something about it."

Simone frowns. "Like he'd remember a week later."

"She would too," Elizabeth says. "They're nervous of us because we come from a jail place. They're always watching whenever anyone's in the store like they think we're all going to steal."

Simone's cheeks darken. "Yeah," she mumbles.

I put my arm around her. "You know what my mom used to say about haters? She'd tell me, 'Forget them, Brianna. You just be your amazing self and prove them wrong.'" I swallow hard. I didn't exactly follow that advice, getting all tangled up with Natalie and her drugs.

"Yeah," Elizabeth says. "We're not thieves no matter what my record says." She smiles slightly. "I'm in."

"Me too," Simone says.

"Cool," I say. "We can only go in two at a time and between Ms. Smith and the manager we're gonna have eyes on us. So let's put our heads together and figure out — " I have that weird feeling like we're being watched. I turn my head over my shoulder and see Patrice staring at us. "Um, can I help you?"

Patrice's mouth opens and closes. She shakes her head slightly and walks away. Coward.

But I can't gloat too much.

She was listening.

And she's got a plan.

I'm dreading tomorrow.

twenty-two

WHEN I'M GETTING ready the next morning, I slip Ms. Whitehouse's card in my lanyard behind my resident ID. I don't know it'll do any good, considering how our meeting went, but it doesn't hurt to be prepped for the worst. Sometimes I wonder if things would have worked out different if I pretended Auntie Nan was my lawyer and demanded her soon as they had me in cuffs, and now I got a big name I can throw around if anyone messes with Elizabeth or Simone.

My stomach's so tight with nerves I can barely eat my scrambled eggs and toast. I keep expecting something to go down, but nothing does. Everyone's on their best behavior. Maybe it's cause it's Friday — no one wants to risk getting barred from the store run today — but everyone seems unusually interested in their cartons of OJ and the butter on their toast, and I catch Patrice looking at me more than once. Her eyes dart away every time and she whispers something in Morgan's ear like she wants to make it clear she's gossiping about me.

I look around the table. Patrice feels like a distraction, but who's really after me and my littles?

When breakfast is over and we line up for the van, Vanessa slides in behind me. "Your free period is 4?" she whispers.

I nod.

"Good," she says. "Mine too. Meet in Computer Room 3A. We need to talk."

My stomach sinks so hard I feel like I'm riding the elevator down to the basement. This can't be good.

The whole morning sucks. People keep shooting me dirty looks. School is the one place I'm not stuck with the girls from the program; we go to Benjamin Franklin High, which is an alternative high school for kids from all sorts of programs and even some from the outside who couldn't make it in a regular high for whatever reason. That should protect me cause kids who don't know me have no reason to pick on me, but it never does, not when it comes to rumors and gossip.

And the gossip is flying today, even worse than usual. Kids I don't even know whispering just loud enough while looking in my direction for me to know it's about me, and they let me hear them call me all sorts of names. They're careful not to use the words everyone knows are hateful but I get the message all the same: they know I'm into girls and they don't like it.

So that was Patrice's plan. Scare Simone and Elizabeth so we're not expecting her to spread rumors about me. Weak.

The worst part is the minute between when I come in a classroom and when the teacher does cause I have kids asking me dumb things like whether it's true me and Ashley got caught making out and that's how they knew she was high and whether she did it cause she was so messed up she thought I was a boy. I can't say it doesn't hurt, but if this is all there is to Patrice's plan, it's nothing I can't handle.

I'm more worried about what Vanessa's got to say. The closer it gets to fourth period, the harder it is to pay attention cause of how hard my heart is pounding. I keep staring at the clock in the corner, aware of how little time is left before I have to face whatever it is Vanessa wants, and for all I know she found out the littles came to me instead of her and she's gonna punish me for it.

Third period finally ends. I drag myself to the computer room, trying my hardest to ignore the whispers. Someone calls, "Sneaking off to see your new lover?" I bite my lip and tell myself I don't care what they think, but it's a lie. I care too damn much when I know they're losers whose opinions shouldn't fucking matter.

There's a teacher in the computer room, but she's grading papers or something at her desk and not really paying attention, other than to look up briefly and say, "Don't forget to sign in so you don't get marked as leaving campus without permission." She points to a paper taped to the desk that has instructions about how to use the screen that'll come up when you log into the computer.

Course they gotta do that. My throat tightens with anger at being watched even during my free period. It's a dumb thing to get upset about, but I can't help throwing myself into the seat next to Vanessa anyway.

She says under her breath, "Relax. We don't need extra pairs of eyes."

I pretend I didn't hear, clicking aggressively to get signed in.

Vanessa puts her hand on my wrist. "The rumors are bothering you. This is why I needed to see you."

I spin my chair around. "You knew? Or did you start them to teach me a lesson?"

Vanessa's eyes narrow. "I would not do that to you. When I punish you you will know it." She crosses her arms and says in a low voice, "Remember, Patrice is allied with our enemies, but she is low level and we have the intel to bury her. If I have not done so yet, there is a reason, and if you put your hurt feeling aside you will see it."

I glare at her, but I don't have the energy to keep that up. My whole body aches with exhaustion. "I'm tired of games and riddles," I say. "What is the plan?"

Vanessa sighs deeply. "You need a stronger wall around yourself," she says. "We are put here to be broken down and we have to show we are stronger than they think."

I press my arms hard against my chest, saying nothing. I don't want to admit she's right. Besides, this is getting me nowhere. I'm no closer to finding the person who messed with Tasha and got Ashley arrested — I'm almost positive they're one and the same — than I was before I walked in here, and that's what's really got me steamed right now.

"You have more of an ear to the ground than me," I say under my breath. "Anything I need to know about the poisoner?"

The teacher up front calls, "Girls. Less talk, more work, please. This isn't a social club."

Course she chooses now to wake up and realize we're not here to do homework. Isn't there anyone who's not actively trying to stop me from learning the truth?

Vanessa clicks her screen so I do too. She stares at it, not at me, while she says under her breath, "Patrice is a distraction. She is not the one in charge of the enemy's plans. Remember that."

I nod slightly as I open the educational portal so the teacher'll think I'm looking at my assignments. "So the rumors aren't the next step in their plan?" I whisper.

"They are only the first step. They are planning something bigger to make sure you're blocked from the truth."

I stare at the reflection on my screen, trying to figure out what that means. "So I'm right Ashley was set up?"

Vanessa nods. "I fell for the first part too," she admits. "The clues lined up perfectly to suggest she poisoned Tasha. But now I see she was getting too close to stopping the drug trade."

"So that's why..." I swallow hard. "But why Tasha? Why not just take Ashley out directly?"

Vanessa shakes her head slightly. "I am too close to it to see it," she says. "I... Tasha is to me what Ashley is to you and the thought of someone poisoning her to punish Ashley ignites such a fire inside me..." She lets her breath out slowly. "But I cannot allow that to interfere with my plans. Tasha will not be avenged if I lose my temper the way some want."

I get what she's saying, but her words are only half sinking in cause my brain's still stuck on the first part of what she said. Her admitting she was wrong about Ashley wasn't on my bingo card at all, but even more...

Is she saying what I think she's saying? She's attracted to Tasha?

No. I have it wrong. I'm reading that into what she's saying cause I don't want to be alone.

Right?

"You and Tasha," I say under my breath, my voice almost as choked as Ashley's was when she was high. "You're..."

Vanessa puts her finger on her lips. "This does not leave this room," she says, her voice hard. "If rumors start I will know who gossiped."

"Course." My heart's pounding. Could Vanessa maybe like me that way?

I let my breath out slowly. It doesn't matter. Ashley's not dead, just locked up. And anyway, I'm not betraying her by moving on with her worst enemy the second she's gone. "Let's just stick to the case. The littles want to focus on the peanut oil. I thought we could talk to the manager to see what they remember."

Vanessa frowns. "I am not sure of this plan," she says. "But more important is that you discussed it outside my presence. Who was listening?"

I swallow hard. Strike 2. I don't know what Vanessa'll do to me if I screw up again, but I don't want to think about it.

"I-I caught Patrice staring," I say, looking away. "But like you said, she's low-level so..."

Vanessa sighs. "This is why I should be at these types of meetings," she says.

"They came to me," I say. "I tell them to tell you and sometimes they don't listen."

"Si," Vanessa says, "but the same mouth that tells them to do the right thing can be used to insist on it and to tell me I need to come somewhere." Vanessa's voice is hard, but somehow she doesn't seem angry. It's like she's... heartbroken. That doesn't make sense but I can feel it.

"I will next time," I promise.

"I hope it is not too late." Vanessa crosses her arms. "Patrice is not powerful but her weakness is someone else's strength. She has already given in to blackmail and sent messages to help hurt Tasha and Ashley. If she knows you are planning to find this answer, she will snitch to the people pulling her strings, and they will make her try to stop you."

I gulp. I hadn't thought of that. "So... abort mission?"

Vanessa shakes her head. "It is too late. We need to pray nothing has happened to the littles while they are in the middle school and cannot be watched by us. And we have to keep a close eye when they get in the van to make sure Patrice leaves them alone." She squeezes my shoulder. "I am not angry at you. But this needs to be a lesson. Never underestimate the damage a coward like Patrice can do."

I nod slightly, but my heart is racing. All sorts of crazy things are going through my mind. Someone locked Simone in the closet that time, so nothing's stopping Patrice from shoving her or Elizabeth into a locker and leaving them to suffocate. Or grabbing one of those sharp knives from woodshop and using it to kidnap the littles. Or...

...or framing them for what happened to Tasha.

That's the most likely. That's what that drawing meant.

"It might be worse than we think," I whisper. I tell Vanessa about the drawing. "I thought it was BS to scare us and so did Elizabeth, but what if..."

"She wants them removed in handcuffs next," Vanessa says. "I can move freely in a way you cannot because of my status. I will meet you at the van when school ends."

She gets up and goes up to the desk. I stare at her back, not sure what she's doing or if I should insist on going with her.

I tiptoe up to the desk and make myself flat against the wall so Vanessa won't see. She rubs the sides of her stomach and says to the teacher, "I'm having cramps." She lowers her voice and adds, "It is that time of the month. Can I go to the nurse and get a pain tablet?"

"Bell's about to ring anyway," the teacher says, while I try to make sense of that. All this secrecy so she can go to the nurse? How does that help Elizabeth and Simone?

Vanessa mumbles her thanks and walks out of the room. I gotta hand it to her — she's a good actress. Too bad there's no drama club putting on a school play for her to be in.

I push that out of my mind so I can follow her. The teacher says, "Hey! You! I gave her permission, not — " The bell rings, stopping her cold. The teacher sighs. "I guess I have to let you go now. But don't try that again or you're getting written up."

"Y-yes, ma'am," I say, then wish I'd been bold enough to pretend not to hear. Someone's out here poisoning people and framing the littlest girls for it, and I'm worrying about a bad report for leaving the room 30 seconds too early.

There's already a crowd in the halls, making it easier to blend in so that Vanessa doesn't see me when she looks over her shoulder to make sure she's not being followed. She slips into the women's room. I wait a sec, then follow. Hopefully I can play it off as a coincidence if she catches me.

Vanessa goes into the stall at the very end of the bathroom and closes the door. I slip into the one next to her, sure she's not just using the bathroom.

Sure enough, I hear her talking in a low voice, but it's all in Spanish so I can't really follow along. I hear my name and the words "contra ella," so she must be telling someone that there's a plan against me. Then I hear Ashley's name and a word that sounds like "arrested."

She's updating someone. It has to be her cop contact.

She sounds disappointed in whatever they're saying. I can't follow the language, but her voice drops and she sighs. Then she says, "*Si, entiendo*," and hangs up.

I sit on the toilet a minute longer even though I'm aware I'm risking being late to class. None of this makes sense.

Bet she reached out for help and the cops turned her down. She should have known they would.

Why in the world is she even helping them? It's not like whatever deal she struck got her out altogether. She's still stuck in this same damn program as the rest of us, trying to survive another day without having the rug pulled out from under her. She's got a leg up on the rest of us cause Mrs. MacGregor and Ms. Carter have to look the other way on minor infractions, but how's that worth it? If they get sick of protecting her she'll still be out on her ass, and with a snitch label following her that could get her killed.

Whatever they have on her, it's gotta be big. She must have downgraded from a felony to a little misdemeanor, something that could land her in Rikers or another adult prison even though she's only 15. Something so bad she has to play along with them if she wants any kind of future.

Who is she, really? I can't judge what she's done cause it's only by the grace of God I'm here and not facing 25 years for getting caught helping Natalie get drugs. But this place is supposed to be for girls who got into minor trouble, not serious criminals, and with Vanessa forced to turn snitch I can't trust she's not dodging a gun charge or something else dangerous.

I take a deep breath. None of this helps me figure out my next move.

Bell's gonna ring any second, too. Better get out of here.

Still, as I slide off the toilet and head for the sink, I can't help wondering...

Is Vanessa a killer? Is she hiding behind the cops when she poisoned Tasha herself?

Doesn't make sense if she was in love with her, but I don't know enough about Vanessa or her world to say for sure she's innocent.

I hurry to wash my hands and get to my next class.

twenty-three

BY THE TIME school ends for the day, I'm wound so tight I can barely breathe. Everything's too normal as the last bell rings. No graffiti on my locker, no bullies waiting for me in the halls, no one elbowing me on purpose when Ms. Smith lets us onto the van.

The only thing out of the ordinary is that when I slide in next to Vanessa and whisper, "We set?" Ms. Smith turns her head around to tell me she wants me sitting in Ashley's old seat like I've been doing every day since Ashley got arrested.

I can't help thinking she's running interference, but Vanessa mouths, "Stay cool," so I cooperate without a word. But my breath sticks in my throat and I doubt I'm gonna be able to relax, at least not til we get to the middle school and I see Elizabeth and Simone are still in one piece.

Nothing much happens there, either, except Patrice shoves Elizabeth when she gets behind her on the way in. Elizabeth says, "Hey!" but Patrice swears it was an accident and that someone pushed her first, so Ms. Smith lets it go with a comment that everyone needs to keep their hands to themselves.

Elizabeth slides into her seat next to Simone. "Did you see that?" she says, annoyed. "That was not an accident."

"I saw," I say, trying to keep my voice even. "Don't let her get to you."

Elizabeth plays with the buckle on her backpack strap, annoyed. I stare at it, my eyes widening.

The little section in the middle is partially open.

"Was that like that all day?" I ask quietly, pointing to it.

"What?" Elizabeth says. I tell her to turn her backpack around so she can see.

She stares at it. "I always close it," she says, her voice shaking. "W-what if Patrice put a bomb?"

"I doubt that's it," I whisper back. "But when we stop at the store, you'd better..."

I trail off cause Elizabeth's already opening her backpack. "This is just like when I was arrested," she says tearfully. "I mean, I was tricked with words that time, so not exactly the same, but those girls got me to put stolen things in my backpack and I didn't know they weren't paid for." Her hand shakes as she undoes the zipper. She stares into the section. "Nothing here," she says. "Wait..."

"Be careful, E," Simone says. "T-they could have put poison that'll hurt you when you touch it. You know, like that drug that causes overdoses. Fen-...fent..."

"Fentanyl?" I say. "I doubt Patrice got her hands on that."

Simone takes a deep breath and holds it.

Elizabeth feels around. Her little fingers curl around something. "There's some kind of plastic in here," she says.

Oh no. I remember the vanilla bottle and what I thought it was.

"Be sly," I whisper. "Don't let anyone else see cause I have a feeling..."

Elizabeth slowly lifts her hand and opens it.

There's a small bottle inside, like a one-dose vanilla bottle, and it smells like peanuts.

"T-this isn't mine," Elizabeth says. "Patrice... she tried to poison Tasha."

"Give me that." I grab the bottle out of her hand and bend down to shove it into my sock. "I'll hide it for now," I whisper, "and when we stop at the store I'll pass it to Vanessa."

Elizabeth's face trembles. "But you could go to jail."

My heart pounds. She's right. I shouldn't have taken that bottle. There I go not thinking again. But I can't let her get caught with it and I can't pass it to Vanessa right this sec, so what the hell am I supposed to do?

We pull into the gas station, but instead of asking who wants to go to the store, Ms. Smith says, "Brianna, can I see you for a minute, please?"

I stand, my heart pounding so hard I feel dizzy. This is it.

The trap. And I just walked right into it.

I walk slowly up to the front. Ms. Smith pats the seat next to her. I sink down into it and she says, quietly, "When Mrs. MacGregor told me you were struggling since Ashley was transferred, I didn't believe it. I thought, not Brianna, she's one of the good girls. But today you seem to be in a troublemaking mood." She crosses her arms. "Sitting in the wrong seat, whispering and looking around like you're afraid you're about to be caught, putting something in your sock... something you want to tell me?"

I swallow hard. The only way out is to snitch on Patrice. If anyone deserves it, it's her, but is it worth saving my own ass if I get labeled a snitch?

Still, I know how this game is played. If I don't cooperate, she'll make me roll down my sock and I'll be in worse trouble for hiding that bottle.

"E-elizabeth's backpack was open," I say, "a-and Patrice put something incriminating inside."

"And then you took it and hid it." Ms. Smith crosses her arms. "Let's have it."

My eyes are wide. "I only have this cause Patrice planted it to get Elizabeth in trouble, I swear," I say.

"No excuses. Show it to me."

I slowly put my hand in my sock and take out the bottle.

Ms. Smith sniffs it. "Peanut..." She frowns. "This the bottle used to poison Tasha?"

"I guess." I put my hands in my lap, aware I need to keep them visible now. "Like I said, it isn't mine or Elizabeth's."

"I understand that," Ms. Smith said, "but the problem is, you're the one hiding it in your sock."

- *Those drugs aren't mine!*
- *Stop giving us attitude. Out of the car! Hands where we can see them!*

I blink hard. "What are you gonna do?"

Ms. Smith sighs. "That's up to Mrs. MacGregor. I have to radio her and find out." She takes out her radio and rattles off a bunch of codes into it. Behind me, people are whispering. Some are wondering what's going on while others have caught on to the fact that I'm in trouble.

My eyes dart to the store and away. Could I make a run for it? Nah. That doesn't even work on TV. In real life, it would have me thrown to the ground and cuffed in seconds. Besides, where would I go? I'm not cut out for life on the run.

"Agreed," Ms. Smith says. "You'll meet on-site? Copy."

She puts the walkie-talkie down. "You're not in big trouble... yet," she says quietly. "This evening you will be my assistant rather than visiting the store yourself. I want you to stay by my side at all times and help escort girls to the entrance and check receipts after they come out."

I bite my lip. This isn't so bad. At least I can look for suspicious behavior. But that can't be all there is to this.

"And after?" I ask.

"You'll sit with me on the way home and when we get there, you'll get off first. Security will be waiting to escort you to Mrs. MacGregor's office."

I raise my eyebrows. "They're keeping it quiet?"

"For now. For what it's worth, I believe your story. But this is the same mistake you made when you were arrested. You can't clean up other people's messes and not face the consequences meant for them, Brianna. I am praying that you are not expelled over this. If God gives you another chance, use it well. Make better decisions. Because otherwise, one of these days you will end up behind bars instead of here, and that would be a damn shame." She stands. "All right, girls. Brianna is going to assist me today. Raise your hand if you want to go to the store."

I look around. Elizabeth and Simone look like they're going to cry, but they each raise their hand. Most of the girls do, except for Molly, who is sitting next to Lisa, staring at her feet.

"What's with Molly?" I whisper to Ms. Smith.

She shrugs. "She rarely goes. Watch for girls buying her things. I got into it with Ashley last week over that, mostly cause she should know better than to buy peanut butter anything no matter what someone says, but also cause Molly always promises to pay back and never does. If I catch it she's getting a write-up cause I'm damn sick of her taking advantage of other girls."

I bite my lip. "You think it's possible whoever really used this bottle sneaked past you while you were confronting Ashley?"

Ms. Smith's jaw tightens. "I don't think you're in a place to accuse me of being derelict in my duties."

"I'm not accusing you of anything. It could happen to anyone. But if Molly's always grifting, could be more to it. Someone could have used the opportunity to get that peanut oil on board while you were fighting the good fight about peanut butter crackers."

Ms. Smith stiffens, but she says, "We don't have time for this." She turns to the girls. "Group 1: Elizabeth and Patrice. Elizabeth, you're with me. Patrice, go with Brianna."

Just my luck. Getting dragged off by Security's gonna feel like peaches and cream after dealing with Patrice.

As my foot hits the step out of the van, it hits me:

Ms. Smith just sent me a message.

She couldn't say openly that she thinks Patrice is the one who sneaked past her with the oil. She's not about to admit to a girl she's supposed to be punishing that she screwed up.

But by making Patrice the first girl I gotta escort, she's saying, *It's this one.*

Am I crazy? Or am I onto something?

Patrice grins at me as she bounces down the steps. "Isn't it good luck we got stuck together?" she says. "Now you can make up for what you said the other day."

I cross my arms. "I think we're even after all the ways you ran your mouth about me today."

Patrice's eyes narrow. "If it were up to me, maybe. But..." She sighs deeply. "Look. I don't hate you. But I do what I gotta do." She starts walking fast enough I gotta take big strides to keep up with her.

Ms. Smith lets Elizabeth and Patrice go in by themselves and tells me to station myself outside the door next to her so we can check their receipts when they come out. Patrice goes in, but Elizabeth turns and looks longingly at me.

"Go inside, please, Elizabeth," Ms. Smith says, "or go back on the van."

"Why isn't Brianna allowed to go to the store?" Elizabeth asks. "If she's in trouble, I should be too. Someone put that bottle in my bag and she was only — "

"Don't," I tell Elizabeth. "I told you, better me than you."

Elizabeth's face falls. "But..."

I lock eyes with Elizabeth and say, "I need you to do what we talked about. I told you this day might come."

Elizabeth takes a deep shuddering breath. "Fine. But you still shouldn't be in trouble."

Ms. Smith starts to say something, but Elizabeth turns and rushes into the store.

"Do I want to know what that's about?" Ms. Smith asks.

"Just me handling Elizabeth." I'm not about to tell Ms. Smith that Elizabeth's my backup investigator if I get arrested, which is where this seems to be headed. "I got a cousin who's autistic so I know how to get her moving when she's stuck."

Ms. Smith's eyes cloud over. I doubt she believes me, but all she says is, "Mmm..."

Elizabeth comes out before Patrice. She comes bouncing over to me as if Ms. Smith isn't there. "Mission accomplished," she says, grinning. "Patrice was in the oil aisle last week for sure." She raises her voice slightly and says, "She should be the one who has to stand here and not be allowed in the store."

Ms. Smith turns and says, "I don't see a bag or a receipt in your hand."

"That's cause I didn't buy anything," Elizabeth says.

Ms. Smith says, "Hmm... I'm gonna have to ask you to empty your pockets to make sure."

Elizabeth's eyes flash. "I don't steal!" she snaps. "I was — "

"Just do it," I tell her. "We don't need two of us going to the office when we get back."

Elizabeth sighs deeply. She turns her pockets inside out to show Ms. Smith there's nothing inside. Ms. Smith says for her to go to Mr. Lancaster, who is pumping gas, and let him know she's getting back on the van. "That girl was one disrespectful comment away from losing her privilege for the next two weeks," she says as soon as Elizabeth is gone. "And you can tell her that once this is over with."

Once this is over with? Am I about to be arrested or not?

The rest of the store run passes slower than molasses. Patrice takes her time inside, but her receipt checks out and she cooperates with emptying her pockets. I ask Ms. Smith if that's always part of the protocol, cause I don't remember ever being asked before, and she says that it is now, so I guess she's trying to make up for missing Patrice last week.

One pair down, nine more to go. This afternoon is never gonna end.

Vanessa's the last to go, with no partner since Molly's not buying anything. I glance at her, not daring to hope she can get me out of this but begging her silently to do it anyway.

Vanessa averts her eyes. A lump forms in my throat that I gotta fight hard to keep from showing on my face.

Me getting caught by Ms. Smith is strike 3. I'm out. Vanessa wants nothing to do with me.

She goes into the store and comes out almost as quick with a bag of cheddar potato chips.

When she shows me her receipt, there's a note on the bottom:

Hang tight & remember, silence is gold.

"Got it," I say, handing her back her receipt.

It's not lost on me that Ms. Smith doesn't make her turn out her pockets like everyone else.

twenty-four

WHEN WE GET BACK on the van, I take my seat next to Ms. Smith without a word, putting my hands in my lap and staring down at them. I know what's coming next and nothing I can do will stop it. I just hope they take me away before Elizabeth catches on and tries to act like my lawyer.

Lawyer. That's it.

As Mr. Lancaster pulls away, I say quietly to Ms. Smith, "Can you tell Security that I want my lawyer? Her name's Nicole Whitestone." I run my finger over my lanyard, not daring to take out the business card to double check I got the first name right.

"That's your right, in the event you are charged with a crime," Ms. Smith says, "but let's hope it doesn't come to that."

I file that away in the back of my mind under *VIOLATING MY RIGHTS* so I can tell Ms. Whitestone if need be.

Soon as the van parks, Ms. Smith tells Mr. Lancaster, "I have to escort Brianna off first. Don't let the others disembark until I give you the all clear."

"Roger that," Mr. Lancaster says. He stares straight ahead like he sees something interesting through the windshield. Guess he doesn't want to even look at me.

I hold tight to the banisters on the way out the van so I don't fall. Security is standing under a tree near the entrance to the building.

Maybe it'll be too far for anyone to see me. I walk slowly, bowing my head slightly, but leave my arms at my sides. I'm done putting them behind my back unless I'm ordered to.

When we get to Security, it's only one guard. She says, "You have the contraband?"

Ms. Smith hands her the bottle. Security has her drop it in a small plastic bag. Then she turns toward me. "All right, Miss," she says. "Turn around, please, and put your hands behind your back. I need to transport you in restraints for everyone's safety."

Just like Ashley. I can only imagine how scared she felt when she was cuffed. I turn around slowly, trying to be grateful that at least I'm sober enough to understand what's happening to me.

Security tightens the plastic cuffs and walks me off. They're not as tight as the metal ones were when the cops arrested me, but I can't balance and need Security to help me stay upright as I'm taken into the building. I keep expecting my heart to pound like crazy, but I'm weirdly calm, like knowing it's a done deal brings me the peace I haven't had since my first day here.

I'm taken to the Security Office. It's tiny and cramped, and they don't take the cuffs off. "We'll only be here a few minutes," Security tells me. "We have to radio Mrs. MacGregor for further instructions."

Leaving me cuffed like this can't be legal, can it? I remember Mom asking me the next morning how long I was cuffed and whether I had any tingling or numbness that would point to nerve damage. My throat tightens, thinking about how she could have prevented all this if she'd just let Auntie Nan act as my lawyer. Some stupid social worker said that was a bad idea cause we're related, but she didn't have to listen.

That reminds me of what I need to do. "Excuse me," I say, being extra polite even though I don't feel like it. "Did Ms. Smith tell you I asked for my lawyer?"

Security raises her eyebrows. "No, she did not. In the event Mrs. MacGregor decides to turn you over to the police — "

"Screw that!" My voice is surprisingly strong and loud. I'm probably signing my paperwork back to juvie, acting like that, but I don't care. "I'm not saying a word to anybody unless my lawyer says it's okay. Not you, not Mrs. MacGregor, and definitely not the cops."

Security picks up her radio. "I'll let her know, but — "

"I'm represented by Nicole Whitestone of the Juvenile Justice Project. Her card's in my lanyard."

Security nods. She picks up her radio and says, "We have Brianna Hunter in custody. She's asking for an attorney. Nicole Whitestone."

The radio buzzes and Mrs. MacGregor says, "I know who that is." There's a pause. I stare at the clock on the wall, tilting my head up and ignoring the way that makes the cuffs dig into my wrists.

I run through what I know about the trap I'm in to try to pass the time without freaking out.

I knew there was a plan to frame Elizabeth or Simone and I knew that Patrice was involved. Like Vanessa said, she's under someone else's control.

But that drawing... the threats against the littles...

They were red herrings. Someone wanted me arrested and out of the picture.

Why?

Cause I was getting too close.

Just like Ashley. We were both set up the same way so we could be neutralized.

Ashley's in Water Bear, and she needs that, but the plan was to get her locked up.

Same with me.

Looking into the peanut oil was a step too close to the truth for whoever is controlling Patrice.

She heard, she snitched, they planned.

Made it look like it was about framing the littles, but I was the target the whole time and I fell for it hook, line and sinker.

If they get away with this, though...

The littles could be next.

The security guard says into the phone, "Yes, ma'am." He hands me the radio. "Mrs. MacGregor wants a word," he says, and presses the button while holding it up to my face.

"Ma'am?" I say.

"Brianna." Mrs. MacGregor's voice is clipped. "I hear you asked for Nicole Whitestone."

"Y-yes, ma'am," I say. "She offered to be my lawyer a few days ago and now's the right time."

Mrs. MacGregor is quiet for a second. Then she says, "How about we handle this internally? No cuffs, no threat of arrest. I'll question you myself and decide what needs to be done. If we do it that way, will you be willing to speak without an attorney present?"

I know I only got a split second to decide, but how can I? The voice in my head screaming NO is the same one that wanted me to fight the charges after I was arrested, so how can I know if I'm doing the right thing or trying to relive that moment and make it come out the other way? Besides, if I take this deal, new criminal charges are off the table. The surveillance video on the van should prove I'm innocent, but Mrs. MacGregor's eager to pin this on someone to save the program, and I can't let it be me.

I don't want to agree any more than I did last time, but they got me where they want me again.

Say No, and I'm risking time behind bars, no sealed record, no future when I get out.

Say Yes and it all goes away, but the system wins.

Unless...

I take a deep breath and let it out slowly. "Only if I get in writing you're not calling the cops on me no matter what."

Mrs. MacGregor hesitates, then says, "Done. Security, release the cuffs and escort her to the conference room by my office."

Security helps me stand so she can cut me loose. "Rub your wrists and let's go."

I can't help grinning as I obey. System 9 billion to Brianna 1, but before it was a shutout.

twenty-five

MRS. MACGREGOR IS sitting at the head of the conference table, her perfectly-manicured hands folded in front of her. "Have a seat, Brianna," she says, her voice weary.

I sink into my seat. "You got that written agreement for me?"

Mrs. MacGregor's eyes widen. Did she think I would forget? But she says, "Of course." She pushes the paper across to me and adds, as I bend over it, trying to read it, "Believe it or not, it would bring me no pleasure to expel you or to turn you over to the police. I said at the beginning that's only something I would do if I absolutely had to, and this case does not rise to that level."

Yeah, right. She just knows it'll look bad for the program if I'm arrested, especially if the case gets kicked cause she has no evidence. Plus, she doesn't want Nicole Whitestone to get her hands on anything that could be used to shut us down.

I cross my arms. "So you believe I only grabbed that bottle because Patrice put it in Elizabeth's bag?"

"The Security Office is reviewing the tapes from this afternoon," Mrs. MacGregor says. "Let me be clear on what needs to happen in this meeting. I need to know exactly why you hid that bottle in your sock and what you intended to do with it. After I obtain that information, I will decide how to discipline you."

My jaw tightens. Why should I be punished at all? I'm not the one who poisoned Tasha or the one who put that bottle in Elizabeth's bag. "It's exactly what I told Ms. Smith," I say. "Patrice put the bottle in Elizabeth's backpack and I figured if someone had to get caught with it, it was better it be me."

"I see," Mrs. MacGregor says. "How do you know Patrice planted the bottle?"

I bite my lip. The only way to answer that is to snitch more. That's not who I want to be, but I can't have Elizabeth getting in trouble when I know that bottle wasn't hers. "Patrice shoved her on the way into the van, then all of a sudden that bottle turned up in her things."

"I see. And then you hid it in your sock. Why didn't you give it to Ms. Smith?"

"Why do you think?" I snap. "Look how you're working harder to prove I did something wrong than on finding out where that bottle came from and who used it to poison Tasha."

Mrs. MacGregor presses her lips together. She breathes in sharply before saying, her voice very quiet, "We are doing both, believe me. But right now you are the girl in front of me, and hiding that bottle in your sock was not an acceptable solution to the problem of Elizabeth claiming it wasn't hers."

"She didn't just claim it. It wasn't."

"I certainly hope it wasn't. I doubt that anyone who had the bottle today was involved in the poisoning, but I will have to question her. But that is between me and her, and has nothing to do with you. Right now, we need to address your inappropriate behavior. You should have turned that bottle in to Ms. Smith. Trying to hide it only made you look guilty."

I glare at her. "I didn't trust her. And it's clear I was right, cause what did she do? Detain me and turn me over to Security."

"She was following protocol." Mrs. MacGregor's voice is too calm. "You need to start taking responsibility for your choices. You continually put the needs of girls you feel affection for above what is best to do, and the trouble it causes you does not seem to make any impact on your thought process."

"Serious?" That pulse starts up behind my eyes. "This isn't about what I did with Natalie and you know it."

"No, it isn't. It's about what you chose to do today that is part of the same pattern. You did it with Ashley also. I can't imagine you have the same feelings for a 13-year-old that you do for a girl closer to your age, but perhaps that is a factor."

She really went there. I'm so shocked I got no words to answer her with, other than a feeble, "It's not like that."

"I hope not," Mrs. MacGregor says, "but whatever the reason is, I suggest you do some thinking about how to get it under proper control." She hits the Print button on her computer. "I have to issue you another written warning because of this behavior. If it happens one more time, I will have no choice but to schedule an expulsion hearing." As she takes the paper off the printer, she adds, "Additionally, for the next week, you are not to use the day room until after dinner. Instead, when you come home from school, you will report directly to the study room. Ms. Vargas will be watching you closely to make sure you are doing homework and not working on personal projects."

I swallow hard. Ms. Vargas already hates me, and now she's gonna babysit me and report back? No way this ends well.

"As happened last time," Mrs. MacGregor adds, "you will be confined to your room for the evening. I will have Ms. Carter bring you your dinner when the time comes. In the meantime, I understand she already gave you a reflection email to write. I suggest you use the time you are spending in your room to do that." She hands me the paper. "You know the drill. You need to sign this paper to acknowledge you have understood this warning and then wait for Security to escort you to your room."

So much for the win I thought I had against the damn system. It was a fakeout. I'm still under arrest no matter what Mrs. MacGregor said about letting me go, and she's not gonna let me forget it.

I sign the damn paper cause I have no choice.

But when Security comes, I don't put my hands behind my back like I'm expected to do.

No one tells me to, though Mrs. MacGregor raises her eyebrows.

Security says, "Okay, Brianna. Straight to your room, no stopping."

I nod slightly, refusing to speak. Let them think they've broken me. Let them think they've won.

It'll be the last time.

I tell myself that over and over as I'm marched to my room.

Security gives me some nonsense about how she hopes I'll stop throwing my future away before she locks me in. The door clicks shut, beeping softly as she deactivates the code so I can't get out til someone decides to free me.

Done. I'm jailed, just like they wanted.

I throw myself hard on my bed, then make myself get up. This needs to be a pity-free zone if I'm gonna survive.

I sit down at my desk and make a sketch of the floor plan from memory so I can try to figure out how to get a message to Vanessa. Her room's all the way on the other side of this wing, right before we go into the main hall. Even with Morse code, I don't see a way to contact her.

I pace back and forth, thinking. I gotta make sure my deputies are ready to take over permanently, cause it's clear that sooner or later, Mrs. MacGregor's gonna decide I'm too much of a liability and ship me to juvie. I'm not happy about that, but I'll survive, long as I know there's still people in here fighting for justice for Tasha.

First things first. I gotta map out everything I know so I can pass it on tomorrow. That's not gonna be easy, especially since Mrs. MacGregor's limiting my time with Vanessa and Elizabeth, but I'll just have to find a way. It's too important not to.

I sit down again and start taking notes on the timeline.

Tasha and them got kicked out of the dining room while Elizabeth was in the kitchen, and then in the day room, Morgan stole Tasha's Epi-Pen and sent Patrice to report it to Lisa and Molly.

Wait. Hold up a sec.

There were only two times Ashley left the potatoes unattended. One was when Elizabeth needed help with the salt and the other was when Patrice knocked Elizabeth down to create a distraction.

And Patrice was there to deliver the message that the Epi-Pen had been stolen. And that means...

...unless someone poisoned the potatoes while Patrice was running her mouth, they were poisoned before Morgan stole the Epi-Pen.

I stare at my paper. This feels like an algebra problem that's not coming out right. But no matter how many times I double check, I get the same result.

The poison came first, then the Epi-Pen was stolen.

But why? Wouldn't the poisoner want to know their plan was gonna work before they went ahead with it? If Tasha got sick but used her Epi-Pen right away, the whole thing would have been solved in two minutes, and that would have been pointless.

But there it is. Poison first, stolen Epi-Pen second.

There's a soft knock on the door, interrupting my thoughts. I hurry to put my notes away as Ms. Carter calls, "Brianna? I'm coming in with your dinner."

The scanner beeps — I guess she can use her staff card even though my lock's deactivated.

I sit up straighter, refusing to turn around til she comes in and says, "Here you are, Brianna. Meatloaf and mashed potatoes. I hope I didn't warm them too much for you."

"I'm sure it's fine," I say, not looking at her.

Ms. Carter sighs deeply. My mattress creaks under her weight as she sits down on it. "You're upset with me. Why?"

I turn slowly. "Like you don't know."

"I don't," Ms. Carter says softly. "Talk to me, Brianna. I know how unfair this punishment seems, and believe me, if I'd been able to be there — "

"But you weren't, were you?" I snap. "You went and did whatever it was that was more important than protecting me."

"It wasn't my choice, and you can take that to the bank." Ms. Carter's voice is hard. "I had to do what I was told, Brianna. I would have rather been in that meeting with you and Mrs. MacGregor than supervising the day room, but I'm not any good to you or any other girl here if I lose my job."

I bow my head slightly. "They can fire you?"

"Hopefully they won't, but yes. My contract says it can be terminated at any time, with or without cause. But don't you worry about me. You need to think about when to fight and when to back off." Ms.

Carter pats my shoulder. "Eat. You need your strength for the days ahead."

"For what? Sitting in the study room trying not to upset Ms. Vargas?"

Ms. Carter sighs. "It won't be that bad. Vanessa will probably develop an interest in homework she never had before, and I daresay her grades could use the extra attention. And there will be plenty of opportunities for you to tutor Elizabeth and Simone."

I stare at her. Is she saying what I think she's saying?

"D-do they know?" I stammer.

Ms. Carter nods slightly. "Gossip about residents who have been detained is against the rules, but since some people were spreading rumors, others needed to know the truth."

"Right." I glance at the sketch I made, then away.

Ms. Carter reminds me again to eat, then says, "I don't agree with Mrs. MacGregor about you investigating. I think you should. But please, please be more careful. As you saw today, it's easy to sideline me so I can't protect you. Now, as long as I am here, I will bail you out best as I can but I can't guarantee I'll always be there to catch you when you fall." She stands. "I hope you understand what I am telling you."

"I do," I say, "but — "

She's already gone. I watch as the door swings closed behind her, locking me in again.

twenty-six

AS SOON AS they let me out, I make a beeline for Vanessa's room. That's probably not real smart. I'm supposed to head to the shower and then get ready for breakfast. But I gotta talk to her ASAP.

She's coming out of her room, holding her shower caddy. "Not here," she hisses, pulling her flowered robe closed tighter around herself. "Too obvious."

My throat tightens. She really thinks I'm trying to see what she has under there? Is that who I am in her eyes?

"Fine," I say. "But I wanted you to know, I'm all in."

Vanessa freezes. I say, my words tumbling out all over each other, "I'm done playing by their rules. You don't have to blackmail me into being part of your crew. I'm 100% in."

"They must have treated you worse than I thought," Vanessa says. "But first rule, you want in, you do what you're told. No more talking in the hall. Get in your robe and we will talk in the bathroom."

I hurry to get ready. The only robe I've got is the one Ms. Carter gave me during intake, and I hate it cause it's made of wool and it makes my skin itch. Usually, I take my chances getting undressed in the bathroom and hoping no one steals my pajamas and they don't get soaked from being too close to the shower. But something tells me that's not acceptable to Vanessa so I throw the robe on and clench my teeth, determined to grin and bear it.

Vanessa has her back to me, about to take off her robe, when I come in. I look away in case she turns around.

"When you get in the shower, sit down against the wall connected with mine," she says quietly. "It will not be easy to hear with both showers on but it is possible."

My first week here, Molly told me not to sit in the shower cause people will think I'm playing with myself. I shudder now as it hits me that she shouldn't have been looking at what I was doing in there.

I hurry to get undressed and slide into the shower.

The water's only lukewarm as usual, but something about putting my body under it while I have a secret convo with Vanessa turns me on big time, even if I'd prefer it was Ashley on the other side and we were only playing out a fantasy. I banish that thought from my head, focusing hard on trying to hear Vanessa.

She says my name, softly, and tells me to tap on the wall three times if I heard her.

I do and she says, "Good. Now listen. I'm sorry I couldn't respond to you before. But the walls in this house all have eyes if you know what I mean, and I couldn't risk the wrong person overhearing."

"I get it." I don't, really. "So out there we're not into girls and in here..."

"Si," Vanessa says, "and even here we must be careful because we are not completely alone."

My heart breaks for her that she feels it has to be this way. But it's not like I have a right to talk. I'm not even out to my mom yet, and in here... forget it. I spend every minute of every day looking over my shoulder to make sure no one's figured out what I am and a way to use it against me.

"Anyway," Vanessa says, "this is not important. Two things. One, after you were arrested last night, they made Elizabeth come answer questions."

Crap. Crap, crap, crap. "Damn," I say. "I was hoping I'd have time to warn her first. They harped on how I should have given up the bottle right away and I could just see they were going to go after her next. She alright?"

"She's not locked up," Vanessa says, "but she came back white as the dough character in the biscuit commercial and all I got out of her last night was she doesn't like being called Roja."

"She doesn't," I whisper back. "Doing that makes it hard to get anywhere with her." I let my breath out slowly, not sure that standing up to Vanessa like that is a good idea. "No disrespect," I add quickly.

"I know. I don't take it this way." Vanessa lets the water rush for a minute. It hits me hard in all the right places, making me start imagining Ashley in here with me, kissing my neck, massaging my shoulders, scrubbing my torso...

I shiver involuntarily before I catch myself. Then I make myself cut it out. This isn't the time or place for that.

Vanessa says, quietly, "You want all in? Tell me something I could use to destroy you." I gulp as she says, "You know already the secret that could land a knife in my back. Now you must give me one in return."

I draw my knees to my chest. "I'm thinking," I say. I don't really have any Earth-shattering secrets, other than me liking girls, and she already knows that. No, it has to be something bigger than that.

I gulp, realizing what I have to do. "All right, fine," I say, "but you tell anyone and I blow your cover."

"That is the idea," Vanessa says. "So we are forced to trust each other. Now stop stalling."

I bite my lip. "The thing I was arrested for," I whisper, "is the one time I was innocent. I could be doing 25 years for drug trafficking now, all cause of this girl I thought loved me." My eyes burn. "I, um, I'd do anything for her," I say, my voice shaking. "Money, rides... and she wasn't even really my girlfriend. I thought she was, but the truth was, she'd only be interested when she was all messed up s-so in a way, I... every time I took her to get coke, every time I gave her 60 bucks... I was buying sex."

I've never said that aloud before. My voice breaks and my shoulders shake.

Vanessa is quiet. I hug myself tight. What does she think of me, knowing what I was, what I am?

Vanessa says quietly, "So she took everything from you and left you to pay the price." Her voice is hard. "I told you, Bri, you are too good for some bitches." She lets her breath out slowly. "Your secret is safe with me, and not only for self-preservation. Because you have been used wrongly enough and you do not deserve to be humiliated further. Now wash away those tears. It is time to be tough, because I have a favor to ask."

I dab at my eyes with a washcloth. "What's up?"

Vanessa says, "Ms. Carter has the full report on Tasha's poisoning. I saw it last night when I was trying to get a sense what punishment you were facing but I didn't have time to read it fully. Get it for me."

I don't know how I'm gonna pull that off, but I mumble, "K." I want it as badly as she does. I just have to figure out how to pull this off without getting myself kicked out of the program.

twenty-seven

I FEEL WEIRD when I walk into the dining room for breakfast. Vanessa didn't tell. I know she didn't. But I can't shake the feeling that all 80 girls in the program know anyway, like they're staring at me and thinking that I'm not just into women, but a whore on top of it.

I make myself hold my head up high anyway. So what if they think it? It's not true, at least not anymore, and I bet half of them have done worse.

Elizabeth comes running up to me. She throws herself at me and hugs me tight. "I'm sorry," she says. "They should have arrested me instead."

"I'm glad they didn't," I tell her, putting my fingertips on her back but not really hugging cause too many people are whispering as it is and I'm not about to have Mrs. MacGregor accuse me of touching Elizabeth inappropriately. "Vanessa said they called you to the office for questioning. You all right?"

Elizabeth stiffens. "I told the truth," she says, her voice hard, "and I said they could arrest me if they wanted, but Ms. Carter said no." She crosses her arms. "Bet nothing happens to Patrice when she started it."

I follow her eyes over to Patrice, who is busy yapping to Morgan about something, Patrice's eyes narrow and she looks away from me.

She's scared. Or guilty. Or both.

"Never mind that for now," I say. "We gotta figure out how she fits into what happened to Tasha. Someone's pulling her strings, but I don't know who or why." I lower my voice. "Maybe the health department report will help. Vanessa wants me to get it from Ms. Carter."

Elizabeth's eyes become slits. "S-she's not gonna give it to us."

"Hope she does," I say thickly, "cause otherwise I gotta steal it."

"Stealing's wrong," Elizabeth whispers. "And anyway, that's how I got arrested. Don't listen to Vanessa that way."

Before I can answer, Ms. Carter passes by and calls, "Take your seats, girls. Brianna, you're up by me."

I drag my feet on the ground all the way to the table, wishing I knew what to do to get my hands on that report.

Ms. Carter says nothing during breakfast, but she keeps looking at me like she wants to. Does she know I'm plotting against her or what?

I bend over my eggs, breathing in the heat while I stir them around the plate. I can feel Patrice's eyes on me. I look up slowly, annoyed. I've had just about enough of that girl.

She looks away again and that's when it hits me: I can use her fear against her. She knows she messed everything up for me and she doesn't like it, but she'll see it as fair if I push back, force her to break into Ms. Carter's office for me.

No! What kind of person does that to a younger kid? Vanessa would. Tasha, maybe. But if I do it....

...I'm no better than Natalie, than Tasha, than any bully you can point to.

This all started with me being disgusted that Tasha was pushing Ashley around and that certain others were using it against her, to frame her.

I swore I'd never be blackmailed like that, but I was.

And now I'm thinking of becoming the blackmailer.

What would Ashley think? She'd never be able to love me the way I love her if I do this.

Besides, it's the same exact thing as with Natalie. Breaking rules. Hurting people. Risking arrest. All so she doesn't leave.

Still, Vanessa needs that report, and it just might have what I need to blow this whole poisoning wide open.

So... okay. First I'll try the normal way, see if Ms. Carter will help.

But if she can't or won't, it's game on.

After breakfast, Simone wants me to supervise her while she sweeps, but Ms. Carter says, "Get started, Simone, and I'll send Brianna to check behind you when you're done." Then she turns toward me and says, quietly, "We need to talk."

I follow her to an empty corner, my heart pounding. Now what?

Ms. Carter says, gently, "The thing we talked about yesterday came true sooner than I expected. I'm afraid this will be my last weekend with the program. Come Monday, I'm being reassigned to a different facility."

I blink hard. "Being reassigned or being gotten rid of?"

Ms. Carter sighs. "Both, I suppose. But I want you to know that I believe in you, Brianna. You have a good head on your shoulders and a bright future ahead."

I bite my lip. How can I make the ask I need to make when she's being so nice to me even after getting kicked out? But if I don't, I won't be able to live with myself.

"I'll help you clean out your desk," I say, "and if you should accidentally leave that health department report out..."

Ms. Carter's eyes widen. "I don't think..."

"Please, Ms. Carter?" I say. "You're leaving anyway, and I gotta know exactly what they said about the poison."

Ms. Carter sighs. "I suppose I could use some help cleaning out my desk. But you are supposed to spend some time in the study room this morning. If you want me to do something for you, you need to get a positive report on your behavior from Ms. Vargas at lunchtime."

Another deal I don't want to make. Maybe manipulating Patrice into breaking into the office isn't so bad, since no one else does anything without extracting their pound of flesh in return.

But if Ms. Carter keeps her word, I can get what I want without selling my soul for once, so I gotta try.

"Deal," I say, and go to help Simone even though a voice in the back of my head says this won't be good enough for Vanessa.

Vanessa's supervising Simone and Elizabeth when I walk back. She smiles slightly and says, "These two like to work hard, especially Roja. Someday when I am free and I have a little store, maybe I give them a job."

"You want to have your own store?" I ask.

Vanessa nods. "I have been in juvie with drug dealers who would be happy to hustle as hard at a legal business as they do to sell cocaine and speed. If I could put a little store and hire them as salespeople maybe they don't need to sell drugs anymore." She lets her breath out slowly. There is a faraway look in her eyes, just for a second, like she's thinking about something that hurt her deeply. Then she sets her jaw and says, "What did Ms. Carter tell you?"

"She's fired," I whisper. "I gotta be good for Ms. Vargas so she'll let me help her clean out her desk and get my hands on the report."

Vanessa's eyes narrow. "Fired I do not like," she says. "But if it gets us this report..."

Simone calls, "Brianna! Come check my sweeping!"

Vanessa nods permission and I go help Simone.

The study room goes better than I thought it would. Ms. Vargas frowns when I walk in and says, "So we meet again. Sit in the front where I can keep an eye on you." But I open my educational portal and do a bunch of review lessons for my history class, trying to pretend she's not there, and when she sees I'm not causing any trouble she chills out.

When the PA system announces it's time for lunch, Ms. Vargas calls me up to her desk. "I like the way you stayed focused today," she says. "Funny how different you are when you aren't with that loudmouth friend of yours."

My jaw tightens. I don't like the way she's talking about Vanessa. But I gotta get that positive report so I play the role she wants, putting my hands behind my back and bowing my head slightly. "I'm sorry I tried to get your password," I say. "I was desperate that day."

"Why?" Ms. Vargas says. "That girl bothering you?"

I shake my head slightly. "Everyone had the wrong idea about who poisoned Tasha, and I thought if I could get my hands on the video chat software I could ask her direct."

Ms. Vargas sighs. "There hasn't been a lot of clear thinking since that day, or maybe even before." She lowers her voice. "A couple days before, there were these three girls in here talking loudly about some salt trick. I thought it was some BS they saw online and I shut them down, but I can't help wondering if those girls were up to no good."

Salt trick? I have no idea what that means. "Who were they?" I whisper.

Ms. Vargas shakes her head. "They're in your cohort, I think. One of them was a big-boned girl. Anyway, I don't want to gossip. I wanted to tell you I'm going to give you a good report and encourage you to think for yourself and not let your friends drag you into trouble."

I'm so tired of hearing that. It's like everyone's stuck on what I did wrong with Natalie and that's who they see me as: the girl who knew better but let some bitch get her arrested.

I'm more than that. Way more.

But I need that good report, so I say, "Yes, ma'am. I will from now on."

-I can barely sit still during lunch. I'm too afraid that Ms. Carter's gonna back out or put some other dumb condition on me getting that report, and I don't want to have to go to Plan B.

I make a point of clearing my plate soon as she tells us too, and taking Elizabeth and Simone's for them too. I don't like being a kissass, but I gotta do everything in my power to make sure Ms. Carter keeps her word, even if it means looking like I'm trying to be a teacher's pet.

Molly follows me to the conveyor belt. "Have you spoken to Ashley since...," she says, fidgeting.

"I wish," I say. "Her therapist talked to me once, but it was just to say

Ashley doesn't want to see me." My voice shakes just a little; I breathe in deep to get it under control.

"Yeah, same." Molly sighs. "I was hoping you had the in, cause I wanted to tell her I'm sorry about everything."

I frown. "What's that mean?"

Molly pushes her hair behind her ear. "Um, well, you know, I made her buy me those cookies and she got in trouble, and then I didn't stand up for her when people were accusing her. And I wish I'd watched her pot better. If I'd seen someone messing with it..."

I cross my arms. This sounds like BS to me. "You know what a salt trick is?" I ask. "I heard someone talking in the hall." The half-lie flows smoothly off my tongue. Guess all the stuff I did with Natalie has its uses, but I'd rather not go there ever again.

Molly goes pale. "Salt trick? Never heard of it. I-I guess maybe someone thinks your friend Elizabeth distracted Ashley on purpose but it's not true." Her eyes are very wide and her fingers won't stop moving. "If you do get in with Ashley, tell her I was trying to protect her." She looks me right in my eyes as she says that. Hers are wide and full of regret.

She's just said something important, but I got no clue what it means.

When I get back to the table, Ms. Carter says, "I could use an extra set of hands. Any preferences who else we should invite to help us?"

I put my hand to my chin, thinking. Elizabeth is good at seeing things other people don't, but she's too rigid and if I step one toe out of line, she won't shut up about it. Simone's quiet and shy so she'll do what I tell her, no questions asked, but does she have the observational skills?

I think of that chess match the other day. Simone tries, but Elizabeth already knows.

It's gotta be Elizabeth, and I tell Ms. Carter so.

Ms. Carter takes care of convincing Elizabeth to come with us. Elizabeth's disappointed that Simone can't come too, but Ms. Carter promises her she'll make sure to say a special goodbye to Simone before she leaves for good.

Mrs. MacGregor sticks her head out of her office as we pass on the way to Ms. Carter's. "Is there something I should know about?" she asks.

I put my finger on my lips to warn Elizabeth to keep her mouth shut. Elizabeth's face goes as red as her hair but she nods.

Ms. Carter turns slowly toward Mrs. MacGregor. "Not at all. These two young ladies are going to help me get some papers in order before I leave tomorrow."

Mrs. MacGregor crosses her arms. "I assume you're keeping the confidential files under lock and key."

Ms. Carter's jaw tightens, but she says, quietly, "Of course, Mrs. MacGregor. I am not the kind of person who would destroy everything we've tried to build on my way out the door."

"I trust you," Mrs. MacGregor says. "I'm just not sure how good an idea it is to let residents — "

"I chose the ones I trust the most," Ms. Carter says. She locks eyes with Mrs. MacGregor, reminding me of the way she used to stare Tasha down. Even Tasha was scared to keep going when Ms. Carter confronted her like that.

"I understand," Mrs. MacGregor says. "As long as you are thinking of the program, I have no objections." She withdraws back into her office.

Ms. Carter lets out a deep, shuddering breath before she unlocks her door and turns on the lights.

Elizabeth and I file in behind her. Ms. Carter tells Elizabeth to close the door. The room feels tight, like being jammed in an elevator with a thousand other people, even though it's only the three of us.

"We have to be very careful," Ms. Carter says quietly. "Mrs. MacGregor is already suspicious of what we are doing in here."

Elizabeth scowls. "We aren't doing anything wrong. Besides, she's not your boss anymore so why do you have to listen to her?"

"She is, for the next 24 hours," Ms. Carter says, "and being transferred somewhere else is better than having no job at all. Let's not tempt fate."

Elizabeth turns toward me, her forehead scrunched up in confusion. "How come Mrs. MacGregor can decide if Ms. Carter has a new job?" she whispers.

I put my hand on her shoulder. "That's a big conversation," I tell her. "All I can say for now is the world doesn't work the way it should and there's a lot more that goes into things than what's right and wrong."

Elizabeth chews on a piece of hair nervously. I take it gently out of her mouth and say, "What do you need us to do, Ms. Carter?"

Ms. Carter unlocks a drawer and takes a few folders out. "These are non-confidential materials," she says. "I need you to look at them and weed out the outdated ones so I can shred them." She takes out a few more, and the last one is marked: *Health Department Report — Tasha Johnson Poisoning*

Elizabeth reaches for it, but I say, "Start with the ones on top, Elizabeth. We got a lot to go through." I lower my voice and whisper in her ear, "We can't move too fast. It's gotta look like a coincidence."

Elizabeth's eyes dart all over the room. "That red light in the corner," she says quietly. "That's the security camera."

So that's that. We gotta make it look like we took the report by accident or Ms. Carter gave it to us.

We sort out a few files, putting half of them in the pile to be shredded. Then I say, cautiously, "Ms. Carter? This Health Department paper? You want it shredded or no?" I pick up the file and hand it to her for her to check over.

She puts her reading glasses on and checks it, then says, "I have everything I need from that saved on the computer." She hands it to me, smiling slightly.

It takes everything I've got not to crack it open and read it right now, but I don't need to be caught on camera doing that. Instead, I say, quietly, "You got any empty file folders?"

"Bottom drawer," Ms. Carter says.

Elizabeth opens the drawer and takes out some empty file folders. I tell her, "Put the documents to be shredded in that folder." I put the folder with the report down on the desk and wink, hoping Elizabeth gets it.

This is gonna need a little sleight of hand. Sure hope it works.

I help Elizabeth put all the shredded documents in the file folder.

Then I put it on top of the report we want. "We need a distraction," I whisper to Elizabeth.

"On it." Elizabeth grins. She opens a small drawer in the middle of the desk and grabs a bunch of highlighters. "Can I have these, Ms. Carter?" she asks, purposely holding them up for the camera.

While she's doing that, I grab the report from under the file folder we just set up. I quickly fold the paper and put it in my jacket pocket.

I won't be able to breathe til I get back with Vanessa without being stopped by Security. If I'm caught with this, I'm gone, and so's the evidence we need to solve this case.

twenty-eight

I DON'T BREATHE PROPERLY til we've sneaked into one of the therapy rooms to talk with Vanessa and Simone.

"We're not supposed to be here," Elizabeth whispers as Vanessa uses her hairpin to bypass the code lock on the door.

"Yeah, well, no one should have poisoned Tasha and all the rest of it," I whisper back. "We gotta do what we gotta do."

My stomach sinks as Elizabeth nods. She's learning the game, but at what cost? She's here cause she got tricked, and I don't want that to keep happening, but I don't want to be another Natalie, dragging her down a bad path, either.

"Go in," Vanessa whispers as the lock beeps and flashes green.

We all slide in and close the door behind us. Elizabeth and Simone sit on the floor next to the couch where Vanessa and I settle in. I almost wish I had my phone cause it feels like a family portrait.

I make myself stop thinking nonsense and give Vanessa the report we stole.

Vanessa's face darkens as she skims it.

"What's it say?" Elizabeth says. "We should get to see cause we — "

I shake my head at her and she cuts herself off.

Vanessa looks up. "I think I understand this, but it is too scientific for me. I need a translation from a doctor's girl." She smiles slightly as she hands me the report.

She knows Mom's a doctor. Course she does. They must have told her everything about me.

It hits me all of a sudden.

Vanessa must have been assigned to investigate me after I was sent here. I can't remember if she was here when I got here or if she came later. It feels like she's always been here, but my memory could be playing tricks on me.

I let my breath out slowly. There's no point to thinking about that right now. Instead, I bend over the report.

It's full of technical language, but the only important section is the final one. "The rest of this is describing what we already know, so we don't have to give ourselves headaches trying to understand it," I tell Vanessa. "The important thing is right here."

I read aloud, "'Sample testing showed that the contaminant was inserted into the potatoes prior to them reaching an internal temperature of 145 degrees.' This is using a lot of words to say the poison was put in before the potatoes were finished cooking. Then it goes on to say that security footage shows Ashley stepped away from the pot to help Elizabeth with the salt and Molly was stirring the pot while she was gone."

Elizabeth gulps. "It's my fault," she whispers. "If I measured the regular way instead of my way and Ashley didn't have to help me..."

"No," Vanessa says. "You were not to blame, Roja."

"Maybe Roja wasn't," Elizabeth says, "but that's not my name, so..."

"She means it to mean you," I tell her, "and you know it. And Vanessa's right. You didn't put that poison in the potatoes and you didn't go in there on purpose to distract Ashley."

"Yeah," Simone says. "I-if it wasn't that, they'd have found something else."

"So," Vanessa says, "the camera shows Molly by the pot while Ashley was away, and it is at the perfect time for her to put peanut oil in it. So this settles it. She is the poisoner."

I stare at her. "Maybe," I say, "but you jumped to conclusions with Ashley when it lined up."

"Even if it's her, she isn't the only one," Simone says. "Morgan took the Epi-Pens and stuff."

"And Patrice framed me yesterday," Elizabeth adds, "and got Brianna in trouble."

"Si," Vanessa says. "And it is Molly who told them this."

"I'm not so sure of that," I say. "She seems too nervous to be the puppetmaster. I'd bet someone else is pulling her strings."

"Who?" Vanessa says. "She was the one with the opportunity. So it follows she manipulated the Epi-Pen theft and frame jobs."

I cross my arms. "Is she the one..." I catch myself before I say 'dealing drugs.' Shit, the littles can't know about that. It'll blow Vanessa's cover. I let my breath out slowly. "She has no motive to hurt Ashley, and that's who got framed."

Vanessa frowns. "This is a problem. But maybe Tasha was wrong it was centered around Ashley. Maybe that was an accident."

She doesn't sound like she believes herself, but I know better than to argue. I glance down at the report. Thinking.

Wait... salt trick... Elizabeth being asked to measure salt...

I know what it means. And I know who's behind this.

"I agree with one thing you said," I tell Vanessa. "We gotta talk to Molly." I leave out that it's not to prove she's guilty. It's to get her to flip on the person who's been pulling her strings.

Vanessa says to bring Molly into the therapy room. I'm not sure that's so great — if we get caught, we'll all get punished and I'll be out. But there isn't any place to go that's not against the rules. I can't use the day room, and anyway, we don't need every girl in the program to overhear. Molly won't be comfortable enough to confess that way. The bathroom's gross and Security might wonder why we're hanging out there, and we can't go in the garden or the kitchen without permission.

So the therapy room it is.

Course, Molly's in the day room. I steel myself to go in there, praying I can get Molly and get out without getting caught, but Elizabeth steps up. "I can get her," she says. "She'll come if she thinks you want to talk to her about Ashley."

"If she doesn't come, I will take action," Vanessa adds. "There is no reason to risk your neck yet. It is brave enough to confront her at all."

Elizabeth runs off. A few minutes later, she knocks softly on the door, using that Shave and a Haircut knock that people use as a passcode and Vanessa lets her and Molly in.

Molly looks around, her eyes darting everywhere. "Elizabeth said...," She glances at Vanessa, then away. "What is this, a trap?"

"No trap," I promise her. Footsteps sound in the hall outside and I tell Elizabeth, "Make sure that door's closed."

Elizabeth checks it, then sits down against it like she thinks that'll actually stop Molly from leaving.

I pat the couch next to me. "Come sit, Molly," I say softly. "Look, we know you poisoned those potatoes. But I'd bet anything you weren't the one behind it."

"I didn't, I swear," Molly said.

I cross my arms. "Don't, all right?"

"Don't what?"

I pace back and forth. "I know what it's like, being so caught up in someone else's nonsense that you feel like the person you really are is slipping away. I've been there. Giving money and rides for drugs to some girl who I thought loved me, knowing every time what I was doing was wrong and dangerous and could land me behind bars, telling myself I was gonna say no and then hearing myself saying yes..."

"I"m sorry that happened," Molly says. "But that's you, not..."

"It's you too," I say. "I know it is. You were only trying to protect Ashley, right?"

"You thought you would get Tasha off her back this way," Vanessa adds. "We all know this, so there is no point to lying. We saw the report. We know the security camera shows you at the pot while Ashley's back was turned."

"There were cameras." Molly's voice is flat, yet she sounds surprised.

"Si," Vanessa says, "and it is only a matter of time before Mrs. MacGregor views them and realizes you need a new arrest."

Molly gasps and puts her hands to her mouth. "I never meant for Tasha to get hurt. I swear I didn't."

"I know," I say, "but it happened anyway, so you gotta make it right. We know most of it, you just gotta fill in some blanks. You told Ashley to help Elizabeth with the salt on purpose, right? So you'd have the opportunity to slip the poison into the potatoes."

"It wasn't..." Molly licked her lips. "That part was Morgan's idea. Her and..." She stops short.

"Say it," I say. "We already know, so you might as well."

Molly shakes her head. "She got me good and stuck," she says. "If I tell she'll make it sound to Mrs. MacGregor like it was all me so I go to jail and she goes about her business."

"Yeah, been there," I say, crossing my arms. "Only in her case, it's an empty threat. We got proof, Molly. We got a report saying exactly when the poison was put in and we got Elizabeth as a witness. She knows who wanted that salt and she knows it doesn't make sense."

"Yeah," Elizabeth says. "Lisa was making salad. She didn't need salt for that."

Molly gulps. "What difference does it make if Lisa told me I should distract Elizabeth? The fact is I'm the one who did it."

"It matters," I say, "cause sometimes people get in your head and get you doing all sorts of things you'd never do if you were thinking straight."

"I guess," Molly says. She turns toward Vanessa. "I thought it was just a harmless prank. I-I know that sounds stupid. But I thought, she'd have her Epi-Pen and that it wouldn't be too bad."

Vanessa says, quietly, "That is stupid. Even with the Epi-Pen, she could have died."

Molly bows her head. "I-I know that now. I didn't realize until it happened..." She blinks hard.

"One thing I don't understand," I say. "Maybe at first you thought it was a prank. But Patrice told you the Epi-Pen was gone. Didn't you think..."

"It was too late," Molly says, her voice shaking. "The peanut oil was already in the potatoes."

"You could have said something." Vanessa sounds more hurt than angry.

"Yeah," Molly says. "But if I had, I might have been arrested and I..."

"So you put your comfort over her life," Vanessa says. "You are lucky

I have Brianna here to stop me from making you feel the pain you caused."

Molly sinks into a couch. "What are you going to do? Are you going to tell?"

Vanessa shakes her head. "We will make sure Mrs. MacGregor gets the report," she says, "and that is all. Now get out of our sight."

Molly blinks hard. She stands slowly and turns toward me. "Whatever you do... if you do talk to Ashley... please don't tell her that I..."

"We'll see," I say coldly. "You'd better go for now."

Molly turns and walks slowly away. I almost feel bad for her, but not quite. Vanessa's right. She could have put a stop to this when she realized how serious it was.

Elizabeth slides over so Molly can leave.

As Molly opens the door, another figure pushes past her and pulls the door closed before we can stop her.

It's Lisa, and she's got a crazy look in her eye.

twenty-nine

LISA TAKES A step toward us. "So," she says, "what lies did Molly tell you about me?"

"This is an interesting reaction," Vanessa says. "To barge in here uninvited, claiming someone lied about you. Who says we were talking about you at all?"

Lisa's eyes snap. "Don't try it, bitch!" she says. "I'm not as stupid and weak as you and your little minions think I am. Ashley learned that the hard way and you will too." She turns toward me. "I don't know why you're hanging with this loser, Brianna. You're too smart for that."

I cross my arms. "No one asked for your opinion."

Lisa scowls. "I know Molly said something. You know she poisoned Tasha, right? She had some stupid idea it would save Ashley. Save her by framing her? Please."

"That was you who did the framing," I say quietly. "We all know it, Lisa. I don't know what you came in here for."

"To talk some sense into you!" Lisa shrieks. "I didn't do anything! It was all Molly!"

"Then why did you tell Elizabeth to get salt when you were making salad?" Simone pipes up.

"Yeah," Elizabeth says. "Why?"

"*Niñas*," Vanessa says quietly.

Lisa whirls around. "You think you're so smart," she says. "If you hadn't been so retarded — "

"HEY!" Vanessa says. "You will not talk to her like that."

"Fine!" Lisa says. "Then how about..." She whirls around suddenly, lunges...

...and before I realize what's going on, she's grabbed Elizabeth from behind, shoving one hand over her mouth. Something sharp and silver glistens in her other hand.

My eyes won't focus at first. When they do, I know what it is.

That broken half-scissor I saw in the art table the other day. Lisa must have hidden it.

Elizabeth's making muffled noises and sobbing softly. She twists and flails, trying to get away.

"Roja!" Vanessa says. "Be still. We will get you out of this. I promise it."

Elizabeth cries harder at the hated nickname.

"There's only one way out," Lisa says. "I'll dump her somewhere before I escape this hellhole for good. She'll be bound and gagged, but maybe you'll find her."

Simone tiptoes toward the door. Lisa tilts Elizabeth backward and says, "STOP! Sit down against the wall or I'll cut her, I swear I will."

Simone looks from me to Vanessa, confused. Vanessa says, "Listen to her, *hermana*. It's not up to you to fix this."

"O-okay," Simone whispers. She sits down against the wall and puts her hands in her lap, then bows her head, blinking hard to keep the tears at bay.

Vanessa and I exchange glances. We don't say a word, but I know what she wants me to do: distract Lisa so she can sneak up behind her.

I bite my lip, thinking. Suddenly, I know what to do. It's the same thing I've seen on TV a thousand times. Only... those people are supposed to be trained to do this. I'm not, and it could backfire badly.

Still, I don't have a better idea.

I turn toward Lisa, raising my hands slowly into the air. "Wait!" I say. "Take me instead."

Lisa freezes. She squeezes the handle of the half-scissor. Then she laughs, bitterly, and says, "You're useless. Why would I —"

"I'm the one you want, and you know it." I don't dare look to see if Vanessa is on the move yet. I hope she is. I take a step toward Lisa myself. "I'm the one who messed up your plan," I say. "You had everything perfectly lined up to make Ashley your scapegoat, and if I hadn't interfered it would have worked. Only I wouldn't stop believing in her and I wouldn't quit fighting to prove she was innocent."

"That's cause you're a freak who thinks of Ashley like she's a boy." Lisa spits on the floor.

I make myself breathe hard so I don't lose my temper with her. She's pushing my buttons and I know it.

"You didn't know what to do when I got Tasha to mess up your story," I say quietly. "She told the whole world Ashley was innocent, and you panicked. That's why you sold her those drugs and made sure Patrice got Security's attention on her."

Lisa laughs. "I don't sell..."

"Yes, you do," Vanessa says. "We've known it for months. And Ashley was setting up a sting. That's why you set this whole thing up in the first place."

"And," I add, taking another step forward, "once she was arrested, you thought maybe you'd pin it on me next, solve your next problem. That's why you had Patrice mess with that bottle. You thought for sure I'd go to jail. Only I found a way out. I kept coming and coming and coming and you couldn't stop me. That's why you grabbed Elizabeth. But the one you want revenge on is me, so let her go and take me instead."

Lisa's eyes dart everywhere. "Fine!" she says. "But I'm not letting her go til I know this isn't a trick." She tilts Elizabeth back again. "On your knees, bitch. Hands behind your head."

The echoes of my arrest are all around me. I make myself breathe as I sink to my knees and slam my hands onto the back of my head.

"You!" Lisa says, looking at Simone. "Get the duct tape out of this desk and tie the bitch up."

"No...," Simone whimpers.

"Do it!" Lisa snaps. "Now or Elizabeth dies!"

“Okay, okay.” It breaks my heart to see Simone put her little hands in the air and stumble toward the drawer to get the tape.

Where is Vanessa? My arms ache but I don't dare put them down.

Simone comes back with the tape. She kneels by me. I can hear her crying softly.

I put my hands behind my back to make it easier for her. She's crying harder as she wraps the tape around my wrists...

And suddenly Vanessa is behind her. She lunges at Lisa and grabs her wrist, twisting hard. Lisa struggles, but Vanessa is stronger and twists hard enough that Lisa drops the scissor. Elizabeth jerks into action, sinking her teeth into Lisa's hand.

Lisa yelps in pain as she throws Elizabeth to the floor."The little retard bit me!" she says, shaking her hand out. "Oh, you will pay!" She struggles, but Vanessa twists her arm behind her back and pushes her to her knees.

"I told you," she says. "Stop calling her this word." She tilts her head up. "Run, Roja!" she says. "You are safe now."

Elizabeth stands frozen. I am too. Am I tied up or not? I have a roll of tape stuck to one wrist, but I'm free enough I can get up.

I run to Elizabeth and scoop her up. She clings to me. Vanessa calls, "I need that tape!"

Elizabeth pulls it off me. It hurts but I don't care. She tosses the tape to Vanessa, then throws her arms around me, hugging me tight and crying.

"You're okay now," I tell her. "Let's go make sure Simone..."

I freeze. Simone's gone.

There's soft beeps outside the door and then Simone comes in, flanked by Security, two of them.

She points. "The girl on the floor had a knife and s-she put it on Elizabeth and made me..."

"We got it," Security says. She gestures toward Vanessa. "Up."

Vanessa gets up.

Security says, "We have to take you both to the office till we figure out what's what. Put your hands behind your back, please."

"Nooo....," Simone says as Vanessa obeys. I stare at her as she allows herself to be cuffed. There's no hint of defiance. Just resignation.

"But she saved us," Simone says as Security turns Vanessa around.

"Is okay, hermana," Vanessa says. "We are family no matter what happens. Remember this."

Two other Security officers drag Lisa away. She's a lot less quiet than Vanessa, screaming, "I'm the victim! She attacked me! What, I'm not cute and perky enough like Ashley so I get in trouble? She did drugs!"

Simone and Elizabeth cling to me, both sobbing. Simone says, "We have to help Vanessa!"

I bite my lip as Vanessa's last words hit me.

She's not coming back.

Her mission's over. That's why she was so compliant. She's being taken to whatever cops she works with and they'll say she was arrested so we don't know the truth.

I hope to God I'm wrong, but I got this sinking feeling I'm not.

"Let's go tell Mrs. MacGregor what happened," I tell the littles. "We can't let Lisa get away with any more than she already has."

thirty

MRS. MACGREGOR WANTS to talk to us one at a time, but Elizabeth asks for me so she lets me sit with her while she tells her story. Elizabeth holds onto the edge of Mrs. MacGregor's desk with all her might while she tells her how Lisa grabbed her and what was going through her head while she was being held hostage.

"I thought I was going to die," she says, "but then I saw Brianna look at Vanessa and I knew they were going to save me."

"You saved yourself too," I tell her. "You stayed quiet and didn't give Lisa any reason to hurt you and when the time was right you used your teeth to get her off you."

Elizabeth looks down at the desk, her cheeks turning redder than her hair.

When she's done giving her statement, Mrs. MacGregor says she wants Elizabeth to talk to Dr. Balsam. "As you know, she is a specialist in helping people who have been through severe trauma."

We've all been through it, I think, but saying so's not gonna help anything. Still, if I ran this place, I'd hire 20 Dr. Balsams.

I put my hand on Elizabeth's shoulder. "You think she needs to go to Water Bear?"

Mrs. MacGregor shakes her head. "I think some sessions with Dr. Balsam on an outpatient basis will be sufficient. I do not want to lose another girl from this cohort if it is at all avoidable." She pages Dr. Balsam to come get Elizabeth.

Soon as Elizabeth's gone to her therapy, Mrs. MacGregor leans forward. "Before I speak with Simone, I want to talk to you privately."

My heart pounds. She can't be expelling me after what just happened. Right? Right?

"I-I'm sorry we went in the therapy room without permission," I say. "We needed somewhere private and it seemed like a good idea at the time."

Mrs. MacGregor smiles sadly. "In normal circumstances, this would be the final straw. But these are not normal circumstances. What you girls did was as brave as it was reckless. I am grateful that Elizabeth was not seriously harmed. But I am also glad that we have finally caught the girls who were responsible for the poisoning." She sighs. "I don't know what will happen to our program now that four girls in our cohort have been arrested, but I hope that the Oversight Board will agree with me that these arrests made it safer for the girls who remain."

"All four are in juvie? What... what's going to happen to them now?"

Mrs. MacGregor sighs deeply. "I don't really have an answer to that, Brianna. I'm afraid in the eyes of the law everyone involved in a conspiracy is considered equally guilty, and I really only have any hope that we can save Patrice. The court may view gossiping and passing on messages as forgivable. But Morgan stole lifesaving medicine, and Molly knowingly put an allergen into a pot of food meant for public consumption. I'm afraid there's no way around significant jail time for such serious crimes."

"I'm sorry, Brianna," the public defender said, her blue eyes wide. "But according to state law, any person who is in a car where drugs are found is considered equally guilty of possession, regardless of who the drugs really belong to."

I blink hard. "So they don't care Molly and Morgan were being manipulated?" I say, my voice bitter. "Don't care they didn't think Tasha would actually get hurt?"

Mrs. MacGregor sighs. "I can't do anything about what the law says.

I can only speak up for what I think would be the fairest outcome in this case. But if you — or any girl — wants to make a statement for the judge to consider before sentencing, I won't stop you."

I nod, thinking about it. I could do more than that. I could ask Auntie Nan... no. Molly and Morgan are being done wrong, but this is too big an ask. I only get so many favors from my family, especially considering how badly I disappointed everyone by getting myself locked up, and I don't want to waste them on girls who messed with me when they were here.

Uh uh. My favors are going toward getting Simone and Elizabeth home. Elizabeth's guilty the same way I am — cause the law says so even though it's not exactly the truth. And Simone's 100% innocent. Auntie Nan can help them.

"I know this is upsetting," Mrs. MacGregor says, "and the last thing I want to do is pile on, but I do have to tell you that Vanessa — "

"She's not coming back. I know." My voice is flat. "I know she was working with the cops. The only thing I don't know is... um, was she investigating me, or was our friendship..."

"I believe Vanessa genuinely cared deeply about you," Mrs. MacGregor says. "There are things you don't know about your case, and I should probably not be the one to tell you. But it's all over now so..." She sighs. "At the time of your arrest, the police had had their eyes on you for some time. The patrol officers, of course, knew nothing other than that you had been caught with drugs during a traffic stop. But your name was quite familiar to Narcotics detectives. They chose not to charge you with drug trafficking because they thought you might lead them to your friend if you were placed here."

I stare at her. "So Vanessa was supposed to get me to tell her dirt on Natalie."

Mrs. MacGregor nods. "For what it's worth, all she could tell her handlers, or us for that matter, was that you were clean and that she believed you had been manipulated by someone who didn't tell you anything other than what she wanted you to know. And that is why, now that her investigation is concluded, I am recommending your early release. I believe you still can benefit from this program, assuming it stays open, but we are recommending that you be released in six months rather than serving your entire sentence."

I breathe in sharply. I'm still stuck for six more months, but I never thought I'd hear the words that I'm going home early.

The next two months are real quiet, but I don't trust it. It's that kind of quiet like when my grandma had a good week right before the cancer took her — like everything's too normal and something terrible's waiting in the wings. I keep my head down and try to get through every one of those days. One foot in front of the other brings me one day closer to getting out of here.

Even after Mrs. MacGregor lifts the day room ban, I stay in the study room after school and help Simone and Elizabeth with their homework. These littles need all the education they can get if they're gonna have a shot when they go home.

But it's not just about school. Half the time we end up talking about drama: who gave who a dirty look in the hallway, who's trying to get out of their chores. Sometimes, I offer to stand up for them, but other times, I make them figure it out themselves. I want them to learn when to speak up and when to let it slide. That's the only way they're gonna survive.

I'm worried about Simone more than Elizabeth. She didn't get sent for therapy with Dr. Balsam even though it's obvious witnessing what happened was just as hard on her as the abduction was on Elizabeth. Sometimes she's her old quiet self, and other times it's like she's trying to make up for Vanessa being gone by turning into her, standing up for what she sees as injustice in the loudest, most disrespectful way possible. That's gonna get her into trouble if she doesn't stop, but I can't seem to get it through her head that she has to watch the words that come out her mouth. I hate punishing her when I know she's hurting, but the only thing that works is sending her to timeout like Vanessa did that time.

Sure hope her Mama can handle this new, sassy Simone. Some of it's her age, but if you ask me, she needs help, and cause of the way the system sees things, all she's got is me.

When my 18th birthday comes around, Elizabeth surprises me with cupcakes she baked herself. "I got my kitchen privilege!" she says happily. "And the first thing I did was make this for you."

Simone isn't old enough to work in the kitchen, but she gives me a hug and whispers, "I'm sorry I keep being rude. I don't even know why I'm so mad."

"I do know," I tell her. "It's cause too many things happened to you and you can't fix it." I put my hands on her shoulders. "We'll figure out a way to get it out your system."

Simone nods, her face trembling. I hug her for as long as she'll let me.

The next morning, Mrs. MacGregor calls me to the office. First she wishes me a happy birthday and tells me that even though I'm technically an adult, the court already gave me permission to stay in the program for up to 3 years. "But it won't be that long," she says. "As we talked about a few months ago, I'm recommending early release. As of today, I am also sealing your written warnings so that the court cannot use them against you. I have no doubt your release will be approved, and you will be going home in January."

I bow my head slightly. My heart's pounding now that this is really happening. I'm glad to be getting out, but at the same time, I don't know what it's gonna be like going home after being here a year. I'm not the same as I was when I went in and I bet Mom and Auntie Nan aren't either. And even Vicki... Mom sends me pictures in the mail, and the small-for-her-age girl with her hair tied back in two bushy ponytails is gone. She's getting tall now, and she wears her hair in one long, strong-as-hell braid. I sure hope her attitude is better than Simone's. I want the same little cousin back who I've missed so much the last four months, but she'll be halfway through eighth grade by the time I get out.

Mrs. MacGregor's waiting for a response, so I mumble my thanks, but my mind's still on Vicki and how once I get out, I have to make sure she never, ever does anything to wind up in a place like this and that she knows that it's not enough to stay clean yourself — you gotta stay away from people who are gonna drag you right into the back of a cop car and then disappear on you.

"My pleasure," Mrs. MacGregor says, as if I answered her properly.

"One more thing, Brianna. This is just between us, but I wanted you to know the state has finished its evaluation of this program."

My head jerks up. "We're staying open, right? I mean, we have to, cause otherwise it wouldn't matter you want me to have early release next year."

Mrs. MacGregor smiles slightly. "We are, but we are on probationary status. Among other things, we need to make certain changes to ensure every girl here is safe." She leans forward. "I know we won't have you much longer, but while we do, I would like your input. You, more than anyone, are a leader in the Tiger Cohort, and I think you have valuable insights into what we need to do to keep everyone safe."

I promise her I'll think about it, leaving out that I'm going to ask my girls what they think. Maybe getting involved in fixing what's wrong in this place will give Simone enough of a sense she matters that she'll stop acting out.

Mrs. MacGregor's phone rings. She answers it and says, "Yes, I was about to tell her. I'm sure she will, but I will ask right now." She covers the receiver and says to me, "Ashley has been asking to see you. Dr. Balsam wants to know if you are willing to meet her in the garden after we're finished here."

My eyes widen. "Course I do," I say, then realize I'm being as disrespectful as Simone. "I mean, yes, ma'am, please."

Mrs. MacGregor smiles slightly and tells Dr. Balsam, "She is very eager to see Ashley. Yes, I will do that."

She tells me that Ashley can meet me in the garden in 15 minutes and gives me permission to wait for her outside.

The garden is beautiful. The warm weather's woken up the flowers and they're starting to come up, and there's a tree that's starting to get new leaves on its skinny little branches. The sun's out, too, but it's not so hot I break a sweat while I'm waiting for Ashley on a small bench between beds.

It's hard to sit still, but I make myself. The last thing I need is for Ashley to see me pacing back and forth when we haven't set eyes on each other in months. It feels like another half year before she finally comes down the path, walking slowly with Dr. Balsam.

Ashley introduces us. I almost tell her we already met, but Dr. Balsam doesn't say anything so I figure maybe it's better not to correct Ashley and leave it alone.

Dr. Balsam explains that she's here to help Ashley in case she gets overwhelmed or upset but that she'll stay out of our way so we can have some privacy. But I'm barely paying attention because I'm taking in how beautiful Ashley is. She's got some more height while she's been in Water Bear, and her brown skin is glowing. But it's her eyes that make my stomach do flip-flops. That sparkle's in them that I haven't seen in months. Tasha snuffed it out, but therapy must have put it back, and it makes her more beautiful than ever.

"H-hi," I stammer.

"Hi," Ashley says back, and then we just stand there, smiling at each other. I'm trying to find the words to say everything I want to say, and Ashley's stuffing her hands in her pockets and swaying slightly.

"Um," she says and gives me another shy smile. Then she turns her head over her shoulder and says, "Dr. B? Can I show Brianna the carrot patch?"

"If you'd like." Dr. Balsam smiles at her. "I'll be right here on this bench if you need me. But I'm sure you can handle this conversation, Ashley. Focus on why you wanted to see Brianna today."

Ashley nods. "Come on," she says.

My heart is beating hard as I follow her down the path to the other side of the garden, where she shows me all sorts of vegetables growing. "Bet you didn't know we grow some of the vegetables we have at dinner right here behind the house," she says. "I planted a whole crop of carrots." She smiles slightly, clearly proud of herself.

"That's cool," I say.

There's another awkward silence and then Ashley says, "Um, I wanted, um... first of all, thanks." She turns toward me. "You fought harder for me during all that poisoning nonsense than anyone's ever fought for me. My lawyer had nothing on you."

My cheeks get hot. "That's not hard. These public defenders are in the business of making sure we plead guilty no matter what the truth is."

"Yeah, well, I was guilty. I didn't deserve to get the cops called on me in my own home, but I was the one who stashed crack cocaine in my room with an eight-year-old in the house." She swallows hard. "If anything had happened cause he found it, I'd never forgive myself."

I pat her hand. "Guess you were pretty caught up in stuff, huh?"

Ashley nods slightly. "I wrote them a letter to try to make amends since they won't take my calls." She sighs deeply. "Anyway, I don't want to waste time on them. I... look, I'm sorry I shut you out so much. It's not cause I don't like you or something like that. I... no one has ever been on my side like you were, and I thought if you knew I cut myself, I'd lose you." Her voice shakes.

"Never," I say. "I know it can't ever work cause we're here but sometimes I wish we'd met in my old high school, when we were both free to..."

Ashley's eyes widen. "You like me that way?"

My heart pounds. What am I doing? No dating while we're in here, and anyway, it's a big risk admitting I like girls, even to Ashley. "Yeah," I say, looking away. "But it's not like we can do anything about it."

"It's not that," Ashley says. "I just didn't think a girl like you would want one like me." She looks away. "You know I've been kicked out of five different foster homes, starting in first grade, right? And I don't want to leave this place cause Mrs. MacGregor can't promise the next one won't kick me out too."

My stomach sinks. How could anyone do that to sweet, beautiful Ashley? "They're missing out, then," I say, "cause you're amazing."

"Nah. That's you." Ashley blinks hard. "I wouldn't be dating material even if we weren't locked up together. I'll tell you one thing, though." She smiles slightly. "Someday when I see you in the news winning some big case for girls like we used to be in the court, I'm gonna tell everyone I know I knew you when."

I laugh.

"Serious!" Ashley says. "What you did to clear my name's only the beginning. Someday you're gonna make it so some girl like me doesn't get locked up in the first place."

I stare at her. "You really think?"

Ashley nods. "If it's okay with you, when you win that big case I'll say we went to high school together. I don't want people judging you cause you ended up here."

I shrug. "I'm never gonna be glad I ended up here, but if it gives me the power to fix it for someone else, maybe I can be happy about that."

"That's what I'm saying," Ashley says. She grins. "Enough seriousness. Race you to the tomatoes."

She takes off before her words even hit my brain. I run after her. We're both laughing by the time I catch her up.

It's the first time I've heard that sound from either of us.

Dr. Balsam calls for Ashley to come back — her outside time's up for today.

She lets us hug, and Ashley touches me gingerly, like she's afraid to go too deep.

Her words echo in my ears as we head back inside, and my own too.

I don't know about being a lawyer. That's Auntie Nan, not me. Besides, I got this record.

But another voice whispers in my ear, *Stop giving up before you start. If you want it, fight for it.*

And that voice is right.

Cause I fought damn hard for Ashley, and for Elizabeth, and Simone. Hell, I'm still fighting Simone's worst self to get the girl she was before to come back.

And if I can do that while I'm locked up, there's no telling what I can do once I'm free.

There are lots of girls on the outside who are gonna need me. For all I know, my cousin Vicki could be one of them.

Time to start fighting for a future where I can be that for them.

I'm torn cause I want to go tell Simone about that garden and get her to talk to Dr. Balsam about helping out. I bet it'd be good for her to focus on something other than how mad she is.

But that's gotta wait, cause if I don't call Auntie Nan right now to start settling my future, I'm gonna lose my nerve.

No, talking to Simone about the garden's gotta wait. Starting today, I have to choose myself before anyone else.

I don't know what Auntie Nan will say or if she'll accept the charges when I'm calling in the middle of the week and not our usual time.

But I have to try.

For Elizabeth. For Simone. For Vicki.

And most of all, for myself.

THE END

a note for readers...

I wrote *Poison in the System* based on my experiences in alternative criminal justice systems as a social work intern. That work sparked a life-long passion for criminal justice reform. Brianna's story is fictional, but the issues she faces—including being retraumatized on a daily basis—are real for far too many kids.

Although the heart of the story is a mystery about who poisoned Tasha, I also wanted to explore the power dynamics and deep flaws in programs meant to "fix" the inequities of the juvenile justice system. Some of what happens to Brianna is based on stories I heard over and over again from clients as a social worker. Other parts are drawn from my own life. It was especially important to me to show how much damage Brianna's addiction to a girl who was emotionally abusive did to her life, because relationship addiction is not taken seriously—even though it's as powerful as any other kind.

Of course, Brianna's story doesn't end when she's released from the group home. We'll catch up with her again in *The Night Quinn Disappeared* (coming this December), when her cousin Vicki turns to her for help after a classmate vanishes.

If you liked this book, you might also enjoy some of my other stories:

• *Reinventing Hannah* – Not a mystery, but a powerful coming-of-age story about a girl who reinvents herself as a bold advocate after surviving a traumatic assault.

• *Open Secrets* – A campus murder mystery involving Brianna's cousin Vicki, her older brother Ken (wrongfully accused), a transmasc freshman determined to uncover the truth, and a 25-year-old scandal the school wants buried.

• *Her Sacred Oath* (coming July 2025*)* – My first adult thriller, about a medical resident whose healing from domestic violence is derailed when she's framed for murder and prescription drug abuse.

• *Shattered Illusions* (coming Sept. 2025) – A sequel to *Open Secrets*. Dani's new beginning unravels when a romantic rival dies at her party—and she's accused of murder.

• *Someone Else's Daughter* (coming Mar. 2026) – Likely featuring Brianna in a supporting role again, this story follows the disappearance of Simone after her release. When police won't take it seriously, the girls must fight for justice again.

Some of these books are already available on Amazon and Kobo; others are still on the way.

If *Poison in the System* moved you, please consider leaving a review on Goodreads or the platform where you bought it. Reviews help the readers who need these stories most to find them.

You're also invited to join my mailing list at https://authorjackori.com/enigma-express/ for behind-the-scenes updates, sneak peeks at new releases, and tips for readers who want to write their own stories that matter.

Finally, while my social work background helped me tell this story with honesty and heart, I am not Black and cannot speak from a first-hand perspective about the injustices many Black people face from the criminal (in)justice system. If *Poison in the System* left you thinking, I hope you'll explore some of these powerful books by Black authors:

• *The New Jim Crow* by Michelle Alexander
• *Pushout* by Monique W. Morris
• *This Is My America* by Kim Johnson
• *Concrete Rose* by Angie Thomas
• *Just Mercy* by Bryan Stevenson

Thank you again for reading Brianna's story. I hope it stays with you.

—Jack Ori

about the author

Jack Ori is a transgender and autistic author who writes mystery/thrillers for teens and adults, often starring trauma survivors and neurodivergent characters. His books tackle social issues like criminal justice reform, homophobia, and finding your voice after being silenced.

Jack is a former social worker with master's degrees in mental health counseling and professional writing. He grew up on Long Island, where many of his stories are set, and he now writes fiction and entertainment journalism full time.

Learn more at authorjackori.com or join his mailing list at authorjackori.com/enigma-express.

also by jack ori

CEDARWOOD JUSTICE

Reinventing Hannah

Open Secrets

Shattered Illusions (coming in September 2025)

The Night Quinn Disappeared (coming in December 2025)

BEHIND CLOSED DOORS

Her Sacred Oath (coming in June 2025)

Someone Else's Daughter (coming in 2026)

www.ingramcontent.com/pod-product-compliance
Lightning Source LLC
Chambersburg PA
CBHW020525310726
48979CB00014B/2212/J

* 9 7 8 1 7 3 4 5 2 1 1 9 1 *